CAMBRIA

A Novel

A.R. TYLER

CAMBRIA

CAMBRIA

First Edition

Published in Canada by Katrina Nerisse Gormley

Toronto, Ontario

ISBN: 978-1-0696007-0-7

Library and Archives Canada Cataloguing in Publication data is not available for this edition.

For permissions or inquiries, contact:

Katrina Nerisse Gormley

Toronto, Ontario, Canada

Content Warning

This book explores mature themes including suicide, drug use, domestic violence, and infidelity, and is intended for adult readers comfortable with morally complex characters and realistic struggles. Reader discretion advised.

CAMBRIA

"There seemed to be something tragic in a friendship so colored by romance."

– Oscar Wilde

CAMBRIA

PROLOGUE

This is not a love story.

At least, not in the way you might expect.

It isn't a tale of sweeping romance and declarations shouted across crowded rooms. There are no cinematic crescendos, no perfect resolutions waiting in the final chapter. What unfolds here is quieter, messier—the story of a young woman stumbling through the strange, unglamorous business of becoming herself.

And yet—there is love. There is always love. There is no such thing as a story without it; it is the marrow of every choice we make, the hidden thread binding every triumph, every undoing. To strip it away would be to tell a story without breath.

So yes, there is a man. There is friendship and longing, the sharp ache of what remains unsaid. There are others too—people she clings to, learns from, loses, betrays, loves in all the flawed and fleeting ways we love when we are still learning how.

But I repeat—this is *not* a love story.

CAMBRIA

And if you're looking for a happy ending, this isn't it. Or perhaps it is. That, dear reader, is not for me to decide. The ending belongs to you—how you read it, what you choose to carry from it, and what you leave behind.

Call it a love story if you must. But I will call it what it truly is: a story about growing up, the choices that define you, and the love you find along the way.

CAMBRIA

June 1989

CAMBRIA

ONE

For as long as she could remember, Cambria could sense a great darkness within her, origins unknown. She did not know what to do with this darkness, nor was she aware how she came to possess it. She must have been born with it. Or perhaps it developed over time, a slow cultivation of things to come.

She could feel it inside her, as though it were a tangible thing, moving around, taking up space where it did not belong. A malignant tumor, growing and expanding, pushing her organs aside when it desired. She could not control it, and that was what she hated most. That she did not control it—it controlled her.

Coursing through her bloodstream and infecting her brain, the darkness found refuge in her mind, swarming her with wild and indignant thoughts. She did not know what else to do but swallow them whole, devouring them, allowing them to eat away at her, piece by piece.

She succumbed to its power, letting the darkness live and breed, wondering just how much damage it could cause if she let it.

But she never did.

A master of suppression, she had spent years learning to conceal this part of her, pushing it down down down until she herself barely knew it was there.

It was hereditary, she concluded. Not the fault of her own but of somebody who came long before her, passing this unfortunate strand of molecules her way. And if she fought it enough, then it'd be relinquished completely.

But she was wrong.

It came out in other ways, bleeding through the cracks that could not be concealed. She was prone to bad decision making, couldn't differentiate right from wrong. She did not learn from her mistakes. She was self-destructive to the point of detriment. After repeating the same mistakes countless times, she questioned whether she'd ever truly learn.

It was grueling, living the way she did. Never able to properly express herself, questioning who she was entirely. She wondered if she'd be this way forever.

All her life, she'd felt so alone, no one to relate to. What she longed for was a companion. Someone who understood her. Someone who did not cast judgment. Someone who was just as lost and misunderstood as she was.

Someone who was the same.

Our story starts with Pine Hills. Tucked between the restless Pacific and stretches of rugged coastline, the town held a quiet kind of beauty, the kind that seeps into you rather than shouts for attention. Life here moved at a rhythm set by the tides and the winds; slow enough for secrets to take root, steady enough for them to linger.

But before Pine Hills, she was just a girl. A girl whose existence was unremarkable, and uneventful.

She had lived her life as grandiose as she could, striving for excellence, never quite sure if she had achieved it. She walked the line between living and surviving, and if you had asked her then what the difference was, she wouldn't have been aware there was one.

But eventually a caged bird will realize it needs to fly.

She had never been a fan of change. She'd always been a stickler for rules and regularity. She loved schedules, and she loved abiding to them. Therefore, whenever change was thrown her way, it caught her off guard. She took longer to adjust than most. And if it were up to her, she'd never change a thing.

You're probably wondering: how did someone who was so intolerant to change end up moving across the country to a place she'd never been in her life?

If only I had the answers.

Something about wanting to start her life anew. Once she turned twenty-two, it was as though her definitive preconceived notion about change had gone out of the window, and suddenly, change was all she craved.

To the average person, it did not make sense. She had been happy and content, living the life she always had, residing in the bedroom she had grown up in, at her parent's house on the east coast, familiar with her surroundings, accustomed to everyday life with her friends, peers, coworkers—everyone around her. And then suddenly, in a blink of an eye, she couldn't stand any of it.

She needed to leave. She needed to escape. If not for her soul, then at least for her sanity.

Her mother was against it, of course. The night she initially proposed the idea led to a heated argument that ended with crimson faces and slammed doors. She could hear her father the next morning, in the kitchen, talking to her mother. Could hear the soft whisper of his voice as he spoke in soothing tones with her, being the voice of reason as he always had.

By the time she had mentally prepared for the impending conversation, her mother's demeanor had already shifted. Cambria found her in the corner of the kitchen, a fresh pot of coffee brewing.

"Good morning," her mother said to her.

Cambria approached slowly, unsure how to gauge her mother's greeting. "Good morning." She looked towards the table where her father sat, holding the newspaper. "Dad," she nodded to him.

"How did you sleep, my girl?" Twenty-two years old and he was still reciting that same line as he did when she was a child.

She shrugged to signify indifference. "Alright." She looked to her mother again, who no longer had her eyes on Cambria, attention on the coffee machine instead.

Cambria slid into the chair across from her father. She looked at them both, then waited as her mother approached the table and sat down. "We've talked, your father and I," she said, looking at her daughter. Cambria braced for the worst. More yelling and screaming. Her mother telling her that she was too young, that it was too far. "You have our blessing."

She nearly fell out of her chair. "What?"

"We've discussed it at great length," her father took the reins. "And we understand this is something you really want, despite how impulsive it may be."

She sat there staring at him, blinking, unsure of what to say, how to respond.

Her mother pursed her lips, hesitated. "I know it will be far. But if this is really what you want, then we support you."

Cambria looked to her father again, waiting for the other shoe to drop. But there was no other shoe. Because somehow, by some miracle, they were okay with it.

And that was how it all began. Cambria, packing her bags, boarding a flight, jetting off to the west coast.

They were right, though. It *was* an impulsive decision. It was a decision Cambria wasn't even sure of, hadn't even fully thought through before implementing. Yet it was all she could think about, her mind obsessing over it until she did it.

Linden Falls was all she had ever known. It had everything she ever needed. It was as though there were a giant glass bubble that surrounded the town, and she never even knew, wallowing in this ignorant bliss. That's the scary thing about being comfortable.

Nothing notable ever happens in the comfort zone.

Perhaps that was how the idea was conceived, lying in her bed that one night, tossing and turning, plagued with insomnia. It was as though she knew she was trapped before the realization had ever hit, and the only thing she could do for her own survival was to get out before it was too late.

Of course, there were things she would miss about Linden Falls. She'd miss her parents, for starters. (She knew she could not live with them forever, but sometimes she wished that she could) She would miss her mother's strawberry pancakes on Sunday mornings. She'd miss playing pickleball with her dad in the summertime. She'd miss waking up in the middle of the night knowing they were just down the hall if she needed them.

But she could always call. She could always write. She'd send them letters and postcards, telling them how her life was going. And they could come visit her, spend the holidays on the beach together.

She'd miss the mall and her high school. She'd miss the places she grew up, and the people she came to know so well.

But those were just memories, no longer tangible things. And those friendships that she once cherished somehow meant so much less than they did back then.

The truth was, her life in Linden Halls had reached a standstill. No longer was she the same girl she was at sixteen, eighteen, twenty-one. The people she cared about back then did not care about her anymore.

Those times were a far and distant thing of the past, and no matter how hard she tried, she could never get them back. But this did not sadden her, rather, it only fueled her desire to leave. She wanted to go somewhere she could learn, grow, *change*. She didn't want to remain the same for the rest of her life.

She wanted to be someone new.

Little did she know that her wish was about to come true. Not only would her move to Pine Hills be like nothing she'd ever experienced, but it would be the catalyst to the rest of her life.

Nothing could have prepared her for what was to come. And when the plane touched down on solid ground, and she was officially on unfamiliar territory, it was only the beginning.

TWO

Her first two weeks in Pine Hills were chaotic and underwhelming simultaneously. She was so far away from home, and everything was so new and unfamiliar to her. Take the streets, for example. Something she had once known so well was now something that confused her. There was so much that needed to be done. She did not know a single person. She felt trepidation, yes, but she also felt, for the first time in a long time, alive.

Pine Hills had similarities to Linden Falls, which was both a comfort and a disappointment. For instance, they had roughly the same population. Pine Hills was technically a city, but it was small. There was the west end, which contained the downtown core, busy one-way streets and small office buildings (but no skyscrapers). And then there was the east side, with the suburbs and rural shopping centers. Cambria had landed somewhere in the middle. She was renting a quaint one-bedroom apartment overlooking the suburban neighborhoods, not too far from the ocean.

A reoccurring dilemma throughout Cambria's life was that she never felt like she belonged anywhere, and she could never quite understand how such a thing could be possible. It was a perplexing phenomenon that could not be explained. That otherworldly feeling of never fitting in; an outlier on the sidelines of life. She always had friends, more than enough. But there was always something missing; a barrier, something preventing her from forming the connection she so desperately needed. And subsequently, the more this feeling persisted, the more connections she attempted to make, collecting friendships like dolls on a shelf, wondering which one would be different.

She remembered hearing the word *monachopsis*—the subtle but persistent feeling of being out of place.

Sometimes she felt as though she were wearing a mask, putting on a show for those around her. She would watch people, study their emotions, memorize their actions. She felt as though life was a stage, and she was simply a performer, switching roles whenever necessary. Like a chameleon, slipping into different skins inadvertently. Each person warranted a new skin, and it was beyond Cambria to determine which role to play with who.

Take her family, for example. With them, she was the doting daughter who worked hard and had goals and ambitions. At school, she was the studious pupil, eager to learn and impress. Around her friends, she was care-free and laid-back. All these characteristics belonged to her, and were indeed herself, but she often wondered which self was the most real. Which self was the true self that belonged to her the most.

She felt trapped in this paradox, of longing to be someone else, but also wanting to be comfortable with who she was. As hard as she tried, she could never succeed. So rather than seeking more, she learned to accept things as they were.

She'd been applying to jobs more than she was sleeping, and within the first week, had zero prospects. By week three, she had five interviews lined up.

On that third Tuesday in Pine Hills, Cambria stood in front of the mirror, adjusting her blouse and skirt. She looked herself over from head to toe. The tiny black heels boosted her height a mere two inches. She tugged her skirt lower down her thighs, then readjusted.

She had seen the ad in the classifieds: *Now Hiring: data entry position for Hargrove & Swanson, university degree required.* She found it comical that they required a degree for a data entry position that most likely paid minimum wage. But then again, for a pharmaceutical conglomerate like Hargrove & Swanson, they probably wanted the most qualified.

Cambria knew nothing about pharmaceuticals, but she had a degree. Albeit in English & Linguistics—but they didn't specify *what* degree, so she hoped this would suffice.

If not, she could always bring out the heels and miniskirt and try her hand at bartending. She'd probably make more money doing that.

The interview was quite rudimentary. They asked the standard questions; she replied in her utmost professional manner. They delved into her life back home, asking what caused her sudden move across the country. By the end of the interview, he was shaking her hand and welcoming her to Hargrove & Swanson.

At last, she was employed.

Training would begin the following Monday. And it turns out she was wrong about the salary. It was much more generous than a meager minimum wage.

One week. She had one week to relax before she'd begin. Now that the stress of job hunting was out of the way, she took this as an opportunity to get acquainted with the city and its people.

She had already met one person who seemed promising — a girl in her building named Mara who was around Cambria's age.

The prospect of making a new friend was both enticing and terrifying. It had never come easy for her, making friends. Or, rather, maintaining them. It was almost as if the majority of her friendships were for show—a group of people to spend time with, eat lunch with, pass the time. But there was no sustenance to these friendships.

Also, there was the fact that she had always preferred solitude over the company of others. So far, no one had come along to change her stance on that.

What Cambria longed for was a bond that was like no other. A partner-in-crime; someone she could confide in and share her darkest secrets. Someone who would always be there for her—and support her—no matter what.

She wanted unconditional comradery.

She traveled near and far (but mostly near) and had never found a bond such as the one she was seeking. But with each new person she became acquainted with, the thought crossed her mind: *could this be it?*

Mara seemed nice. And she was willing to have a conversation with her—that was more than most.

They had met in the apartment lobby on Cambria's first week in Pine Hills as she was struggling to open her mailbox.

Mara suddenly appeared. "Do you live here?"

Cambria startled and placed her hand over her chest.

"Didn't mean to scare you."

"It's fine, I'm jumpy. And yes, I just moved in."

"Let me help you with that," Mara took the key from Cambria's hand and pressed her body hard against the box, twisting the key into place.

Cambria took in her appearance. The girl was shorter than she was and had auburn hair cascading over her shoulders. The lock clicked, and the mailbox opened. "You're a saint," Cambria said as Mara handed her back the key.

"You'll get used to it. But I will warn you, it's not the only pain in the ass in this building."

"Oh, great, good to know."

"You betcha." Mara side-stepped awkwardly, about to leave, then turned back around. "I'm Mara, by the way. I live on floor eight."

"Cambria," she replied. "I'm on seven"

"We're practically neighbors. Where'd you move from?"

"East Coast. Nowhere near here."

"You've come a long way."

"Yep. But I'm excited to get to know the place. Any recommendations?"

Mara grinned. "Tons. And I have a feeling you and me are going to get along. You like pizza and beer?"

"Love."

"I like you already."

Cambria didn't drink beer, but she liked pizza, and that was close enough.

That Friday—which happened to be the last day of June—Mara made plans for them to go out.

Had Cambria known what was in store for her that night, perhaps she would have done something differently. Or maybe not. Maybe she wouldn't have done anything differently, fully aware of where it would lead her.

Years later, she would look back on this night, playing it over in her head, a vicious cycle on repeat. And every single time, she would come up with the same conclusion: it was the start of the rest of her life.

Because after that, nothing was the same.

Mara finished work at five and told Cambria to be ready for eight. She wasn't entirely sure what their plans entailed, so she dressed casual in tight-fitted jeans and a red blouse. At this point in her life, her hair was long and dirty blond, bordering a sandy brown. She had never once dyed it—it had come to be like that all on its own. Her father's hair was dark brown, and her mother was blond, so she assumed she'd end up with one or the other. But this? She wasn't sure what to call it. She swept it up into a low ponytail and tied a bow in it.

Mara knocked on her door not a minute past eight. She waltzed in, marveling at the apartment's vacancy. "I love what you've done with the place," she said as she traipsed through the living room.

Her presence made Cambria slightly nervous. She'd always struggled with small talk. "I'm still working on it."

She stopped and looked at Cambria, smirking. "Ever heard of furniture?"

"You know, I've never really been a fan."

"Where do you eat?"

"Counter."

She raised her eyebrows and nodded. "It's nice. Homey. I like it."

"I'll furnish it eventually. Scavenge whatever people have left out on the curb."

"Careful, my friend got scabies from doing that."

"Oh."

"Do your parents have money?"

Cambria shrugged. "Money's not an issue for them."

"Have they seen this place?"

She rolled her eyes. "Are we leaving or are we going to stay and talk about my apartment all night?"

Mara laughed and swung her purse over her shoulder, heading out the door, Cambria following close behind.

They started the evening off with dinner. Mara took her to a restaurant called Benji's where they served flaming saganaki and margaritas that were bigger than their heads.

As Mara spoke, Cambria listened, simultaneously watching every single person who entered the restaurant. There was an eclectic mix of individuals walking through that door, and Cambria wanted to study all of them.

The elderly couple in the booth next to them who held hands for their entire meal. The woman standing at the bar wearing a short black dress and six-inch heels. And in the far back corner, a man sitting in solitude, a cup of coffee on the table in front of him, his eyes cast down to the book he was deeply immersed in. For him, the rest of the room didn't exist.

"What's the craziest thing you've ever done?" Mara asked, their empty dishes scattered across the table between them.

"Um, how crazy are we talking?"

At this, Mara laughed. "Why do I have a feeling you can't answer that question?"

"Maybe because I can't."

"I knew it. I can just tell."

"Am I really that predictable? That *boring*?"

"You're not boring! You just haven't lived yet. But maybe that's about to start. Maybe this move is exactly what you needed. Why *did* you move here, anyway?"

"Change of scenery."

Mara burst into a fit of laughter. "Honey, please. If you wanted a change of scenery you could've went on vacation. You packed up your entire life and moved three thousand miles across the country. Hey, maybe *that's* the craziest thing you've ever done."

"Honestly, I think you're right."

Mara sat back. "You're in Pine Hills now, baby. Your life officially begins *now*."

After dinner, Mara brought her to a bar called The Tap, which was infamous in Pine Hills for having more than fifteen beers on tap per night.

They got a round of drinks and settled into a booth. Mara peppered her with questions which Cambria tried her best to answer. And when she wasn't answering Mara's questions, she was listening intently to the stories she shared.

Mara was an extremely interesting person who had already lived a hundred lives. Cambria felt inexperienced compared to her and wished she had better stories to share.

As they stood at the bar, sipping their cosmos, a man tapped Mara on the shoulder. She spun around and her eyes widened in surprise. There was a girl there next to him. "No fucking way," Mara threw her arms around both of them.

"Mara Henley," the man said as he pulled back and looked at her. "Of all the gin joints. How long has it been? Three years?"

"Longer," said the girl next to him.

"Why have I never seen you guys here?" Mara asked them.

"Probably because we don't come here," the man replied.

Cambria watched like a mouse in a corner.

"Oh, come on," Mara said. "Tap isn't *that* bad, is it?"

"The last time I was here, someone was arrested for bringing a portable barbeque inside."

"Okay, well, times have changed," Mara grinned cheekily. "Guys, meet my new friend, Cambria. She just moved here from the East Coast, like, a week ago."

"Three weeks ago," Cambria corrected her.

"Damn, shorty, you're *new new*. I'm Oliver." The man shook her hand. "Mara and I go way back. And this is my girlfriend, Lily."

"Pleasure to meet you," Lily said. "Any friend of Mara's is a friend of ours."

"What on Earth brings you here tonight?" Mara pressed.

"A friend of a friend," Oliver said. "Who I guess I could just call my friend now—he suckered me into coming. Do they still do half price shots on Fridays?"

"No idea," Mara replied. "But you should stick around and find out."

After catching up with Oliver and Lily, Mara was on the hunt for boys. They did a couple shots and grabbed another drink, then scanned the bar, eyeing potential suitors.

That was how they ended up seated in a booth near the entrance with two bachelors, Mara deeply engrossed in conversation with the one she wanted to bring home. Cambria, on the other hand, had no interest in his friend. He asked her dull questions that only bred small talk, which made her want to die. Normally she was good at keeping up a cheerful façade, but this time she couldn't even be bothered to fake it. She wanted to crawl out of her skin, or out the window.

Just when she thought she couldn't stand it a moment more, Oliver walked by their booth.

"OLIVER!" Cambria shouted.

He stopped and his eyes found hers. "Hiya, kid."

"I need to talk to you!" The conversation around her halted abruptly. "Help me out of here." She was seated nearest to the wall, Mara beside her. She reached her hand out to Oliver and he grabbed it, helping her out as she maneuvered past Mara.

"You okay?" Mara asked her.

"Yeah, I'm good. I just need to talk to Oliver."

Mara gave her a strange look. "Okay, weirdo."

Oliver kept hold of her hand and led her around the corner. "What's up? Everything okay."

"You saved me!" She threw her arms around him. Suffice to say, she was drunk. "Thank you."

"Uh, for what?"

"From a dreadful conversation. I had to get out of there; I was going to kill someone. Or myself."

Oliver laughed. "No problem, sweetheart. Come with me."

She followed Oliver as he weaved through the crowds of people. The bar was three floors—they were on the main. He headed towards the staircase and led her downstairs.

This floor was completely different from the one they were just on. The lights were dimmed, the music was loud, and people were dancing.

"These are the assholes I mentioned earlier," Oliver said of his two friends.

They both turned and focused their attention on Cambria. "Who's this?" the one asked.

"This is Cambria," Oliver said. "She just moved here a week ago."

"Three weeks ago," she corrected him. "Nice to meet you guys."

"Theodore," the one said, shaking her hand. "But everyone calls me Theo."

"I'm a bit drunk right now," she said. "So hopefully I remember that."

"Jackson," said the other, taking her attention. "I'm sure you won't forget that."

And just like that, everything was about to change.

THREE

Of course, in the moment, seldom do we recognize when life is pivoting on a single event. It isn't until years later that we scan our memories and spot the true catalyst.

Cambria, though, had a flicker of awareness that night. She knew something significant was unfolding—just not about the person she thought. Years later, she would wonder: what would have happened if she hadn't gone out with Mara that night? If they'd chosen a different bar? If she had never moved to Pine Hills?

"Where'd you move from?" Theo asked, inquisitive eyes on hers.

"What a unique name you have," Jackson remarked. "*Cambria.* I like it."

"I'm not from anywhere near here."

"What does that even mean?" Theo asked.

"Linden Falls," she said meekly. "You've probably never heard of it."

"You're right about that," he laughed.

"Is that near Sacramento?" Jackson asked.

"No," she said. "Not even close."

"What brings you to Pine Hills?" Theo asked.

Cambria hesitated, unsure how to respond. "I'm still trying to figure that out."

Before she knew it, she was back on the main floor, seated in a booth with Theo and Jackson, the three of them thick as thieves. Cambria struggled to remember the trajectory that led them there. They were on the dance floor. Theo was spinning her around. Then… someone wanted shots?

Oliver was with Lily on the third floor. Mara was nowhere to be seen; maybe she had already gone home with that guy. Cambria hoped his friend wasn't wandering around looking for her. At least she now had Theo and Jackson to hide behind.

She wasn't sure what her alcohol tolerance was, but at this point, she had surely surpassed it. Everything in her was telling her to stop drinking, yet every time they came back with more, she couldn't say no.

The conversations were flowing faster than the drinks. She had not known these men for the better part of an hour yet already felt as though they had been friends for years.

Cambria had never experienced anything quite like this before.

Normally, when she met someone new, there was the awkward dance of small talk and sidestepping questions. But nothing about this interaction felt awkward. If anything, she found herself more than willing to pour her heart out to these two strangers whom she just met. She felt a familiarity with them that she could not explain.

But most importantly, she felt comfortable with them. Comfortable, at ease, and at home.

That night was a hazy blur—tequila, arm-wrestling, laughing, dancing. It was like looking through a kaleidoscope, everything distorted, but in the loveliest of ways. When she looked at Theo and Jackson, she really *saw* them. Everything made sense in her head. She felt seen and understood. Theo's hand on his cold beer. Jackson setting down three shot glasses, smirking at her, testing her, seeing if she'd do another.

Theo's hand in hers as he pulled her onto the dancefloor and spun her around. How everything else blurred, and she could see nothing but him.

It was two in the morning when they left the bar, Cambria and Theo. It wasn't something they discussed, rather, something that just happened. As if they did this all the time.

The air outside was warm and inviting. Theo led the way as he hailed a cab and they got inside. Three blocks north, two blocks south, then she lost track. Eventually the cab pulled up to a condo and Theo handed him cash.

After climbing nine flights of stairs (the elevator was down), they reached Theo's place, at last. He unlocked the door, and she followed him in. He quickly surveyed the space, then tossed some clothes into the bedroom and placed a few dishes in the sink. "Sorry," he said as they sat on the sofa. "I don't normally bring people back here."

"By *people*, you mean women."

"Well, yes."

"I find that extremely hard to believe."

He held her gaze. "Why do you say that?"

"Have you looked at yourself?"

He laughed. "Stop."

"I'm serious. Surely you have girls flitting in and out of here all the time."

He found this amusing. "I really don't. You're the first one in… well, some time."

This, she found even more hard to believe. "You're doing things to my head," she laughed.

"Am I?"

She studied him. "Why is that? That you don't bring women home often."

"I don't know. I guess I take this kind of thing seriously."

"So it's me, then."

"Yes." He held her gaze. "There's something different about you. I can't quite put my finger on it."

"I'm not anything special."

"Don't be modest."

She was quiet for a moment. "I don't normally do this sort of thing either."

"What changed your mind?"

She titled her head slightly, observing him. "You."

His eyes were intense on hers. "Tell me something," he said.

"Like what?"

"Anything."

She thought about this. "I've never been to the mountains."

"The mountains," he repeated. "You want to?"

"Yes. Very much so."

He smiled at this. "I'll take you."

"I don't even know you."

"That's not true. I think we know each other quite well at this point, wouldn't you say?"

This made her smile. "Touché."

"There's still one question you haven't answered."

"And what's that?"

"Why you came here. To Pine Hills."

With a look of satisfaction, she smiled at him. "Prepare to be disappointed, then."

"Why?"

"Because," she said. "I haven't even figured that out myself."

FOUR

As the days went by, Cambria felt herself getting more adjusted in Pine Hills. The streets that once confused her she now understood. She'd become familiarized with the coffee shop down the street from her building, using this as an excuse to get out each morning.

And each morning, she would think the same thing: This is my life now.

That night at Theo's didn't go quite as she expected.

They talked well into the early hours of morning, drinking each other's words. He was just as enthralled by her as she was with him. But around six a.m. when she returned from the bathroom, he was sound asleep.

She covered him with a blanket, then did her best to tidy up, moving their half empty glasses and still-full bowl of chips into the kitchen. She took one last glance at him before slipping out, just as the sun was beginning to rise.

It was as she was down the street, trying to navigate her way home, that she realized two things. The first was that she didn't have a clue where she was or how to get home. The second was that she had no way to contact him.

They never exchanged numbers.

The most perfect night, and that would be the end of it.

As she made her way home that morning, something on the ground caught her eye. She bent down and picked it up, inspecting it between her fingers. It was a man's ring, plain gold band, with a date engraved on the inside: *IV. XXIII. MCMLIX.*

She looked up and surveyed the area. The streets were desolate at this time. Nobody was scouring the ground, searching for a ring.

Not wanting to just leave it there, she pocketed the ring, hoping she could eventually find whoever it belonged to.

Her weekend consisted of running errands. She stocked the fridge with fresh produce. She took the bus downtown and found a furniture store, buying herself a new lamp and coffee table. She cleaned her apartment, took out the garbage. She even went for a run by the water.

It was as she was here, taking in the view, that she felt herself missing home for the first time.

Cambria had, for her whole life, relished being near water; it felt like home. No matter where she went, she would always find herself back here inexplicably. A homing pigeon, coming back to the same spot.

Her mind flashed to a time of the past: running across the beach, stripping off her clothes, diving in headfirst; her body submerged beneath the icy water.

She closed her eyes and felt the breeze on her skin. There was a calming presence, being here. When the silence is so loud it screams at you, the only noise you hear is the waves crashing into shore.

She'd choose this over city life any day.

Monday morning arrived like an anxiety attack. Cambria was looking forward to finally getting a paycheck, but she was nervous as hell to start all over again.

Only a fifteen-minute bus ride from her apartment, Hargrove & Swanson's Pine Hill location was smaller than she imagined. It was still glorious, nonetheless. Four floors of office space as well as the manufacturing facility. Her itinerary began with a tour of the building. She, along with the rest of the new hires, attended an introductory session on the inception of Hargrove & Swanson. It was after this that they were shown to their departments to begin training.

Back at home, Cambria worked as a bookkeeper at the library. It was the first job she could find after graduating university. And while she had no complaints, she also knew that it wasn't sustainable.

Her duties at H&S consisted of receiving customer data, medical histories, and account information, and inputting it to the system. It wasn't difficult to adjust to her new role. Once she got the hang of it, she felt herself enjoying it.

It was after lunch, as she was making her way to the elevator, that she saw him. She almost didn't recognize him, considering last time they'd seen each other she was seeing double.

"Jackson!" she called, getting his attention. He looked far too professional in his office attire.

"Girl from Friday!" he saw her and made his way over. "What are you doing here?"

"I work here. Well, today's my first day."

"You're kidding. What are the chances?"

"You didn't mention that you work here."

"I guess it never came up."

"Maybe it did and we both forgot," Cambria laughed. "Enough tequila will do that to me."

"You're probably right on that."

"Small world," she remarked.

"What department are you in?"

"Admin Services. Yourself?"

"Marketing."

"How long have you worked here?"

"Just over a year. It wasn't the job I was looking for—it kind of fell into my lap. How are you liking it? How's your first day?"

"No complaints so far. Everyone's been super nice."

"Yeah, the people are great." He checked his watch. "Listen, I have a meeting to get to, but come find me once the day is done, we should grab dinner. I'm on the fourth floor, near the windows."

"Okay, sure. I'll see you then."

"And—sorry—what's your name again?"

"Wowwww, you forgot already? Wasn't it you who was complimenting my name?"

"Cambria."

She smiled. "I knew you'd remember."

She spent the remainder of the day biding her time until five o'clock, wondering what dinner with Jackson entailed.

When the day was over she found him at his desk, and they made their way downstairs to the parking lot. He drove a red 1988 Mercedes, which wasn't surprising. It had been gifted to him by his parents on his last birthday. When he asked her what she liked to eat, she replied, "anything."

They ended up at a pub on Third, Jackson holding the door open as they crossed the threshold. He was greeted—by name—by nearly every patron they passed on their way to the table. "Come here often?" she asked.

They each ordered a burger and fries with milkshakes, Jackson informing her that they're the best in town. She dipped a fry in her milkshake, then took a bite of her burger.

"How many people have you slept with?" was the first thing he said to her.

She nearly choked. "*What?*"

He stared at her blankly, then repeated the question, slower this time, as if that made a difference.

"Do I have to answer that?"

"No." He took a drink from his milkshake.

She raised an eyebrow. "How many people have *you* slept with?"

"Thirty-seven."

"Actually?"

"No."

Frowning, she said, "well are you going to tell me the real answer?"

"No."

She furrowed her eyebrows even more.

"I'll tell you mine if you tell me yours," he said.

"Aren't you curious."

She had him there. "Fine," he dipped a fry in ketchup. "I don't even know, to be completely honest."

"You've lost track?"

He didn't respond, choosing instead to take an enormous bite of his burger.

"Why do you think that is?" she asked him.

"Irrelevancy," he said with his mouth full.

She laughed at this, finding it amusing. "Why do you sleep with so many people?"

He swallowed. "Good question."

It was silent as he continued to chew. "You don't know?" she asked.

He swallowed again, then set his milkshake on the table and focused his attention on her. "I think because it makes me feel good. Makes me feel… wanted. You like feeling wanted?"

"Who doesn't?"

"Exactly." He sat back in his chair. "Did you have fun with Theo the other night?"

She held his gaze, unsure what he knew. "I did. And you too, of course."

"I meant after."

She didn't know how to respond. "How do you two know each other again?"

"We've been friends since high school."

"Right. You're very similar."

"You think?"

"Yeah, you're like two peas in a pod."

"It's funny you say that—I don't think Theo and I are alike at all."

"Really?"

"Not at all."

"Then why do you get along so well?"

"Don't you know? Opposites attract."

"You guys are *not* opposites."

"If you think that, you clearly don't know either of us."

She held his gaze a moment. "Okay. Fair."

"Are you seeing him again?" he asked.

"No, actually. I have no way of contacting him."

"He didn't give you his number? That's surprising."

"He fell asleep. On the couch. We spent all night talking. I didn't want to wake him, so I left. And it wasn't until I was on my way home that I realized." For some reason, Jackson seemed satisfied at hearing this. That was, until, Cambria said, "You could give me his number…?"

He held her gaze. "You'd want that? To see him again?"

"Yes. I think I would."

"Alright," he said. "I can hook you guys up."

She smiled, pleased with herself. "Thanks. Oh, by the way, take a look at this." She dug through her purse until she found the ring, then set it on the table between them. "I found this on the sidewalk Saturday morning while I was walking home."

Jackson picked it up, inspecting it in his fingers. "Looks expensive."

"Look on the inside."

Jackson brought it closer to his face and squinted. "April twenty-third, 1959." He looked at her. "Probably someone's wedding ring."

"Yeah, seems like it."

He handed it back to her. "You gunna turn it in to lost and found?"

"I wish. I've got no clue what to do with it."

"Keep it," he said. "It's yours now."

"And what am I supposed to do with a man's wedding ring?"

"Give it to your future husband," he told her. "When you find him, of course."

Jackson Harding was fascinating. But more importantly, he felt inexplicably familiar—something she had never experienced with someone she'd just met.

He shared stories; she shared secrets. She told him everything without holding back, and somehow, even this early, she knew he would not cast judgment.

He made her feel understood. He made her feel *accepted.*

Jackson had two brothers and a sister. His parents came from old money. He grew up getting nearly everything he asked for. He loved his job, but his true passions were cars and music—he could tell you almost anything about either.

Everything he said was delivered with such certainty. Cambria felt that Jackson could talk her into almost anything. If he had a strong enough argument for why she should jump off a bridge, she'd probably do it.

Jackson was intelligent but egotistical. You could hear it in what he said—and in what he didn't. He was confident, funny, carefree, and well put-together. He could walk into a room and command everyone's attention. And he could converse for hours—a skill Cambria envied, given that she struggled with basic socializing. She constantly over-anticipated what words would come next, focusing more on what was coming than what was actually being said. And then there was her crippling fear of silence. Silence between two people should never be loud.

And somehow, she had not met a single person who let her speak as freely and for as long as Jackson did.

She was, dare I say, enraptured.

And the best part? He seemed just as intrigued with her as she was with him—which baffled Cambria, given that he was a somebody, and she was a nobody.

"I feel like I already know you," she said to him suddenly. "Or, have known you. Does that sound weird?"

"Not at all," he replied. "Because I was thinking the exact same thing."

Jackson paid for their food, and they left the pub. He told her having the grand tour of the city was a mandatory part of her initiation. "And your ever-so-knowledgeable—and attractive—tour guide, is moi."

The city wasn't huge—it had a population of 120,000—but there was plenty of land to cover.

They started in the city center, then made their way outwards to the suburbs. Each neighborhood they passed came with a story from Jackson's past. He showed her his old elementary school, and high school. He showed her where he and his friends used to drink, as well as the parking lot where he lost his virginity. After an hour of driving, they ended up at the waterfront. It was interesting that he, too, seemed to gravitate here.

"We used to have bonfires down here," Jackson explained as they parked the car and got out. "We'd pick up a case of beer, smoke some weed. Spend entire evenings down here as if it were home. I'd bring my guitar, and I'd play that thing for hours."

"Do you still play?"

"Sometimes. Not really."

"How come?"

He shrugged. "Things aren't like they used to be."

They ended up at an abandoned house. He told her about an older couple that once lived here. The city had been trying to get them to sell for years. They owned all the land in this area, and developers wanted to tear it down and build a neighborhood. But they never could, because the couple remained adamant on preserving the land.

Once the wife died, his children pleaded with him to sell and take the profit, but the man refused.

He eventually passed, and everyone expected the land to be torn down for construction to begin. However, what nobody knew was that the man had privately allocated ownership to a conservation group. They then took the necessary steps to ensure the land could not be touched.

"Do you want to go inside?" he asked her.

"Absolutely." She followed close behind him as they made their way to the side of the house, where there was an opening for them to get through.

Thc placc was a disastcr. Dust and dcbris covcrcd thc floor, along with wooden boards with rusty nails sticking out. The walls were marked with graffiti. In the corner were blankets and pillows. "Who comes here?" she asked.

"Different people. All looking for the same thing, I presume."

"What's that?"

"Solitude."

She took in her surroundings. "Do you ever come here?"

"No. I haven't been here in a long time. But I wanted you to see it." He looked at her. "What do you think?"

"It's… interesting."

"You haven't seen the best part."

"What could possibly be better than this?" She gestured around them.

He smirked and turned on his heel, heading up the stairs. Cambria followed him. They reached the master bedroom, and it somehow remained more preserved than downstairs. There was a bed against the back wall, curtains over the window. "This place was beautiful, once upon a time." He turned to face her. "Humans destroy everything."

"Were his children angry?" she asked. "That he didn't sell?"

"Extremely." Jackson walked across the room to the window. "I get it, they wanted the money. And it was a lot. But," he looked at her again. "I get it from his side too. And I think, if I were him, I would've done the same thing. Because at the end of your life, money means nothing."

She walked over to him. "I heard this quote once," she said. "*At the end of the day, the king and the pawn go in the same box*."

"It's true," he said, then looked out the window towards the night sky. She followed his line of vision. "See that star over there?" he asked, pointing.

"Yes."

"That's Polaris."

"The North Star."

He looked at her. "You're familiar with it?"

"Not really. But my—" she stopped.

He squinted his eyes. "What?"

"Nothing."

"What, your ex was into astrology?"

"Ha, no. But I do know that it's the forty-fifth brightest star in the night sky. It's been used as a navigational tool in the northern hemisphere for centuries."

"Good on you."

She returned her attention to the sky. "It's beautiful."

His attention remained on her. "So are you."

She could feel his eyes on her, burning into her skin. Finally, she turned and met his gaze. The look on his face was steadfast and unrelenting. They remained this way for a moment, neither breaking away.

They were communicating, though no words were exchanged.

Then he said, "you probably already know what I'm going to say."

She was quiet a moment. "No, I really don't." But she did.

"Can I kiss you?"

She looked away, facing the night sky once again. She located the star. "I shouldn't," she said. "Theo."

He nodded once, then turned to face the sky as well. "Fair enough. He did get to you first, after all."

She faced him again. "I like you, Jackson. I think we'd make great friends."

"Friends," he repeated. "Okay, deal."

And just like that, their night came to an end. They headed back down the old, rickety stairs in which they came, out into the cool evening air. They drove off in his car, and Cambria took one last look at the house, shrinking in size the further they got. Then she looked at Jackson. And it is there where her eyes remained.

CAMBRIA

FIVE

Tuesday evening, she stood in her kitchen, staring at the phone on the wall, willing herself to pick it up and dial the number.

She wasn't sure why she was so hesitant. If his willingness to bring her back to his place was any indication of his interest in her, then she had nothing to be worried about. Yet still, she couldn't bring herself to pick up the phone.

Just then, it rang, startling her. She picked it up.

"Did you call him yet?" It was Jackson's voice on the other end.

"You just about gave me a heart attack."

"I tend to have that affect on women."

She rolled her eyes. "I was just about to. Or—was trying to."

"What do you mean *trying*? It's not that hard to make a phone call."

"Apparently it is."

"Why?"

"I don't know. I'm nervous."

"Why are you nervous?"

"Because I'm an insane person."

"You have nothing to be worried about."

"What do I even say?"

"Ask him if he wants to see you again."

"What if he doesn't?"

"Shut up. Call me when its done."

"Okay. Wish me luck."

"You don't need it."

She hung up the phone, took a deep breath, then picked it up again and dialed Theo's number.

Just when she thought there would be no answer, he picked up. "Hello?"

"Hi, Theo?"

"Yes…?"

"It's Cambria. How are you?"

"Cambria? Hey. I'm good. Sorry, wow—I'm surprised to be hearing from you right now."

"I got your number from Jackson. I hope that's okay."

"Jackson?"

"Turns out we work together."

"No way. What a small world."

"Yeah, crazy right?"

"And you thought to ask him for my number?"

"Well, yes. I didn't realize until after I left your place that I had no way of contacting you."

"I woke up and you were gone."

"You fell asleep."

"I'm an idiot."

"You're not. It happens. I could tell you were tired."

"I can't believe you called. I've been beating myself up over it, thinking I let you slip away all because I couldn't stay awake."

"I guess it's a good thing I ran into Jackson then."

"Yeah, thank God for Jackson. Never thought I'd hear myself saying that."

"I really did have a good time with you Friday night."

"Me too," he said. "I'd love to see you again, if you'd want that."

"I'd love that."

"Are you doing anything this Friday?"

"I am doing nothing at all this Friday."

"How would you like to come to a party with me?"

"A party sounds fun."

"Great, I'll pick you up for eight. What's your address?"

Friday seemed an eternity away.

Nonetheless, her first week at Hargrove & Swanson went well. She ate lunch with Jackson in the cafeteria every day. It was nice to have someone there that she knew, a comfort to her she didn't realize she needed. They were quickly becoming fast friends, already interrupting and talking over each other, unable to get their words out fast enough.

They did not once speak about Theo.

When Friday arrived, he stayed true to his word and picked her up at eight. His car smelt of aftershave and cologne. He looked different than she remembered—better.

They arrived at Grayson Welch's house, a close friend of Theo's. It was a large, stunning home that immediately captivated her. They parked on the street among other lined-up cars and made their way to the front door, where Theo pushed it open without knocking. Cambria was instantly overwhelmed by the sheer number of people inside. Sensing her discomfort, he took her hand and led her through the crowd until they reached the kitchen.

The kitchen was even more beautiful than the rest of the house. A marble island countertop stood in the center, cluttered with red solo cups. A double-decker oven gleamed nearby, as well as a refrigerator larger than her closet. In fact, the kitchen alone was bigger than her entire apartment. She looked around as Theo poured them both drinks. He handed her a cup, and she took a sip, eyes wandering as she took in the lively room around her.

"I want you to meet Grayson," Theo said. "Stay here." He took off and left her standing alone at the island. She took this as an opportunity to pour herself a shot of tequila.

Theo returned a moment later, his friend in tow. "Cambria, this is Grayson. Grayson, Cambria."

They shook hands. "I've heard great things," Grayson said to her.

"I wouldn't take his word for it," she replied.

"Can I join you on that?" Theo nodded to her shot glass.

"Absolutely. Grayson, you too?"

"I don't drink."

"He's joking," Theo told her. "Grayson's an alcoholic."

"It runs in the family," he grabbed two more shot glasses and filled them. "Lime?"

Theo plucked a slice from his fingers and handed it to Cambria. She licked her hand, then poured some salt. The three of them clinked their glasses together, then took the shot.

Grayson wiped his mouth with the back of his hand. "Have you met my snake?"

"You have a snake?"

Just then the backdoor opened, revealing a cluster of people smoking on the balcony. And there was Jackson. "Cambria?" he looked taken aback. His eyes flickered from her to Theo. "I didn't know you were coming tonight."

"Cambria didn't mention it?" Theo said to him.

"I guess it never came up," she said.

Jackson stubbed out his cigarette and walked inside. "Surely you're going to take this girl on a proper date."

"I'll take her wherever she wants."

Cambria looked from Jackson to Theo, Theo to Jackson. Did Theo know that Jackson had asked to kiss her?

Surely not. She doubted Jackson would have said anything.

Unless he did?

"Anyways, I'll let you two get acquainted," Jackson said, patting Theo on the shoulder as he passed. Cambria sensed a hint of condescension. "Catch you guys later."

As Grayson promised, Cambria met the snake: a Ball Python named Fendi. She was a crowd pleaser at parties. Everyone seemed to adore Fendi. Cambria watched as the snake was passed to one of the girls. Fendi coiled around her arm, wrapping its body gently around her neck. The girl nestled into the snake, placing a kiss on its head.

Meanwhile, out in the backyard, people were removing their clothes and jumping off the balcony into the pool.

Theo had left her to her own devices, and she found herself strangely lost without him. She didn't know a single person here, aside from Jackson, but she had no idea where he was. And as much as she wanted to socialize, she was afraid.

She found herself amongst a crowd of girls who were smoking joints and taking shots. A girl with white-blond hair pulled into a tight ponytail was pouring Cîroc into people's cups. Cambria shook her head and declined.

"Do I know you?" the girl asked her.

"I don't think so."

"What's your name?"

"Cambria."

"I'm Naomi," she flashed her a kind smile. "Have some."

"Okay." She lifted her cup and Naomi filled it.

"You came with Theo, right?"

Cambria took a drink, cringed, lowered it. "Yes."

"How do you know each other?"

Suddenly, she realized, everyone in the group was staring at her. "We met at The Tap. Last Friday." Having everyone's eyes on her made her uncomfortable.

"Are you dating?" one of the other girls asked.

"Um, I don't know," Cambria replied. "I think we're just hanging out for now."

"You're really pretty."

She was overwhelmed. "Thank you."

"What do you think so far?" Naomi asked. "Of Theo."

"He's really nice," Cambria blushed. "I like him."

"Can you see yourself in a relationship with him?" Naomi continued.

The question caught her off guard.

"Don't ask her that," from one of the others. "She barely knows him."

"True," Naomi said. "Well, his last girlfriend was a psychotic cunt who cheated on him, so I'm sure he can only go up from there."

"When was that?" Cambria asked.

"A few months ago, maybe? It's hard to keep track when it comes to Theo."

"Really?" Cambria said. "He made it seem like the opposite."

"Theo? Please. He's a Casanova. But he's too modest, he'd never admit it."

"He's not that special," from one of the other girls.

"You're just bitter because he turned you down," Naomi laughed. "Several times."

"It was *twice*. Two times."

"Still more than once."

Cambria excused herself from the group and made her way to the kitchen, looking for Theo. She continued her search throughout the house but came up blank.

She approached a group of people who were gathered around a keg-stand, asking if they'd seen him. "I think he went out front," someone told her.

Thanking them, Cambria turned and made her way to the front door. She pulled it open just in time to see Theo remove a cigarette from another girl's mouth and put it in his.

Without a word, Cambria closed the door and retreated inside. Somehow, the house felt safer than it did out there. But she didn't know anyone, all these people were strangers to her.

She needed Jackson.

Jackson, who had serendipitously become an integral presence in her life here. Who had taken her under his wing and given her the grand tour to Pine Hills. Who had been more than kind, more than welcoming, and more than apparent in his intentions with her. And yet for some reason, Cambria had chosen Theo.

Had she made the wrong choice?

She went to the backyard. Out onto the balcony, down the steps. And there she found him. But it was too late.

He sat shirtless at the edge of the pool, dripping wet. And on his lap was a girl with dark hair the color of charcoal, dressed only in her bra and underwear, equally as wet, her lips pressed to Jackson's.

CAMBRIA

SIX

Cambria stood there observing the scene in front of her, momentarily stunned. So much had unfolded in the short span of not even ten minutes and she was trying to process it all. The conversation with Naomi, followed by Theo sharing an intimate moment with a girl out front. And then the icing on the cake: Jackson, poolside, making out with some girl.

Before they could see her, she turned and made her way back up the steps, returning to the safety of the kitchen. She needed to leave. She needed to be home.

She was almost at the front door when he intercepted her. "I've been looking for you," said Theo. "Where'd you go?"

"I needed air."

"Can we talk?"

"I'd like to leave."

He stared at her. "Let me explain. It's not what it looks like."

"It's fine, Theo. I just want to go home."

"We were just having a cigarette. That's all."

"You can do whatever you like. We're not dating."

He made a face. "Why would you say that?"

"Because it's true. If you want to talk to other girls, you can."

"I don't want to talk to other girls. I want to talk to *you*. I came here with *you*."

She held his gaze, unwavering.

"I'm sorry for leaving you," he continued. "I shouldn't have done that. But she's just a friend. I promise I won't leave you again. Are you okay?"

"I'm fine."

"How much have you had to drink?"

"Too much."

"Okay. I can either take you home, or you can go upstairs to the spare bedroom and lie down, since I'm not really in a state to drive right now."

He didn't really give her much of a choice.

Together, they ascended the stairs to the second floor. Theo led the way, down the hall, to a vacant bedroom. He turned on the bedside lamp, then left to fetch her some water. When he returned, she was lying down, already on the fringes of sleep.

When she awoke an hour later, she felt sober and clear-minded. She spotted Theo in the corner of the room, slumped against the wall, asleep.

She sat up slowly, then reached for the glass of water he had left for her on the nightstand. Once she had quenched her thirst, she stood and made her way to Theo, kneeling in front of him.

She took this as an opportunity to study his face. He looked so tranquil. How could she stay mad at him? It was a misunderstanding.

Gently, she woke him.

His eyes opened and found hers. "Am I in heaven?" he said.

She laughed modestly.

"Are you an angel?"

"Good morning to you too."

"What time is it?"

"Almost two."

He rubbed his eyes and sat up. "How are you feeling? Better?"

"Yes."

"Good. I was worried about you."

They both stood.

Once they were face-to-face, Cambria said, "How many girls have you been with?"

He blinked. "What?"

"You told me you don't do this often."

"I don't."

"That's not what I heard."

"Who told you that? Naomi?"

Cambria didn't respond.

"Don't listen to them, all they do is gossip. I wouldn't believe anything they told you."

"Even that you were cheated on?"

He pursed his lips together. "She said that?"

"Yes."

He shook his head. "Yeah, it ended pretty badly."

"I'm sorry."

"Not really something I want to be discussing at this very moment," he scratched the back of his head. "I'd rather just focus on you. Are we good?"

"We're good."

"Okay, good. I'm sorry again."

"You don't have to apologize. I get it."

He smiled, then put his hand out for her to take. "Shall we?"

They made their way downstairs, where the crowds of people had significantly thinned. He brought her to the kitchen and got her another glass of water. She perched herself on one of the barstools while Theo began rummaging through the cupboards.

Grayson appeared with his girlfriend, Meredith. "Looking for something, Boudreau?"

Theo turned to face him. "Do you not have any food in here?"

"Should be leftover pizza in the fridge." Grayson slid into the seat next to her, adjusting Meredith on his lap. "Cambria, darling, you good?"

"I'm fine, thanks," she gave him a smile and took another drink of water.

"Did you have a good night?" Meredith asked. "You disappeared for a bit there."

"She had a bit too much to drink," Theo said as he sat down with the pizza box. He opened it and handed her a slice.

"Happens to the best of us," Grayson reassured her. "As long as we didn't scare you off."

"No, not at all," Cambria said. "You guys are great."

The back door opened and a few more people sauntered in, Jackson amongst them. The girl from the pool was hanging off his arm. He immediately locked eyes with Cambria.

"There you are," Grayson remarked as Jackson approached. "Heard you almost broke your neck."

"I think that's a grave exaggeration." Jackson pulled out a chair, took a seat, pulled the girl onto his lap. Cambria felt something inside her stir.

"And who do we have here?" Theo asked between bites.

"This is Natalia," Jackson said.

"Natalia, pleasure to meet you—I'm Theo. And this is Cambria."

"Hi," the girl said.

"Hi," Cambria replied.

"How'd you get duped into being Jackson's plus-one?" Theo pressed.

She laughed, a deep, raspy laugh. "No duping required. I'm happy to be here."

"Where'd you find this one again?" asked Grayson. He had just opened another beer.

"At Tap," Jackson said. "Last Friday."

Cambria looked at him inquisitively. He caught her eye and held it. She had this peculiar feeling that nothing was going how it should be.

The conversation continued, and Cambria tried to act normal, feel normal. But she could not be placated.

She looked at Natalia once more and felt the unease growing. This didn't seem right. Everything felt off. And then there was Jackson, who kept looking at Cambria as though he were speaking to her in a language she did not yet understand.

The night finally concluded just after three. Theo was sober enough to drive at that point, so he and Cambria said goodbye and headed out.

"Thank you for coming tonight," he said as they idled outside her building.

"Thank you for bringing me. I had a good time."

"Did you, though?"

She laughed. "For the most part, yes. Your friends are really sweet."

"Grayson's the best. You're going to love him."

"I believe that."

"And about earlier… We're okay?"

"Yes, we're okay. I just want you to be honest with me."

"And I have been. You can disregard anything else Naomi told you. Trust me on that."

"Okay."

"I like you, Cambria. I don't want to mess this up."

"I like you too."

He gave her a soft smile. "I'd really like to kiss you now."

She blushed. "Then kiss me."

She couldn't remember the last time she'd been kissed.

SEVEN

Cambria's history with love had been… how do I say this?

Non-existent.

She was twenty-two years old and had never truly been in love. Okay, she'd sort of been in love. When she was in high school she fell in love with her guy best friend. Whether he also considered her his best friend was debatable. But he was funny, and sweet, and kind. He was a bit dorky but also hot. He was charming, and polite, and respectful—everything a mom would want in a son-in-law. He played lacrosse but was also captain of the debate team. He hosted an annual camping trip each summer. And he was smart! He wanted to be a lawyer, or a pilot. Cambria fell head over heels for him. It took her six months to decide if she should tell him or not. But she'd once heard someone in a movie say that you should always tell people how you feel, before it's too late. And because that sentiment hit a little too close to home for Cambria, she gathered all the courage her little body could carry and she told him how she felt.

He rejected her, of course. Okay, reject is a harsh word. But he didn't feel the same way, and that was basically the same thing.

Cambria never spoke to him again.

She also believed she had been in love with this boy from middle school who had basically the same effect on her. But it's so hard to tell when you're that young. She knew she was infatuated, that's for sure. She had heard a quote somewhere that said if you have a crush that lasts over three months, it means you're in love. So, by that standard, she was definitely in love with both of them.

Cambria had never been sure what she wanted in life, in terms of a partner. People made everything seem so straightforward. You meet someone, get married, buy a house, have a baby. But as she got older, she realized how intangible this was.

How was she supposed to meet someone let alone get married?

She believed she was destined to be alone forever.

But now, for the first time in a long time, Cambria felt herself opening up to the idea of love. She had become so accustomed to being alone that she had memorized the sound of silence. She had forgotten what it was like to be so infatuated with someone that her stomach fluttered at the mere thought of them, when sleepless nights were spent thinking only of them.

Cambria had never been one to fall fast, but she could feel herself falling for Theo. He was intoxicating. But along with all these new and exciting emotions came the feeling of uncertainty and trepidation. As much as she wanted to let go and fall completely, she was hesitant, fearing the worst: that his feelings weren't reciprocated in the same way. That he would get bored and leave. It had been a long time since she'd let anyone in, and she was scared of getting hurt.

But she was tired of being alone. She longed for the company of another. A hand to hold, a kiss to anticipate. And Theo was all those things. He was hope and eagerness and relief.

After Grayson's party, they began seeing each other regularly. Coffee dates and dinner dates; nights spent at his place. She'd wake up in the mornings, his side of the bed still warm. She'd roll onto her back and stare up at the ceiling, smiling to herself.

He was so careful with her, as though she were glass. Tentative hands soon became eager, and with time, a warm familiarity blossomed between them. She found herself anticipating the feel of his lips on hers, spending her days lost in daydreams of only him. At night, she'd be back at his place, back to the comfort of his bed. That was all that mattered to her—the feeling of being wanted by him.

What Cambria liked most about Theo was that he was intelligent, and he was kind. She found herself getting lost in his words, mesmerized by the cadence of his voice.

But most of all, her favorite thing about Theo wasn't what he did or said, but rather, how he made her feel.

The demands of Theo's work schedule as an electrical apprentice were unpredictable and challenging. His hours changed daily and weekly—some days he started early and finished by afternoon, while other shifts began in the evening and stretched through the night. This made coordinating their time together a constant challenge.

While this was all happening with Theo, there was something happening with Jackson too—a friendship.

They had spent nearly every day together since she started at Hargrove & Swanson. Most days they'd go out for lunch together, equally as agreeable to getting pitas. Sometimes they'd go to a restaurant, other times they'd grab takeout and eat in his car. Cambria began noticing they had all the same favorite foods. No matter the day, they always agreed on a spot.

Jackson was perpetually in a good mood. In fact, in the few weeks that she'd known him, Cambria had not seen him falter even once. And best of all, his mood was contagious. If Cambria was feeling sad or having a bad day, she knew, without a doubt, Jackson would cheer her up.

He was always trying to make her laugh, and she knew he felt satisfaction when he did, but she also knew she was funnier. He was witty and sardonic, but so was she, and therefore, they bantered well together. They had the same fucked up sense of humor.

Sometimes it felt like he could read her mind, saying something just before she had the chance. They'd cut each other off, talk over one another, finish each other's sentences.

Cambria didn't feel this way about Mara. Mara also didn't banter with her like Jackson did. Everything with Jackson was so easy, she never even had to try.

After weeks of casually hanging out during and after work, he finally invited her to his house to meet his family.

If Cambria thought Grayson's house was impressive, then Jackson's house was something else entirely. She knew his parents came from money, but she wasn't expecting this.

She came from a middle-class household. Her parents had decent paying jobs, but their salaries weren't extravagant. Her house was quaint and average. She could sneak out the window of her second-story bedroom no problem. She had memorized every creak in the floorboards and could navigate the entire thing with her eyes closed. Jackson's house, on the other hand, looked like it required its own navigational system.

They got out of the car, and she followed Jackson up the front steps. Inside, Cambria took in the spacious foyer with its fifteen-foot ceilings. Around them were elegantly furnished living and sitting rooms, with a glimpse of the kitchen down the hall. Directly ahead, a spiral staircase curved gracefully both upstairs and below. She turned to face him. "You didn't tell me you were rich."

"I'm not rich," he said. "My parents are rich."

He brought her to the kitchen, where his mother stood at the island chopping vegetables, and his father sat at the table drinking something dark. "This is Cambria," Jackson announced. "The girl I told you about."

"Which one?" his father said at the same time his mother beamed, "the infamous Cambria." She placed the knife on the counter and grabbed a towel to dry her hands.

Cambria grinned. "Infamous? Is he that obsessed with me?"

His father barked out a laugh and his mother smirked. "You're funny."

"As if," Jackson said. "It's the other way around."

"Oh, yeah, you wish," Cambria countered.

"It was you who stalked me to my place of work."

"Oh, shut up," she quipped. Then to his mother she said, "he's so annoying."

His mother raised her eyebrows—not quite *impressed*, per se. More like *intrigued.* "I'm Leanne, good to finally meet you. We've heard good things."

Cambria smirked at Jackson. "Your mother isn't really helping your case."

Jackson ignored her and went to the fridge.

"Your home is beautiful," Cambria said to Leanne.

"I'm Dave," his father had stood and walked over. "But seriously, which one are you?"

"Oh, would you stop?" Leanne said to him, then looked to Cambria. "Are you staying for dinner?"

"Uh," Cambria looked to Jackson, who was walking back over with two beers.

"Yes," he said.

"Yes," she smiled at Leanne.

"We're putting the barbeque on around seven."

"Alright, let's go," Jackson handed her a beer and walked off.

She smiled one last time at his parents, then followed him. "Your mom seems nice," she said once they got to his room. They sat on the couch and put their beers on the coffee table in front of them.

"I think she likes you."

"Really? You can tell?"

"Yeah. And my dad too."

Cambria felt smug. "You must bring so many girls back here."

"Yeah, sooo many. And I have sex with all of them right where you're sitting."

"You probably do," she said, grabbing her beer. "Do they all get an introduction to your parents like I do?"

"Yeah right."

"Are you still seeing whatshername?"

"Natalia," he said. "I see her occasionally."

"Is it serious?"

He shrugged. "I don't know."

Cambria took a drink. "You never told me you met her the same night you met me."

He raised his eyebrows but didn't respond, placing his beer back on the table.

"It was after, I presume," she continued. "Right?"

"Hmm?" he looked up at her.

"It was after. I left. That you met her."

"Yeah."

"Cool," Cambria nodded, looked at the wall, cleared her throat, looked at Jackson. "Hey, can I ask you a question about Theo or is that weird?"

"That's weird."

Cambria sulked. "I guess I could just talk to Mara. She's probably better with this stuff anyways," she looked at him. "Like, girl talk, I mean. But I'd rather talk with you. Plus, you're friends with him."

"Do I *have* to?"

"Oh my God, can you just shut up? I need to talk." She paused for a moment, then looked at him. "Do you think he's into me?"

"Why are you asking me this?"

"Cause… I want to know what you think."

"Does he not seem into you?"

"I don't know. Yeah, I guess he does."

"Then what's the problem?"

"Has he said anything to you?"

"About what?"

"Me. Like, me and him."

"No? Why would he say anything?"

"I don't know—I guess guys don't talk about their feelings. But if you had to guess… you'd say he's into me?"

"How am I supposed to know that? Why don't you just ask him?"

"I'm not going to ask him—that's weird."

"Go ask Mara, then."

"He's just so confusing sometimes. Like, he acts all lovey dovey with me. But then says he's not looking for anything serious. And it's like… okay, who said I was? It's so hot and cold with him."

"That sounds like Theo."

"Really?"

"Yeah. He's a strange one."

"You're also a strange one."

"Well you *like* the strange ones," he winked.

At the dinner table, Cambria was introduced to Jackson's two brothers, Landon and Kyle, as well as his younger sister, Victoria, who was elated at her presence. "It's nice to have another girl around here," Victoria told her. "Too much testosterone."

"Three sons," Cambria remarked. "That must've been a lot growing up."

"Them?" Dave said. "They were angels."

"He's joking," Victoria told her. "They were devils."

"Speak for yourself," Kyle countered.

"Do you have any siblings?" Leanne asked Cambria.

"You must," Victoria chimed in. "I can tell."

The question caught her off guard. "Uh," she said. "I did."

The room went silent after that, no one sure how to respond.

They were parked at the beach; Jackson smoking a cigarette in the driver's seat. The sun had just dipped below the horizon and the sky was red. She could feel it in the air around them that the silence was loud. He was being respectful, but she knew he was waiting for her to say something.

"My brother killed himself," she finally said.

Jackson looked at her but remained silent, allowing her the time to speak.

"It was six years ago," she continued. "He had a lot of issues I guess you could say. He saw doctors and specialists, but no one could help him. I guess some people just can't be saved."

He waited a moment to ensure she was done before responding. "Were you close?"

"Um," she scratched her arm. "Not really."

"How'd he do it?"

"Overdose."

"Did he leave a note?"

"Yeah."

Jackson was quiet for a moment. "Is that why you don't do drugs?"

She didn't respond.

"My best friend killed himself," he told her.

She was quiet while she processed this. Then she looked at him, and he looked at her. "When?" she asked.

"Eight years ago. We were seventeen."

"How'd he do it?"

"Blew his brains out."

Cambria winced. "What was his name?"

"Trevor."

"Did you forgive him?"

"No. Did you forgive your brother?"

"There's nothing to forgive."

"How old was he?"

"Twenty-two," she said. "I was sixteen. Which means he would've been twenty-eight now."

"I'm sorry."

She shrugged, never sure how to respond when someone said that. "He's the one who was into astrology. He told me about Polaris."

"Oh."

"Yeah."

They were quiet again. Then Jackson said, "you're the same age now that he was when he died."

She nodded solemnly. "Yeah… I know."

She thought back to that morning two months ago, the morning of her twenty-second birthday, when she woke up and everything dawned on her.

She needed to leave.

She needed to *live.*

CAMBRIA

EIGHT

Rare was it to meet someone whose soul mirrored your own. With no one else could she slip into such comfortable silence. He was the only person with whom she could do nothing and still feel completely at ease.

With certainty, Cambria knew she could tell Jackson anything without fear of judgment. With him, she could let her guard down and simply be herself—her true, genuine self. Between them existed a likeness she found with no one else, and from that likeness grew trust and solidarity.

He became her sole confidant.

When they weren't together (which was scarcely), they were with their respective partners. Cambria couldn't understand why Jackson was with Natalia. She seemed like the type of girl he would avoid, not date. Yet still, his spare time that wasn't spent with Cambria was spent with her.

And then there was Theo. Due to his unpredictable schedule, Cambria never knew when she was going to see him. And when he wasn't working, he was at the gym. But when he'd have some consecutive days off, they'd spend them together.

A good majority of their time was spent in bed. She became addicted to him in the way all girls do when they're falling in love.

There were things she didn't know about him, but that was okay, because they were both still learning, and she understood that came with time. She did know a few things: his favorite color was green, he loved working out, his parents were divorced, and he didn't see much of his dad. She also knew his most prized possession was his car. She'd sit cross-legged on the grass, reading a book while he worked under the hood. He'd call her over and quiz her on the parts. She didn't know a thing about cars, and didn't care to learn, but she knew it made him happy. They went car shopping together, and he helped her choose a blue 1985 Honda Accord. The night she picked it up and got the keys, they drove for hours until the gas light came on, and she realized how liberating it was to just get in your car and drive.

He was always leaving at the crack of dawn for work, and despite how tired she was, she always woke up with him, not wanting to miss out on a single second. And the last thing she felt before her eyes closed and she drifted back to sleep was his lips on her forehead.

This was what she had been waiting for, yearning for—years spent wondering if she'd ever find it. And here it was at last: the delicacy, the intimacy, the reassurance that says, 'You are cared for. You are enough.'

But then came the droughts—the long stretches when he was elsewhere, out of town or on a job. And during those dry spells, Cambria sought solace elsewhere.

Eventually there came to be more time spent without Theo than there was with, and before she knew it, she was spending nearly all her waking hours with Jackson.

It was never difficult to find something to do because they had the same hobbies and interests. Anything that Cambria liked, Jackson liked. Albeit the two could watch paint dry and still be content together. Seldom did they disagree or argue. He was so easy to get along with, and sometimes she felt he were made just for her.

They went to Walmart and bought bicycles. After that they were relentless, taking their bikes anywhere and everywhere they could. She couldn't store it at her place, so she kept it at Jackson's. Not like she ever biked without him anyways.

Theo didn't understand the bike thing. "You have a car," he said. "Just use that."

"I don't want to use my car," she tried to explain. "I like cycling."

They did everything together. Movie nights on Tuesdays (Jackson always picked but she never complained). Concerts of all his favorite artists. Fairs and amusement parks, with popcorn and cotton candy, always. Fridays were for the pub. And then they started doing Wine Wednesdays. "You two drink too much," his mother remarked after they had just opened another bottle of cab sav.

"No we don't," Jackson said, turning to Cambria. "I don't think we drink enough, actually."

"I agree," Cambria said. "We hardly drink at all."

"I can't even recall the last time we drank," Jackson continued.

Leanne stared at them, unamused. "You were drinking last night."

"Yeah, but that was beer," Jackson said.

"Yeah, I don't think that counts," Cambria added.

"You're both alcoholics."

One night after too many drinks, they hailed a taxi and went back to Cambria's place. Jackson was barely able to get himself from the car to her apartment. Stumbling inside, she helped him walk to her bedroom. He collapsed on the bed, and she left to get him a glass of water and a cool cloth. When she returned, he was hugging both pillows to his chest, eyes closed.

She placed the water on the nightstand and started removing his shoes. Then she stood over him and placed the cloth on his forehead. He opened one eye and looked up at her.

"You alive?" she asked.

"I'm fine."

She laughed audibly. "You are far from fine, Jackson. What the hell is wrong with you? Do you not know your limits?"

"I know them," he said. "Very well."

"And yet…"

He didn't respond.

"What would your girlfriend say if she saw you right now?"

"You're my girlfriend."

"Shut up."

Jackson scarcely talked about Natalia. So scarcely, in fact, that Cambria nearly forgot she existed. It caught her off guard sometimes, the fact that he had a girlfriend. She had grown so used to sharing her daily life with him that it startled her to remember he also had other people and commitments.

He smirked. "You clean my room and wash my dishes. You take off my shoes and put cloths on my head. You're basically my girlfriend."

"You couldn't pay me to be your girlfriend."

"If monetary incentive is all it takes…"

She covered his face with the pillow, suffocating him. He knocked it away, staring up at her, grinning.

People often mistook them for a couple, and Cambria could see why—they did almost everything together. From Sunday barbeques with his family to Wine Wednesdays at her place, bike rides, and picnics at the lake. Just the other day they fell asleep outside after staying up until two in the morning having a bonfire in Jackson's backyard. They dozed off lying opposite each other, and Cambria woke to the sun rising, Jackson's feet in her face.

But to Cambria, all these things didn't feel romantic—they felt platonic, in the best way.

It was like having a brother all over again.

"It's crazy that we just met," Cambria said to Jackson. "It feels like I've known you since the beginning of time."

"Maybe you have."

"Do you believe in reincarnation? What if we knew each other in a past life?"

"With you I do."

"I've never believed in soulmates. But maybe soulmates aren't just lovers. Maybe soulmates can be best friends."

And that's exactly what Jackson was—her best friend.

NINE

What goes up must come down. And while Cambria knew that gravity could be a fickle thing, she never expected it to come as quickly as it did.

Theo called her over one Sunday afternoon in late August. She was sun-kissed and starry eyed from spending the weekend at Jackson's cottage with friends. Theo, as always, couldn't make it because of work. Cambria assumed the invitation to come over was to make up for lost time.

She was wrong.

Theo was leaving—moving four hours north for his job. The company was expanding, and he had been chosen as the first of many to relocate. It was a promising opportunity, but what did it mean for him and Cambria?

It meant they were done.

At first, she objected, insisting they could make it work despite the distance. But Theo disagreed. It was too far, he said, and he'd be too busy—no time for a girlfriend or a relationship. It wouldn't be fair to her; she deserved someone who could give her more. "Don't make this more difficult than it needs to be," he said to her, and she would always remember those words, the way he said it, so blasé, as if their time together hadn't meant anything at all. And how in that moment, she realized this was an entirely different conversation for him than it was for her.

"You know I care about you," he told her. "I wish you nothing but the best. And I hope we can still be friends."

Friends. As if Cambria could ever be friends with him. After all those mornings she woke up at dawn to see him. Midnights driving in his car. Laughing as they cooked together because Theo always managed to make a mess. Days on end spent in bed, the rest of the world disappeared. To be friends was an insult, and she didn't even want to bother trying.

Yet on the night before he left, she found herself at his place, once more, one last time. She told herself it was just to say goodbye, but she knew that wasn't true.

If anything, this was closure. Or perhaps that was just a lie she told herself.

The next morning, while he was still asleep, she collected her things, and without saying a word, slipped out the door, just as she had that very first night.

Theo's absence hit harder than she thought it would. The days dragged on, her thoughts occupied of nothing but him. Surely this was irrational. She didn't even spend this much time thinking about him when he was here, yet suddenly, as soon as he was gone, that was all she could think about. Theo and that look he would give her. Theo and his blue eyes. Theo and his hands around her waist.

She tortured herself, conjuring every memory she could. Her mind repeatedly went back to the night they met; how nervous he was to bring her home, talking on his couch until the early morning. And then everything that followed, cutting herself open to give him her heart.

As if he'd even want it.

She knew his facial features by heart, could recall them at any given time, memorized every crease and dimple. She could close her eyes and feel his hands on her skin, a phantom touch. His scent lingered on her duvet. And if she concentrated hard enough, she could still hear his voice.

They'd taken only one photo together, the solitary proof that he was here. She kept it in a book on her nightstand.

It was painstakingly obvious that Cambria was in love with Theo. Yet somehow the thought had never occurred to her until after he was gone.

It was also clear these feelings were not reciprocated. To Cambria, Theo was everything she'd been longing for. But to Theo, Cambria was nothing but a summer dalliance. Perhaps she had known this all along, but it was easier to pretend otherwise.

Cambria had wanted Jackson—needed Jackson—but he'd been busy with Natalia. Subjected to involuntary solitude and desperate for emotional support, Cambria had no other choice but to seek solace elsewhere, in Mara.

"He's nothing special," Mara told her as they sat on her bed eating a tub of ice-cream. "He's just a boy. You'll move on and be fine."

And while Cambria knew that was true, she also knew it would take somc timc to gct ovcr this onc.

"Will you miss him?" Cambria was lying on Jackson's bed, pillow to her chest, as he smoked a cigarette out the window. They had just finished dinner with his family, and the sun was beginning to set.

Jackson exhaled and turned to face her. "Yeah, I'll miss him."

"Do you think you'll stay in touch?"

"I doubt it. Theo doesn't seem like the type to stay in touch."

"That's disappointing."

Jackson took another drag and shrugged. "Yeah, well. What can you do?"

"You could go visit him."

"Maybe I'll do that. And bring you with me."

"No, thanks."

He laughed. "Are you *heartbroken*?"

"Fuck off."

Another drag. "He did a real number on you, didn't he?" She didn't respond. "Aw, do you love him?"

"Shut up."

"Do you?"

"I don't want to talk about this with you anymore."

"Why, because I'm right?"

"No, because you're being a dick."

"You need me."

"Mara was a better substitute."

"Oh, you were hanging out with *Mara*? *How was that?* Are you going to ditch me for her now?"

"She's nicer than you. And gives better advice."

"What advice did she give you?"

"I'm *not* talking about this with you."

"I thought girls liked to talk about this shit."

"Fuck off."

Jackson laughed and stubbed out his cigarette, joining her on the bed. "Who's your favorite person to hang out with?"

"You."

"Good."

"Isn't that obvious?"

"I guess it is."

"Unfortunately you can't say the same about me."

"What do you mean? Of course you're my favorite person to hang out with."

"Natalia."

He rolled his eyes. "She's been pissing me off lately."

"Trouble in paradise?" she raised one eyebrow. "Dare I ask?"

"It's always something with her. So melodramatic."

"I'm melodramatic and you still like me."

"Yeah, cause you're Cambri. You don't count."

She loved when he called her that. "I don't count? What does that mean?"

"That it's fine when you do it."

She smirked. "Cause I'm better?"

"Settle down."

"You know," she said, looking at him. "I feel the same way with you. You're the exception to every rule. Everyone pisses me off but you."

"That's cause I'm the best."

"You are. And cause you're my person."

He smiled at her. "You're my person too." He held her gaze for just a moment too long, then said, "You know what you need? To get drunk."

TEN

Each year at the end of September, Grayson Welch hosted his annual end of summer party. These parties were the talk of the town. Cambria heard rumors of previous years, things that had happened that no one would confirm or deny.

"What's with all the secrecy?" Cambria asked Jackson.

"It's not secrecy," he replied. "It's uncertainty. No one actually knows." She'd heard stories of cops being called, fires being started. "They do tend to get a little out of control," he told her.

Cambria had (wrongfully) assumed they'd be going together, she and Jackson. But he was already going with Natalia. And you know what they say—two's a party, three's a crowd.

Cambria had only interacted with Natalia a handful of times, mostly social gatherings with the rest of the friend group. On only one occasion did she spend one-on-one time with her when the three of them went to the mall together. Jackson got distracted looking at golf clubs and Cambria and Natalia were stuck together in Sephora.

She didn't have much of an opinion about her. She was nice enough, but Cambria still couldn't see the appeal. She knew Jackson better than anyone, and she couldn't comprehend the apparent connection. There was also the fact that Jackson had spent the last three weeks doing nothing but complain about her.

When pushed for details, he didn't provide much. The most she could gather was that in only a three-month span, the relationship had become toxic and turbulent. It was hard to picture Jackson angry. She'd barely seen him raise his voice, let alone yell at someone. Yet somehow, that's what their relationship consisted of.

She didn't like that Natalia was bringing out the worst in him.

"If your relationship is so bad," she said to him one day, "why not break up?"

"Trust me, I've thought about it."

"What's stopping you? Why stay in a relationship if all you do is fight?"

"It's not *all* we do. We're fine for the most part. But the fighting can get pretty bad."

"Yes, I'm painstakingly aware."

He took a drag of his cigarette. "She just makes me so angry sometimes. She's bossy and controlling and demanding. I can't live my life without her making snide remarks about everything."

"Have you tried talking to her?"

"Yeah, and it gets me nowhere."

Cambria gave up. She didn't understand either of them, and her suggestions were futile. Hence why not attending the party with Jackson bothered her more than it should have.

Instead, she brought Mara, who seemed to only serve as a substitute for Jackson. Albeit Mara did have better taste in clothes.

It was nice spending time with Mara. She had forgotten what it was like to have girl-time. They got ready together and Mara did her makeup, arriving at Grayson's house just after nine. A good majority of their friend group was already there, and Cambria took this as an opportunity to introduce Mara to everyone.

"I want to meet Jackson's crazy girlfriend," Mara said.

"Shh," Cambria hushed her, surveying the room to ensure they weren't in ear shot. "Don't say that here."

"Why, do people actually like her?"

"Well, yes. I think."

"Are they here yet?" Mara looked around, and Cambria did too.

"I don't think so. But we probably won't even see Jackson anyways if he's with Natalia."

"What a buzzkill. He should break up with her."

"You're telling me."

"What does she think of you?"

"Good question. She's cordial with me. But I get the feeling she probably hates me."

"Can you blame her? If my boyfriend was spending that much time with another girl I'd definitely hate her."

"It's not like that," Cambria protested. But Mara already knew that.

They socialized and made their way around the party. Mara recognized some people she knew, so Cambria left her to her own devices, heading to the kitchen for more alcohol.

An hour passed and still no sign of Jackson.

By this point it was past eleven and Cambria was pleasantly intoxicated. Her lips were numb, and the room spun slightly when she walked. She was all hiccups and giggles, barely able to get a full sentence out.

She ended up at the pool, thinking it would be a phenomenal idea to go swimming in this state. She stripped off her clothes until she was only in her bra and underwear, then dove in headfirst without hesitating.

Swimming to the shallow end, she joined a group of people who were smoking a joint. "Can I have some?"

She was passed the joint and took a hit. She took a few more, coughing, then passed it along, the effects kicking in almost immediately.

Suddenly she didn't feel good anymore. She swam over to the stairs to sit, resting her head on the edge of the pool.

"You okay?" she heard someone ask.

She looked up. She did not recognize this person or know who he was. "I'm fine."

"You don't look fine," he said.

"I think I'm going to be sick."

"Actually?"

"Cambri." She heard her name and knew it could only be one person. She lifted her head to see Jackson hovering over her. "Louis, kick rocks." He knelt so he was closer to her level. "What the fuck are you doing?"

"I was swimming."

"Clearly. Where are your clothes?"

"Honestly, I don't even know."

For some reason, he looked annoyed. "How much have you had to drink?"

"Too much."

"What did he say to you?"

"Who?"

"Louis?"

"Who's Louis?"

Jackson shook his head. "Alright, let's go." He stood, then helped her out of the pool, looking around for a towel to cover her.

Once she was wrapped up, Jackson scoured the pool deck for her clothes. He returned a moment later holding them.

"I've been looking for you," Cambria said to him. "I didn't think you were going to come."

"I've been here."

"Where?"

Jackson stared at her, not answering her question. Instead, he said, "We broke up."

This was the last thing she was expecting him to say. "What? When?"

"Just now."

"Where is she?"

"No clue."

"What happened?"

"It's been problems nonstop since we got here. She said I was flirting with other girls. I told her she was being insane, which pissed her off even more. Then she sat on another guy's lap to spite me. I dragged her out of there and we started going at it in the living room. Grayson told us to take it outside because we were causing a scene. We proceeded to go out front and basically scream at each other for an hour." He shook his head. "I'm done. It's over. She's fucking crazy and I can't put up with it anymore."

She didn't know what to say. "I'm sorry."

"Don't be sorry. Let's just get out of here."

"I came with Mara. I have to find her."

"Can you put your clothes on first?"

"I can't, I'm wet."

They made their way up the balcony stairs, back to the kitchen. Cambria anxiously surveyed the room, fearing Natalia would suddenly appear.

"She's not here, if that's who you're looking for," Jackson said. "She left."

He went to grab them each a water bottle for the road while Cambria found Mara. "You're okay if I head out?"

Mara had been in the middle of playing beer pong with Oliver. "I'm fine, don't worry about me. Are *you* okay?"

"I'm okay. Jackson, on the other hand…"

"You'll have to update me tomorrow."

"I will."

"Was it because of you?"

"What?" the question caught her off guard.

"The break-up."

"No. God, no."

She met Jackson on the sidewalk, and they walked down the street to where his car was parked. She wanted to ask him if he was good to drive but thought better of it.

They drove home in silence, not even the radio on. Cambria looked over at Jackson, whose eyes were focused on the road. She wanted to say something but was scared to break the silence, so she said nothing.

They crept into the house quietly, trying not to wake his family. Much like her house back home in Connecticut, she now had Jackson's memorized. She could navigate it with her eyes closed. Up the spiral staircase, down the hall, turn left: Jackson's room.

Her happy place.

He closed the door behind them. Cambria had put her clothes on before they left the party, but now everything was drenched. Jackson went to his closet and grabbed a hoodie and a pair of track pants, handing them to her. Not wanting to leave the room and risk waking anyone, she said, "Can you turn around?" and he did.

Once she had on warm and dry clothes, she sat on the couch, grabbing the water bottle and chugging half. Jackson lay on his bed, hands behind the back of his head, staring up at the ceiling. Cambria didn't know what to say. She wanted to say, *are you okay?* But it was quite obvious that he wasn't. "Why are you on the couch?" he said.

She didn't respond. Instead, she grabbed the water bottle and lay on the bed next to him. They both stared up at the ceiling, not saying a word, their breathing synchronized. "Do you want to talk about it?" she asked, breaking the silence.

"Not particularly."

More silence. "I'm high."

Jackson turned so fast to look at her. "Whaatttttt? High on what?"

"Weed."

"Cambria Nickson. I thought you didn't smoke. Or do drugs."

"I don't."

He laughed. Then he laughed even harder. "Now I want to be high." He stood, reaching into his dresser drawer, and pulled out a bag of weed and a pipe. She watched from her spot on the bed as he opened the window. "Want some?" he said as he exhaled, coughing once.

"Okay." She got up and went to him. He held it to her lips and lit it for her. Cambria used to smoke weed in high school. It helped her concentrate. It was also fun. But then her brother killed himself by overdosing on drugs and she was a bit apprehensive to do anything remotely close after that. She knew you couldn't die from weed. But still.

"You alright?" he asked as she coughed.

She nodded, then grabbed the water bottle and finished the remaining half.

After they both had a couple more hits, they fell backwards onto the bed adjacently, staring up at the ceiling once again. Cambria could feel her senses come alive, Jackson's presence beside her. It had been so long since she'd been high, so long since she'd felt like this. She had forgotten how good it felt, your body numb, your mind clear. She stared at the stucco ceiling, studying its patterns, getting lost in the design.

"You see me," Jackson said. Cambria turned to face him. "She doesn't."

Cambria didn't respond. Instead, she removed the piece of gum that had been in her mouth and stuck it to his forehead. He let it sit there for a moment, then put it in his mouth. "You're disgusting," she laughed.

"You love me."

"I do. I really do. I'm so glad we met. You're my best friend."

"You're *my* best friend."

She smiled to herself, and they continued staring at the ceiling. "I wonder if our mouths produce saliva when we sleep," she said.

"I think they do."

"Then why are our mouths dry when we wake up?"

"Good point."

"My mouth isn't producing saliva right now."

"Neither is mine. Definitely not."

"What would you eat right now?" she asked him.

"Anything."

"I could go for a burger. Or pizza."

"Frenchie's burgers."

"Yeah. With that hot sauce you like."

"Fuck. Now I'm hungry."

"We could get food," she suggested. "Or make food."

"I don't want to get up."

"Me neither. I'm strangely comfortable right now."

"Me too. I don't want to move."

Her head felt light. She smiled to herself unknowingly.

"I really did think you and Theo were it."

She turned to him. "Really?"

"Yeah. Theo doesn't normally do this. He's had like, two girlfriends. And so, I actually thought… What if you were it for him?"

"But you guys never talked about it?"

"No. I told you, we don't talk about that stuff."

"Maybe you should have."

"Why? It's not going to change anything. He's gone."

"I know. And I also know it wouldn't have made a difference. He doesn't feel the same."

"You win some, you lose some. You live and you learn."

She faced the ceiling again. It was easier to converse this way. "What's your favorite part about being a man?"

"Having a dick."

"Aside from that."

"Being able to walk into a room and command power."

"In all of your life, when has that ever happened to you?"

"So many times."

"I bet you can't name one."

"Shut it."

"Do you ever wish you were a woman?"

"Fuck no. Do you ever wish you were a man?"

"I wish I had a man's ability to command power." He looked at her. She looked at him, and contemptuously said, "and I'm sure you do too." He rolled his eyes. "I like being a woman. Women create life."

"I think men play a small part in that as well."

"Yeah but women do all the work. Men can take credit for being a sperm donor and that's about it. No offence."

"I guess you're right."

"I used to complain about my mom. Then I grew up to be just like her. And now I understand. She was right. About everything. I should have listened."

"Do you get along?"

"There was a time when I hated her. But then I grew to love her. It's complicated."

"I've never hated my mom."

"What about your dad?"

"Nope."

"Me neither. My dad's the best."

"Do you want kids?" he asked.

"No. I don't know. I don't think I do."

"Why?"

"I'm scared."

"When have you ever let that stop you before?"

"Um, basically my entire life."

"Okay, but you can't let that be a deterrent for having kids—everybody's scared."

"But there's so much you lose, so much you have to give up."

"That's one way to look at it." He held her gaze. "I look at it as something you gain."

She considered his words. They would stay with her for a long time. "Do you want kids?"

"I do. I want a big family, like my parents."

"Oh, God, I don't know if I could do three boys."

"Honestly, me neither."

"If I did have kids, I'd want a girl. I'd name her Winter."

"That's a nice name. It's unique. Like Summer, but opposite."

"Yeah, exactly. Summer is beautiful and so is winter. But I'd spell it with a *y*."

"Different. I like that."

"Would you want a girl?"

"If I had a girl, it'd be game over for me."

"What do you mean?"

"She'd take my heart, and all my money. I'd give her the world. And I'd kill anyone who hurt her."

Cambria had never thought about it like that. And suddenly, Jackson had just given her a new perspective.

The room was quiet. The only thing she could hear was the sound of her own heart beating. She remained silent, trying to listen for Jackson's. She reached over and placed two fingers to his neck, feeling for a pulse. While still staring at the ceiling above, he, too, reached over and put his two fingers to the side of her neck.

He turned his head so that he was facing her. She did the same. She stared into his eyes, so dark, like blackholes. She could get lost in them. So lost she'd never find her way out.

Perhaps she already was.

Then he kissed her. Just like that, like there was nothing to it.

December 1989

CAMBRIA

ELEVEN

There was something in the air during Christmas time—candy canes and nostalgia. Cambria loved Christmas. Started counting down the days on the twenty-sixth of December. One of those people that wish for Christmas in July and start their shopping in August.

Lunacy.

When she was young, she'd wake before the rest of her house, creeping down the hall to Lincoln's room. Together, they'd congregate at the Christmas tree—sizing up boxes, shaking them—until their parents woke up and joined them.

They had their tradition. Presents. Bacon and eggs with orange juice. A family walk. Church, even though she never considered herself religious. More presents. Christmas dinner.

Now, she sat alone in her apartment, drinking chai tea at the kitchen table. She had decorated, but scarcely. A miniature tree sat in the corner of the living room, wrapped in red garland and a handful of ornaments that Mara helped her pick out. A snow globe sat on her coffee table, an angel in her kitchen.

It was the tenth of December. She had a flight back home to Linden Falls on the twenty-first, where she would visit with her family until the twenty-eighth. As happy as she was in Pine Hills, there was something about going back to the place you came from.

And quite honestly, she needed it.

Cambria's life at the moment remained mundane and uneventful. She was making decent money at her job and shoveling it away into savings. Her free time was spent either reading books or watching television alone. And on the days that Mara was free, drinking martinis in her kitchen.

Life was so amiss without Jackson.

Cambria had only come to know life *after* Jackson. Anything prior to meeting him was irrelevant. She found it difficult to fathom time before him. It was hard to believe that, just six months ago, they didn't even know of each other's existence. And now, he was her entire world.

What a dangerous thing, bestowing that power on someone—it makes losing them all the more painful.

Well, she didn't *lose* him. She still had him, kind of. But things weren't like before.

Before Grayson's party.

Before the kiss.

Let's go back to that moment, shall we?

Cambria allowed Jackson's lips to linger on hers for only a moment before she pulled away. She stared at him, bewildered. It shouldn't have been that much of a surprise—anyone with half a brain could've seen that coming. How Cambria did not was astonishing but understandable—it wasn't blind ignorance, but rather, earnest naivety.

But suddenly, then, everything flashed before her—how everything seemed to make sense except timing itself.

What if it had been Jackson instead of Theo?

What if it had been Jackson all along?

She stared at him, lips slightly parted, eyes locked on his. She tried to formulate words, but nothing came out.

Mistaking her silence for apprehension, Jackson mumbled, "sorry," and pulled away. She watched as he stood, searching for something—anything. He grabbed the water bottle, but it was empty. He stared at it, contemplating, then threw it in the bin. "I'll be right back," he said, then left the room. Cambria remained on the bed, immobile.

When Jackson returned, she still had not moved. "You alright?" he asked.

At his words she came to life. "Yes, sorry." She sat up, adjusting herself.

"Do you want me to take you home?"

"Sure. Okay. Thanks."

He opened his closet, grabbed a hoodie, and put it on.

Watching as he did this, Cambria said, "Do you want your clothes back?"

He looked at her. "Why are you asking me if I want my clothes back?"

She didn't respond.

They drove in silence. This made twice in one night, and Cambria did not like it. Jackson was the only person she could sit in comfortable silence with, yet right now, all she wanted was the opposite.

For him to say something, do something.

Still feeling the effects of the weed and alcohol, she stared out the window, choosing instead to focus her attention elsewhere. But even that was difficult to do in the presence of Jackson.

At last, they arrived in front of her building. Jackson idled for a moment, neither of them breaking the silence. He turned off the car. "I shouldn't have done that," he said. "I was high. Not thinking clearly."

She didn't know how to respond. "It's okay."

More silence.

"You won't tell anyone, right?" he said.

"Who am I going to tell?"

"I don't know."

"Are you mad at me?"

"No, I—" he paused. "It's fine. Mistakes happen. We can just move on."

Mistakes. She should've said something then. Should've corrected him. But she didn't. A decision that would ultimately haunt her.

And then there was Jackson, staring at her as if she possessed some sort of answer. They had their own language, but even this she did not understand. He had a way of doing that—making her question everything. "Okay."

They held each other's gaze for another elongated moment before Jackson broke away, deciding to give her a pat on the knee. "So, we good?"

"Of course."

"Do you need me to walk you up, or…"

"I'll be fine. Thanks."

"Okay. Well, goodnight." He flashed her a smile. But it didn't look happy. It looked sad.

"Goodnight, Jackson."

He got back together with Natalia the very next day.

As if none of it happened. As if the whole fight and the party and the kiss never occurred. A figment of her imagination.

And therefore it must have been, she concluded. None of it happened. And even if it did, it didn't matter now anyways. He broke up with Natalia and then got back together with her. And if he was willing to do that so easily, Cambria knew how their relationship would go. Breaking up, making up—a vicious cycle that would never end.

And she was right.

There was no point in getting hung up over *what ifs.* She needed to move on and put the past where it belonged.

The months that followed weren't the same. Cambria still hung out with Jackson on a somewhat regular basis, but their interactions had dwindled significantly since becoming more involved in his relationship with Natalia. "We talked about everything," Jackson explained. "And we both want to make this work."

Even to the average person this would be perplexing, but to Cambria it was beyond her wildest comprehension.

On top of that, Jackson got a new job working as supervisor of the marketing department at Ford, which meant he was no longer at Hargrove & Swanson. Nothing had been the same since.

Work without Jackson was like an ocean without water. She no longer had something to look forward to each morning. She ate alone at her desk each day. And when five o'clock arrived and she made her way to the parking lot, she still searched for red, a natural reflex. But alas, he wasn't there. And never would be again.

As much as Cambria liked to tell herself that nothing had changed between them, she knew that wasn't true. On the surface, all appeared normal. But Cambria knew. She could feel it in the air, the shift between them. She saw it in the subtleties, how Jackson maintained this faux professionalism between them that never existed before. He began prioritizing Natalia. He stopped discussing the details of his relationship. Their hugs didn't linger like they used to. And the times when she'd be over at his house, he'd lay on his bed, smoking a cigarette out the window as they watched TV, and she'd remain on the couch, fearing the implications of joining him.

She hadn't been on his bed since that night.

And so, she went along with it too—whatever game this was they were now playing. When he drew back, she drew back. If he could be indifferent, then so could she. And thus, this new friendship was born, that had all the semblances of the old one, but with a few modifications.

Cambria's mind was plagued with thoughts of Theo. She had assumed this erratic behavior would cease after he was gone, but it did not. His absence only made things worse. It was a reminder of what she could've had, almost had.

Her mind was free of Theo only when she was with Jackson—hence why she tried to occupy her time this way as much as possible. It never occurred to Cambria that there may be a reason she didn't think about Theo when she was with Jackson.

To remedy this predicament, she kept herself busy. Whether that be attending yoga classes, hanging out at Mara's, or consuming more movies and TV shows she ever had in her life.

Cambria missed home. She didn't like to admit it, but it was true. She thought admitting it meant defeat. That it would somehow mean she failed in her endeavours. What she didn't yet understand was that she was allowed to miss home. She was allowed to miss the place she came from. She was allowed to miss her parents. And once she accepted this for what it was, it made her all the more eager to make her return.

The flight seemed to go by painstakingly slow. Seven months since she first made this trip, yet it felt as though she had lived an entire lifetime since then.

Her parents picked her up from the airport. As they drove home, Cambria stared out the window from the backseat of her mother's old station wagon. She watched the snow as it fell from the sky, blanketing the landscape before them. She had missed the cold, crisp air of the east coast.

The days that followed were spent visiting family: Her maternal grandparents, her paternal grandparents, her aunts and uncles and friends of the family. They exchanged gifts and ate elaborate meals.

For her entire life, Cambria had felt that as long as she was with her parents, everything would be okay. It was a feeling she had forgotten, being so far away. But now she felt it again: invincibility.

On the morning of the twenty-fifth, Cambria slept in. Her mother came into her bedroom and coaxed her awake, hot coffee and biscuits waiting. They gathered in the living room and opened presents, trying not to feel the absence that had always been so evident on this day. Instead, she focused her attention on her parents. How in love they were, even now, after thirty-three years of marriage.

Cambria had never looked at her parents and longed for what they had. But she did now. Her heart wasn't completely back to how it had been, and everything still hurt. She looked at her parents that Christmas morning and for the first time she recognized what they had. And for the first time in her life, she wanted it.

When it was time to return to Pine Hills, Cambria cried. She didn't cry often. In fact, she hardly cried at all.

She stood outside the airport with her suitcase clutched in one hand. "It's okay, honey," her mother said as she pressed another tissue to her daughter's eyes. "You can come home anytime. This isn't forever."

Cambria knew it wasn't forever, but this was her life now. Across the country, thousands of miles from her parents and everything else she had ever known. Yet even as she said her goodbyes, even as she sat on the plane, looking out the window into the great abyss, Cambria knew she wouldn't be coming home again for a very long time.

As much as it pained her to leave Linden Falls, it wasn't her home anymore. She had a new home now. And it was time to get back to it.

TWELVE

Upon her arrival, Jackson was parked outside the airport in his red Mercedes waiting for her.

"How much did you miss me?" she asked him.

"Too much. Don't ever leave again." He rolled down the windows, turned up the music, and just like that, she was home.

They went straight to Jonah Tremblant's house for a holiday soirée. Christmas in California just wasn't the same as it was back home. The air was warm and there was no snow on the ground. Cambria wrinkled her nose at Jackson as they stood on the front porch and rang the doorbell. She was wearing jean shorts and one of Jackson's hoodies. They both sported a red Santa hat.

Jonah answered the door, and Cambria thrust a bottle of wine at him as they entered. Everyone was gathered in the living room, the faux fireplace on for décor. The boys sat on the couches while the girls all sat crossed legged on the floor. Naomi, who was handing out candy-canes, was wearing red knee-high Santa socks. Off to the side stood Grayson, who was watching Ian struggle to fix the cabling on the TV. "Look what the cat dragged in," Grayson remarked as they walked in and squeezed onto one of the couches. "And so, she returns."

Heather: "How was home?"

Cambria: "It was good. I had a good time, yeah. Was nice to see everyone. But I'm glad to be back."

Grayson: "Where's Nat?"

Jackson: "She's out of town for the holidays. Palm Springs."

Cambria was aware that, had this not been the case, she probably wouldn't be here.

"What's your vote," Naomi said, pointing at them with a candy-cane, "Frosty or Grinch?"

Jackson: "I don't care."

Cambria: "I'm fine with either."

Naomi rolled her eyes. "You guys are not at all helpful."

Grayson: "Not like we'll ever get the TV working anyways."

Ian: "I'm doing my best."

Jackson: "Where's the booze?"

Cambria: "He's fiending."

Jonah: "Drinks and snacks are in the kitchen. Help yourselves."

They stood at the kitchen counter hovering over the cheese platter. Cambria dished out two plates, then grabbed a bottle of wine. She poured one glass that they shared between them.

"My stomach hurts," Jackson said as he took a drink.

"Is it wise to be drinking?"

"Yes, obviously."

"You're insane. Do you want Tums?"

"You have?"

"No, but there's probably some around here somewhere." She began opening cupboards. "Jonah, do you have Tums?"

"Second cupboard on the right!" he called out from the living room.

She brought the Tums over to Jackson, twisting off the cap and giving him one. "Thanks, mom." He popped it into his mouth, chasing it down with wine.

"When does Natalia get back?"

"Next week. Tuesday, I think."

"She's not here for New Year's?"

"Nope."

"What are we doing? Grayson's?"

"Yep. He hosts every year."

"He seems to host everything every year."

"Basically." He took another drink, then handed her the glass and she did the same.

"I guess I'll need to figure out an outfit. What will the atmosphere be?"

Jackson was staring at her peculiarly. "I need to talk to you about something."

"Sounds serious." She placed the glass on the counter. "Is everything okay?"

"Everything's fine. It's just… it's about us. And our friendship. I don't really know how to say this."

"You're scaring me."

"I'm sorry. It's Natalia. We had a talk about some stuff."

"Pertaining to me?"

"Well, yes. Solely pertaining to you."

"Did I do something?"

"I think we just need to cool it a bit, you and me."

She stared at him, uncomprehending. "What do you mean?"

He took in a big breath. "Natalia thinks we hang out too much."

"We barely hang out anymore."

"Yeah, well, we still do."

"What are you trying to say… That we can't hang out anymore?"

"I don't know what I'm trying to say."

"Jackson! What's going on?"

He grabbed the wine and finished the glass. He reached for the bottle and filled it to the brim as Cambria watched in silence. He glanced up, met her eye, handed her the glass.

She took it hesitantly, took a drink. "Where is this coming from?" she handed it back to him.

"I guess there's some stuff I haven't told you. Back in September, when we got back together, she said that part of the problem is how much time I spend with you."

"Is that why you've been so distant?"

"Yes."

"Okay… but we're best friends."

"I know that. But… She thinks you have feelings for me."

"What!? Did you tell her I don't?"

He didn't respond.

"Jackson…"

"Well, do you?"

"No! Of course not. Why would you even think that?"

"I don't know, it's a valid concern, I guess."

"So you agree with her?"

"I don't know what I agree with. All I know is that my girlfriend is very unhappy about our interactions."

"Well maybe you should tell your girlfriend that she has nothing to worry about and that I'm not trying to steal her boyfriend."

He scratched the back of his neck. "Okay."

"Okay? That's it?"

He hunched over, resting his forehead on the countertop. "I don't know what to do."

She watched him like that for a moment, not saying anything. Then she pulled him back up so that he was facing her. "Talk to me."

"I'm just trying to ensure everyone's happiness."

"Except mine."

He didn't respond.

"I feel like I'm being punished. Like I did something wrong."

"You didn't do anything wrong."

"Then explain it to me. I don't understand."

He held her gaze for a moment. "So, you don't have feelings for me?"

"No! You're my best friend, Jackson. I love you, but not like that."

"Okay."

"Do you believe me?"

"I believe you."

But even as he said it, she knew he in fact did not believe her.

As Cambria lay in bed that night, tipsy from the alcohol in her system, she was distracted by thoughts of Jackson.

They had managed to come to a resolution. He promised he'd talk with Natalia and try to find some sort of solution. But until he did that, Cambria would be walking on eggshells. The last thing she wanted was either of them thinking she had feelings for him. Because if the consequence was losing Jackson, she didn't want it. He was her closest friend, partner in crime, sole confidant. Without him she'd be lost. She wouldn't even know what to do with herself anymore.

She could understand where the confusion came from. Since the day they met, Jackson and Cambria had spent approximately seventy-five percent of their free time together. She was close with his family. They slept over at each other's houses. They'd go grocery shopping together. Spend evenings alone over a bottle of wine. Fall asleep in his backyard by the fire. But if she swapped out Jackson for Mara and looked at the situation that way, it wasn't at all incriminating.

It was a tale as old as time, that men and women couldn't be *just friends*. Cambria never had a guy best friend before Jackson. She didn't think she was the type. But looking back, she hadn't been the type for female friends either. She wasn't the type for any friends, really. Not until Jackson. When she met him, something just *clicked*.

What she needed to do was distance herself. Just enough to eradicate any suspicion he had about her. Prove to him that it wasn't like that, and that she'd be perfectly fine without him, even though that wasn't really the case. She just needed him to believe that.

For the first time, Cambria considered the possibility that she may actually have feelings for Jackson. The notion was absurd. But was it true?

She knew they had a connection like no other. She knew he was her favorite person. And she knew how she felt when she was with him. But was that infatuation, or companionship?

It was hard to tell. She found it difficult to envision anything romantic between them, mostly due to how platonic and familial they were with each other. But then there was the kiss at the end of September, and she didn't really have an excuse for that one. Because no matter how hard she tried to deny it, deep down, she knew she liked it.

She tried to justify that as well, blaming it on the fact that Theo was gone and she was lonely and heartbroken, and Jackson was *there*, and he had just broken up with his girlfriend, and tensions were high, and *they* were high.

As Jackson had said, it was a mistake.

Her head was spinning. She didn't know what to think anymore, how to even determine something like this. It's easy to confuse feelings of camaraderie for enamor when you're as close as they were.

There was only one way to tell whether she truly had feelings for Jackson or not. And that was to fall in love with somebody else.

If the feelings for Jackson dissipated, then Cambria knew she was safe, the whole thing chalked up to loneliness—infatuation by proximity.

However, if she fell in love with someone else and these feelings for Jackson persisted… well, then she'd be doomed.

THIRTEEN

On the evening of December 31, 1989, Cambria sat in the kitchen of the Harding residence having drinks with Jackson's family while he was upstairs getting ready.

Cambria: "I swear he takes longer than I do."

Leanne: "He's quite high maintenance. I'm not sure why."

Landon: "He gets it from you."

Leanne: "He does not."

Victoria: "I'm not high maintenance."

Landon: "You brought a Vitamix to Greece."

Victoria: "I don't think that's high maintenance. I just needed my smoothies."

Her mother gave her a look. "Perhaps you are."

Dave opened another bottle of merlot. "Just let the boy take his time. He needs it."

Kyle: "Has to look good for Cambria."

Cambria: "Oh, shut up."

Landon: "Would you marry Jackson if he asked you?"

Cambria: "He has a girlfriend."

Kyle: "Yeah—you."

Leanne: "You know we love you, Cambria."

Cambria: "Jackson's going to kill you guys."

"Who am I going to kill?" Jackson suddenly appeared in the kitchen. He was wearing black dress pants and a navy blue button-down, a dark blazer draped over his arm.

Leanne: "You look nice."

Jackson: "What are you guys doing? Talkin shit?"

Cambria: "Obviously."

Jackson: "You ready to go?"

Cambria: "Let me just finish my drink."

Jackson pulled out a chair and sat next to her. "Why are you wearing lipstick?"

"Because it's New Year's and I want to look nice."

"It looks weird."

"Does it?"

"It does not," Leanne told her. "Don't listen to him, you look beautiful."

"You never wear lipstick," he continued.

Cambria rolled her eyes and finished the last of her wine. "Let's go," she stood. She was wearing a dark ruby gown, tight fitted to her body, sweetheart neckline. Her hair was done up lavishly. She could feel Jackson's eyes on her, trailing the length of her body.

"Nice dress," he said to her.

"Thanks. I could never get away with wearing this back home. There's usually six inches of snow on the ground this time of year."

"Well, you definitely won't be cold tonight."

They arrived just after eight. The house was full and bustling, as it normally was whenever Grayson Welch hosted a party. On their way to the kitchen, they saw a crowd of people congregated around Fendi, who was being passed around. They both grabbed a cup and filled it, joining the others who were standing around the table playing beer pong. "Where's Gray?" Jackson asked Ian.

"Upstairs dealing with a situation."

"Already?"

As the ball was thrown back and forth into cups, Cambria reflected on the year. It had only been seven months since she moved to Pine Hills, but it had felt like a lifetime. January to April was a distant memory now, a time she didn't recognize, a person she was no longer. She had been working a job she loathed, living in her childhood home, with no plan, no direction. She was comfortable, but stagnant. And then there was the morning of her twenty-second birthday, when she woke up, the realization dawning on her—she didn't want to end up like her brother. She had been suffocating without even realizing it, and she'd needed to escape.

She thought back to an earlier conversation she had with Jackson, when he asked her if she had any resolutions for the New Year. "Not currently," she replied. "I can't think of anything."

"That's surprising. What do you want to change about your life?"

"Nothing. I love my life right now."

"Nothing at all?"

She pondered this. Recalled the conversation they had at Jonah's that night. "I think I need to fall in love."

"With who?"

"Somebody. Anybody."

"You miss Theo?"

"Fuck off."

"It's a serious question."

She was quiet for a moment. "I could say no. But we both know I'd be lying."

"I know."

"I feel like an idiot."

"You're not. It's okay to miss someone. It's okay to love someone."

"Not someone who never loved you back."

Now, she looked around the room, scanning the sea of people for something, anything.

By eleven o'clock, Cambria was hammered. Not only had she played (and won) three consecutive games of beer pong, but she had also finished multiple vodka sodas and taken several shots of rum. The room was spinning, and Jackson had four eyes, two heads.

"I'm going to go lay down," she told Jackson.

He gave her a puzzled look. "Where?"

"I don't know."

She wandered off, pushing through the crowd, until she reached the foyer. Opening the front door, she peered outside to see if anyone was out there. It was empty.

She slipped on a random pair of shoes and walked outside, closing the door behind her.

The air was cool and refreshing. She closed her eyes and breathed, finally able to hear her own thoughts again. Opening her eyes, she looked around, unsure of what to do, where to go. She had no clear objective when she had opened that door, and now, she was hesitant.

Walking across the lawn, she dragged her feet. She decided to sit, then lay back to face the sky. Everything was spinning, but she felt good. Happy. Content.

She smelt cigarette smoke and instantly thought of Jackson. She closed her eyes and inhaled, even though she loathed the smell.

"Are you alive?"

Her eyes shot open. Hovering over her was a stranger. "I'm alive."

He took another drag and exhaled, looking at her inquisitively. "What are you doing out here?"

"I'm not sure."

"Just catching some rays?"

"Yeah, that's what I'm doing."

"What's your name?"

"Cambria."

"That's a beautiful name."

"And you are…?"

"Lawson," he extended his hand. She contemplated it a moment, then shook it.

With his hand still in hers, she pulled, hard, and he stumbled down, nearly on top of her.

"Where'd you come from?" he laughed as he readjusted and lay next to her.

"That's a great question."

"You don't know?"

"There are just so many answers."

He found this amusing. "How much have you had to drink?"

"Enough."

He offered her the cigarette, and she declined.

"Where'd *you* come from?" she asked.

He took another drag. "Stratton."

"What brings you here?"

"I came with a buddy of mine. He knows the owner."

"Grayson."

"That's his name?"

"Yes."

"I like the snake."

"Everybody does."

"You still haven't answered my question."

She gave him a look. "And I'm not going to." She faced the sky again. "It's so beautiful."

He followed her gaze and looked up. "It is. And only twenty minutes till countdown."

"And then it's 1990."

"A new decade." He looked at her again. "Did you come here with someone?"

"Jackson."

"Is that your boyfriend?"

She laughed. "No. Just a friend."

"Does *he* know that?"

"He has a girlfriend."

"She here?"

Cambria didn't respond.

"Ah," he took another drag. "I see."

"It's not like that."

He caught her eye. She held his gaze. "Will you come inside with me?"

She thought about it. "Okay."

He stood first, then extended his hand and helped her up. Once they were standing, she realized how tall he was.

They remained that way for a moment, simply staring at one another. Lawson flicked his cigarette but didn't break eye contact.

And then they went inside.

Jackson now a forgotten thought, she followed Lawson through the house to the living room, where everyone was gathered for the countdown. Someone handed her a glass of champagne. The TV was on, displaying Times Square. And then before she knew it, the countdown was beginning.

Five, four, three, two, one.

"*Happy New Year!*" The room erupted, whistles and cheers and claps all around. She looked at Lawson, and he looked at her, and then he kissed her.

They pulled back and stared at each other, remaining that way for a moment. Then she brought her hands to his neck and pulled him to her once again.

FOURTEEN

She woke up in a bed unfamiliar to her. Next to her was Lawson, sound asleep. She looked around the room, observing her surroundings, then spotted her dress on the floor.

Cambria didn't do this—she didn't go home with randos. Theo had been an exception, and they didn't even sleep together that night. That in itself was bold, considering she'd never had sex before she met him.

Carefully, without making a sound, she slipped from the sheets and grabbed her dress, remnants from the night before coming to her in pieces. They had waited two hours for a taxi. It was a forty-minute drive to Lawson's place in Stratton. They didn't get there until almost five in the morning.

He offered her coffee. She couldn't help but laugh. Then she kissed him, right there in his front hallway. He brought her upstairs to his bedroom, where he took his time undressing her. And then, while they were having sex, she got her period.

Lawson thought he had hurt her. She laughed at that too. "Well, at least I'm not pregnant."

He gave her a look.

"I'm joking, I haven't had sex in months."

"Do you want to stop?"

"No. Do you?"

And so, they didn't.

Now, she stepped into her dress and pulled it up to her hips.

"What are you doing?"

She turned, surprised to see him awake. "Good morning."

"Take that off."

"Do you have something more comfortable?"

"I'd prefer you in nothing at all."

She laughed modestly, then grabbed one of his t-shirts from the floor, choosing to wear that instead. She slipped back into bed next to him.

He lifted the duvet and pulled her close. "Were you going to sneak off and disappear on me?"

"No," she said. "Maybe."

"Did you not have a good time?"

She smiled coyly. "I did. It's just… I've never done this before."

"Done what?"

"One night stand."

"Who said this was a one-night stand? I could be your future husband."

She laughed. "You're forward."

"I'm just being honest. And for the record, I have difficulty believing you on that."

"I had a good time with you last night."

"Can I make you breakfast?"

"Okay."

She spent the entire day with him. And the day after that. And by the time she was finally back in her own bed two days later, the only thing on her mind was Lawson.

Lawson Wolf was something else. He was charming, charismatic, and bold. He knew what he wanted in life, and he chased it relentlessly. When he had his sights set on something, he was guaranteed to get it. And what he wanted, was Cambria.

After New Years, they couldn't get enough of each other. The day after returning home, he called her and asked when he could see her again. He took her out for dinner the next night. And the night after that, roller blading. And after that, the movies.

Suddenly Cambria had forgotten entirely what it was to be lonely.

They had nothing in common but got along all the same. He came from a completely different life than her, one consisting of abuse, drugs, and alcohol. His parents had divorced when he was fifteen after his mother left for another man, which didn't phase Lawson at all, seeing as his father had been beating him since he could walk. That was probably why he never told his father that he walked in on his mother fucking another man when he was ten years old. His father deserved it. But Lawson didn't deserve any of it.

He had an older sister, but they didn't have much of a relationship. She was married and had a family of her own. Their father had beat her too, but she didn't like to talk about it. Therefore, Lawson had no one. And when you have no one, you turn to whatever you can. And in Lawson's case, that was drugs and alcohol.

He got expelled on three different occasions, yet somehow managed to graduate high school with a 3.7 GPA. He went to college, followed in his grandfather's footsteps, and began making a life for himself. He had no one to rely on but himself. And that was the way he preferred things.

He wanted to be honest with Cambria, so he told her everything, even the bad stuff. *Especially* the bad stuff. And trust me, there was plenty.

But Cambria didn't judge him for his past—she welcomed his candor with open arms, intrigued to hear everything he had to say, as if each intimate detail he shared was a step closer to him. And that was all she wanted.

She felt herself opening up to him in a way she never really could with Theo. Perhaps it was that perpetual dissonance that had existed between them. That wasn't the case with Lawson. He wanted to know everything there was to know about her. He was so fascinated by her, just as she was him. He made her feel special, unique, and I think that was the most important part of all. With Theo, she had felt like his equal. But Lawson put her on a pedestal, making her feel like something else entirely. And subsequently, they became inseparable.

Eight consecutive days they spent together. She didn't know it was possible to feel this way about someone after only knowing them such a short time. He was spellbinding, and she was head-over-heels.

There was just one tiny problem that Cambria couldn't quite reconcile.

On that very first day they spent together, when all she had to wear were his trackpants and t-shirt, they had been sitting on his couch watching TV when Lawson brought out a small dime bag containing a white substance.

Cambria had never seen cocaine before.

He dumped the contents onto a plate and used a credit card to grind it into a fine powder.

"Is that what I think it is?" she asked him.

"It's coke. You want some?"

"No." She looked at him. "Isn't it a bit early for that?"

"A buddy of mine just got a new batch and needs me to try it to make sure it's pure."

"You're just… sampling it?"

"Yeah, exactly. Don't worry, I'm not an addict or anything."

"Okay, good." She hadn't told him about her brother, and perhaps she never would.

He grabbed his wallet, pulled out a hundred-dollar bill, rolled it into a tight cylinder, then leaned over and snorted the line.

They did not speak of it again. And he hadn't done it since.

She finally saw Jackson after a two-week hiatus, which was probably the longest amount of time they'd gone without seeing each other. "Where the hell have you been?" he said once they were together again. "I never see you anymore."

They sat on her living room sofa, a bottle of wine between them, since it was Wednesday. "You're one to talk."

"What's that supposed to mean?"

"You're joking, right? I hardly ever see you because you're always with Natalia."

"I'm not sure what you want me to say. She's my girlfriend."

"Do you really not see the hypocrisy?"

"Why are you bringing hypocrisy into this?"

"I'm just saying."

"Okay, so where have you been?"

"I've been seeing someone."

"The guy from New Year's?"

"Yeah—you remember that?"

"Of course I remember. He looked like an idiot."

"Alright. Well, his name's Lawson. And he's a really great guy."

"Lawson? What kind of name is that?"

"What kind of name is Jackson?"

"Uh, the best kind?"

She had to laugh at that. "Why are you being an asshole?"

"I'm not trying to be. I just don't like that you've been spending so much time with a guy you barely know."

"I spent a lot of time with you when I barely knew you."

"Yeah but that's different."

"How?"

"It just is."

"Alright. Any more unsolicited advice you have for me?"

"What's he like?"

"Funny. Hot. Charming."

"Barf. He has a crooked nose."

"You sure remember a lot of details about a guy you didn't even meet."

"I saw you kiss him."

"You did?"

"Yeah."

"You never said anything."

"What was I supposed to say?" It was quiet for a moment. "You really like him?" he asked.

"I think I do."

"Is it serious?"

"I don't know."

"Just… be careful."

"I'm not sure why you're telling me to be careful. There's nothing to be worried about."

"I have a bad feeling about this guy."

"You don't even know him."

He gave her a look. "Exactly."

Cambria wouldn't let Jackson's ambiguous warning get in the way—she was determined to prove him wrong. And so, when they made plans to go bowling the following week, she took it upon herself to remedy the situation.

She sat in the passenger seat as Lawson pulled into the parking lot and put his truck in park. His eyes scanned the building before them. "I've never heard of this place," he said.

"Thursdays is half price. And they have cheap drinks."

"Is your friend here already?"

"I'm not sure, I don't see his car."

"*His*?"

Cambria may have neglected to mention that they were meeting Jackson. And she may have also neglected to tell Jackson that she was bringing Lawson.

Perhaps not the wisest idea, but she'd never been a fan of wise.

They exited the truck and made their way inside the bowling alley. Cambria had scanned the parking lot rigorously for Jackson's red Mercedes but by the time they got to the front door, she still hadn't spotted it.

As soon as they walked through the doors, they came face-to-face with Jackson, who was coming from the bar, a drink in each hand.

He stopped in his tracks upon seeing her—them.

"Jackson!" she exclaimed, almost too eagerly. "This is Lawson. Lawson, this is Jackson."

The two stared at each other for an extended moment, neither of them saying anything. "Well, this is unexpected," Jackson remarked. "I would shake your hand, but—" he shrugged.

"Is that for me?" Cambria asked.

He looked at her, and she could tell, immediately, that she had fucked up. "Yes." He handed her the drink.

"Thanks."

Lawson extended his hand and shook Jackson's.

"Cambria's told me good things," Jackson said.

"Really?" Lawson said. "She hasn't mentioned you at all."

The silence was palpable.

Jackson had reserved a lane. He walked ahead of them, Cambria and Lawson holding hands as they trailed behind. "You didn't tell me your friend was a dude."

"Didn't I? Oops."

"How do you know this guy?"

"He's my best friend. I told you about him on New Year's."

"He's the one with the girlfriend?"

"Yes."

"Well where is she?"

"Uh, not here?"

"That much is clear. Isn't this supposed to be a double date or something?"

"I'm really not sure what this is supposed to be."

The evening went as well as you can imagine. And by that, I mean it went terribly. Jackson spoke roughly seven words to Cambria. Lawson made small talk. He was good at that, Cambria noticed. She was sure he could conversate with anyone, about anything. But his charm and charisma did not work on Jackson, who had a rebuttal to everything he said, even when Cambria knew, under normal circumstances, he would agree. She sat there with her drink in her hand, wishing she had something stronger, just to get through the night.

When it was finally over, Jackson couldn't get out of there fast enough, citing off some excuse about needing to go to Natalia's. He left without another word.

"That was weird," Lawson said.

"You think?"

"You'd have to have half a brain to think that went well. I think he hates me."

"I think he likes you."

"I think he's in love with you."

"Don't be ridiculous."

Lawson laughed and kissed her on the cheek. "You're so naïve it's adorable."

FIFTEEN

Cambria had never known what it was like to be wanted. When it came to love, her record was clean. She knew she'd been in love, but always with people who didn't love her back. She'd yet to experience requited love.

For most of her life, Cambria settled for being ordinarily adequate. She watched others soar—getting into Ivy Leagues, building careers, living lives filled with ambition and success—while she felt stuck, a silent witness to her own mediocrity. She believed her best was never quite enough.

Then came Lawson. He was the first person to make her feel like she might be more than the sum of her doubts. That maybe, just maybe, she was worthy of something greater. With him, she glimpsed a possibility she had never allowed herself to imagine—a love that was returned, a bond that was real.

She craved his attention with an intensity that surprised her, deeper than anything she'd felt. And for the first time, Cambria began to believe that love wasn't just something for other people—it could be hers.

By mid-February, Cambria knew nothing except Lawson. Her life had become so absorbed by him that she nearly forgot about everything else.

Sure, they might've been moving quickly, but wasn't that how it was supposed to go? An all-encompassing love that sweeps you up and carries you to new heights.

They stood in his kitchen preparing dinner. Cambria was cutting up a baguette and ricotta, Lawson was searing the meat. Cambria finished with the bread and cheese, then grabbed a head of romaine from the fridge. She washed the vegetables, then began chopping them up, starting with the cucumber and tomato, finishing with the red onion. Lawson topped up her glass of wine, then took a swig from the bottle.

He stood behind her, watching over her shoulder. He placed his hand over hers as she cut the asparagus, then took the knife from her hand, placing it on the counter. She turned around and looked up at him. "You're so beautiful," he said. He had told her this almost every day since they met, yet still, she did not believe it.

She probably never would. But that was her own problem.

He leaned in and kissed her. Gently at first, then, within seconds, the kiss deepened, and his hands were around the back of her head. She wrapped her arms around him, pulling him closer. He pushed the cutting board to the side, then lifted her onto the counter, laying her backwards as he kissed her neck. He made his way down her body, kissing her chest, her breasts, her stomach, her thighs, removing her jeans with ease. Then he pushed himself inside her and fucked her right there on the counter.

Once they were finished, they continued with their dinner preparation. Cambria grabbed her jeans from the ground and slipped them on, then pulled the cutting board in front of her. Lawson opened another bottle of wine.

Over the past six weeks, Cambria had learned nearly everything there was to know about Lawson. He had laid his past bare in painstaking detail, never shying away from the darker corners of his life. He wasn't a good man—she knew that—but for reasons unbeknownst to her, she did not care. Her desire to be loved outweighed any moral compass she may have had. Besides, those things were behind him now, left in the past where they belonged. He was a changed person (so he claimed). Still, Cambria could see the parts of him that once existed, bleeding through his personality, seeping into their relationship. Sure, there were red flags and warning signs, but nothing she couldn't fix. And Cambria was certain that the love she could give him would remedy any of that.

All her life, she had walked a fine line between wrong and right. She knew what was bad for her yet wanted it anyways. She had always played on the safe side, but that didn't mean the other side didn't pique her interest. She craved reckless precarity but had never been given the opportunity to taste it. Back home, she was the good girl: obedient daughter, rule-follower, predictable in every way. How boring. She wanted danger. She wanted the thrill of uncertainty. And Lawson was all of that, distilled into one intoxicating man. The only difference between them was that he acted on his thoughts, whereas Cambria suppressed them.

She quite enjoyed the benevolent role she'd curated for herself, never wanting to be seen as aberrant, much like her brother. He was the bad one, the troublemaker, the one everyone had doubts about. She, on the other hand, was the good one, the law-abider, the stickler for rules. Yet she could not deny what felt true to her core.

There was something alluring about it. Perhaps that was why she was so drawn to Lawson in the first place; he embodied everything she had always wanted to be but never could.

Here he was, living an accomplished and successful life, while also acknowledging his faults and wrongdoings. Cambria longed to do the same. To break free from the restraints society had cast on her, the rigid compulsion to be polite and graceful, and instead, simply be bad.

When it came to Lawson's drug use, Cambria was unsure how to feel. Since her brother's death, she held a vendetta against drugs. Albeit she could acknowledge it wasn't the drugs that killed him—he did that himself. The drugs were a byproduct, not a cause. He had been broken long before that.

She wondered if she and her brother were the same in that sense.

It often plagued her mind, the differences between them, what had divided his fate from hers. They had been raised by the same parents, in the same household. What changed? What went wrong? Where did their lives diverge?

There was only one thing that separated them now, and that was life from death.

She tried to do everything not to be like him, not to end up like him. But being around Lawson dredged everything up again.

She believed his cocaine use that very first day was a one-off—until it continued happening. As it turned out, Lawson used cocaine nearly every single day. In the mornings, before work. In the afternoons, with his coffee. In the evenings, no matter what they were doing—whether that was going out for dinner or watching TV.

Suffice to say, he had a bit of a problem. But he didn't seem to think so.

What she was unaware of at the time was the laundry list of other drugs he was also doing recreationally. Weed, ketamine, uppers, downers—you name it. By the time she discovered the rest, it was already too late. She was falling for him, hard, and any self-respect she once had was now gone. Therefore, she did not protest. She did not express her concerns. She did not tell him that his behavior was problematic. And as more time passed, she felt her reserve slipping farther and farther away. As badly as she wanted her dignity, she feared what would happen if she spoke up. The worst outcome for her at that time was Lawson leaving her.

She tried to justify it, telling herself that everybody has their flaws, and there were people who were much worse. Instead, she focused on the positives, such as how she felt when she was with him. That was the only thing that mattered, the silver lining in his flaws.

When Cambria really weighed out her options, she realized there were none. That's what they call Hobson's choice. She could either leave

Lawson and be single and alone, just as she'd been for her entire life, feeling empty and devoid of anything and everything. Or she could stay with him and continue feeling wanted and revered.

"I've never felt this way about anyone," he told her one evening as they lay in bed, post sex.

She was dumb enough to actually believe him.

SIXTEEN

A Sunday afternoon outing to the grocery store resulted in an unwanted run-in with a stranger from the past.

Lawson was browsing the shelves as Cambria pushed the cart down the aisle. What she liked most about Lawson was that he always needed to be touching her. Whether that was keeping his palm on the small of her back, holding her hand, or slinging his arm around her shoulders. She relished any moment their skin made contact.

"Lawson?" a voice said. Both their heads turned at the mention of his name. And there, standing in the middle of the aisle, was a petite blond with big brown eyes. Lawson did not respond. Cambria looked at him questioningly. "Got your claws in another one already?" the girl said.

"Do I know you?" Lawson finally spoke.

The girl laughed. "You've got to be fucking joking. Are you seriously going to play that card right now?"

"I have no idea what you're talking about." He turned to Cambria, "let's go," he grabbed her hand and began to pull her.

"I'd be careful if I were you," the girl said, looking directly at Cambria. At this, Cambria stopped abruptly. "He's not who you think he is."

"I'm sorry?" Cambria said.

"Just watch out," the girl said. "And be careful."

"What are you talking about?" She could feel Lawson pulling her and fought every urge in her body to resist, ultimately allowing him to lead her away. Cambria looked back at the girl in the aisle, who stood there staring at them as they left. "What the fuck was that?" she said to him once they had turned the corner.

Lawson would not look at her, just kept walking, his hand still in hers.

She let go, dropping his hand, stopping in her tracks. "Lawson," she commanded, her voice stern. "Answer me."

He looked back at her. "Not here."

"Why?"

He looked frustrated. "I'll tell you once we get outside."

They abandoned the groceries, leaving the cart in the aisle where the confrontation had happened. Once they were back in his truck, Cambria stared at him, waiting for a response.

He took a moment to think. "That was my ex. Heather."

"Why did you pretend not to know her?"

"Because she's crazy."

"That's… weird. Why would you pretend not to know someone?"

"I just told you," he snapped. "Do you not listen?"

"I don't understand. Why was she telling me to be careful?"

"Because she's a fucking lunatic, that's why. She'll do anything she can to ruin my life. She obviously saw me in there happy with you and is jealous."

"When did you guys break up?"

"A while ago."

"How long is *a while ago*?"

"Over a year ago." This was a lie. They broke up at the beginning of December, only a month before he met Cambria. But she did not know that, and therefore, believed anything he told her.

Later that night, they lay in bed, tangled beneath the sheets. He stroked her skin with his finger, pressed his lips to her shoulder and kissed it. "You're so perfect," he said.

"No, I'm not."

"Your skin is so smooth. How do you keep it so smooth?"

"Moisturizer," she said, "and Victoria's Secret body lotion."

He laughed, finding this amusing. Then he said, "I think I'm in love with you."

This caught her off guard. She wasn't expecting him to say it so soon. She was, of course, feeling the same way, but would never be the first to say it.

Such words had never been exchanged with Theo. That love was the worst kind: unrequited.

"You *think*?" was her response.

He smiled demurely. "Sorry. I *am* in love with you. I love you, Cambria."

She couldn't contain her own smile. "I love you too."

And just like that, everything changed. All the hardships, all the heartache—they meant nothing, suddenly reduced to a blip of the past in a split second.

Nothing else mattered. For the first time ever, she was experiencing a love that was requited.

When she was young, Cambria imagined growing up, getting married, and starting a family, as if those were her only objectives in life. To think about anything otherwise did not occur to her. It wasn't until she reached young adulthood that she realized these ideals had been injected into her hypodermically. For the first time in her life, she realized she was an autonomous being with the ability to think for herself. And when she really thought about it, the idea of marriage and children simply did not appeal to her the way it once did. Cambria envisioned great things for herself, for her future, and she feared that having a child would hinder her.

With that being said, she wasn't *completely* opposed to the idea. Sometimes she thought about it, being a mother. It would be neat, she concluded, having a carbon copy of herself. Someone to care for and raise and shape into a full person.

Regardless, she liked knowing she had options, and that ultimately, it was her choice, not the choice of anyone else.

When she tried explaining this to Lawson, he seemed utterly perplexed. "So, you *don't* want kids?"

"I never said that. I just haven't made up my mind yet. And I like to weigh out my options."

"But women are supposed to have babies. Heather was always going on about how badly she wanted one."

"Having babies is fine. But not having babies is also fine."

"So there's a possibility that you won't have kids?"

"I don't know. Is this an important question to you?"

"Kind of, yeah. I want to start a family. I've always wanted a son. To teach him everything I know. I want to give my kid a better life than my parents gave me. I'd make sure he had everything he ever wanted and never went without. I'd be the best father in the world to him."

"Or her," Cambria said.

"What?"

"If you had a daughter."

"Sure," he said, an afterthought, as if having a daughter had never occurred to him. "I guess a girl would be alright."

Cambria smiled to herself. "A girl would be perfect."

Cambria came home from work and took a bath. She lit some candles and put on music as she lay in the tub with her eyes closed. Once she was done, she wrapped herself in a towel and walked to the kitchen, filling a pot of water to boil, then reached for the phone to call Lawson. He was supposed to be at her place for six. It was now six fifteen.

There was no answer.

She proceeded to make herself dinner, despite the fact that they usually ate together. After pouring herself a glass of wine, she brought her plate of pasta into the living room and got situated on the couch while she turned on the TV. Her eyes flickered to the clock on the wall. It was now 6:45.

He kind of had a habit of doing this, showing up late, and in some cases, not at all. He'd claim later that something came up, or that he forgot. Other times, he'd show up hours later, citing the same excuses; he got caught up at work, had to take an important call, had fallen asleep, lost track of the time.

Seven o'clock came and still no word from him. She waited and waited, growing impatient and frustrated. The later he was, the more upset she became.

He finally arrived shortly after eight, fluttering into the room with a flurry of excuses. His neighbor's house had flooded, he said, and their dog escaped, and Lawson was the only possible person who could have helped. And then, while on his way over here, was stuck in traffic.

He apologized profusely.

Cambria stood there staring at him, unsure of what to make of the situation. "It's fine," she said. "Not a big deal."

"I love you," he said, his remedy for everything. He kissed her, and as he pulled away, his gaze lingered on her for just a second longer. That look always made her forget everything else. That look could make her do anything he asked.

He followed her into the living room and flopped down on the sofa. He closed his eyes, stretched his neck. Cambria sat on the loveseat next to him. She stared at him, waiting. He didn't move. Didn't speak. "I was thinking…" she began. "There's supposed to be a nice sunset tonight.

Can we go to the beach?" She watched his face as she spoke. He gave no indication that he even heard her. "Lawson?"

He stirred slightly, then opened one eye and looked at her. "Not tonight, babe. I'm exhausted from work."

"I thought you had today off."

"No, that's tomorrow you're thinking."

"You told me on Monday that it was today."

"No," he said, sitting up now. "Lucien had an appointment today, so I obviously couldn't have taken it off. I told you it was tomorrow."

"Alright, sorry." She sat with her thoughts, unsure of what to say next. "What should we do tonight then, if we can't go to the beach?"

"Why are you saying it like that? I get that you wanted to go to the beach, but you don't have to give me fucking attitude. I told you I'm exhausted."

"I'm not giving you attitude. It was a simple question."

He rolled his eyes, flopped back on the couch. "Can we just watch a movie or something?"

"Sure," she acquiesced. "What do you want to watch?"

"Anything but another rom-com."

"Alright. I'll let you choose then."

"Can you make me something to eat? I'm starving."

"Well maybe if you had arrived on time like you were supposed to we could have eaten together."

"Oh, here we go again with the attitude. What is with you tonight?"

She was stunned. "You showed up here over two hours late and then demand I make you dinner."

"I wasn't demanding, I was asking. And if it's that much of a fucking hassle to make your boyfriend dinner then I'll just go out and get something myself."

She stared at him, deadpan. "Will noodles suffice? That's all I have."

"Sure."

She went to the kitchen and filled a pot with water yet again. She stood off to the side, leaning against the counter as she waited for the water to bottle. She peeked into the living room to catch a glimpse of Lawson. He was still lying on the couch with his eyes closed, hands behind his head.

She had the slight urge to strangle him.

Once the noodles were finished, she dumped them into a bowl and gave it to him. He set the bowl aside and pulled her onto his lap. "You're the best, thank you."

It was the first time she faked a smile.

Cambria anticipated the times they would spend in bed. Sometimes when they had sex, it felt like they were making love; the way they'd stare into each other's eyes, his hands in hers. In those moments, she felt the most connected to him. But other times, she felt as though she were just an instrument, her sole purpose being something he could fuck. She would lay beneath him, gazing up as he clenched his eyes, wondering why he wasn't looking at her, what he was thinking. Then he'd come, just like that, and it'd be over. She wouldn't feel better again until he rolled over and cuddled her.

When he suggested they stop using condoms, they did. When he told her to go on birth control, she did. And when he told her it would feel even better if he came inside of her, she allowed him that luxury as well.

It seemed, to Cambria, that everything was about what Lawson wanted. But she couldn't deny that it did feel better without the condoms, having him bare inside her. And when he did eventually come inside of her, it was everything he had told her it would be, subsequently bringing them closer.

He took care of her. He treated her well. And she loved the feeling of being venerated. Being so far from her parents, it was a comfort knowing that if she ran into any problems, Lawson would be the one to step in and save her.

That's what he was there for, after all. He had told her this countless times. That it was his job to protect her. That he would never let anything bad happen to her. And just as often, he liked to remind her that if anyone lay a finger on her, he would kill them.

On a Saturday afternoon in March, they decided to bake cupcakes. Lawson turned up the music, and they danced around the kitchen. Cambria wrapped her arms around his neck, and he pulled her closer. They continued to dance like this, then Lawson grabbed beneath her thighs and lifted her. She wrapped her legs around his torso, and they kissed. She could've seen fireworks.

Once he set her down, she peeked in the stove to check the cupcakes. Lawson opened the fridge and grabbed a beer.

"A bit early to start drinking, no?" she laughed. It was one o'clock in the afternoon.

"I'm a grown adult, are you seriously trying to tell me when I can and can't drink?" She stared at him blankly. "Besides," he continued, "we're going out in a few hours anyways. Figured I'd have a bit of a head start."

"What do you mean *we're going out in a few hours*?"

"To dinner?"

"What are you talking about?"

"We're going out for dinner tonight."

"No, we're not."

"Yes, we are. Did you forget?"

"We never made dinner plans. Mara asked me last week to go for drinks tonight."

"Mara," he scoffed. "That pigeon-eyed bitch always wants something from you."

Cambria furrowed her eyebrows. "First of all, don't insult my friend. Second, she doesn't *always want something from me.* We barely see each other anymore—that's why she asked me to get together tonight, to catch up. Which you would've known if you had asked me what I was doing tonight rather than just assuming I'm always readily available at your beck and call."

He threw the can of beer against the wall, a loud noise erupting as it hit. Cambria flinched. "What the fuck is that supposed to mean?"

She stared at the can as it leaked onto the floor. She returned her attention to him. "You just assumed we had dinner plans tonight, even though you made no mention of it."

"We talked about it on Thursday."

"No, we didn't. What the fuck are you talking about?"

"Is your IQ really that low that you can't remember a conversation from two days ago?" She was stunned, speechless. "You're so fucking stupid sometimes," he turned around and left the room. She heard him going up the stairs.

She stood there, unable to move.

He returned a moment later with her purse and overnight bag. He walked directly to her and dropped them at her feet. "Take your shit and get the fuck out."

"Lawson—"

"No. You don't get to talk back and disrespect me in my own house."

"I wasn't talking back. We were having a conversation—"

"Go have fun getting shitfaced with Mara."

"Are you serious?"

He stared at her.

"You're fucking crazy," she said.

In one quick motion, he slapped her across the face.

She was too stunned to react, to say anything at all. She simply stood there, mouth agape, hand to her cheek from where it stung, staring at him.

"Get the fuck out," he said to her one last time.
And so, she did.

SEVENTEEN

She sat at the table across from Mara absently stroking her cheek where Lawson had struck her earlier. Mara, as usual, was dressed elegantly, despite being at a dive bar. She sipped from her drink intermittingly as she spoke.

"Are you even listening to me?"

Cambria snapped out of whatever daze she was in. "What? Yes."

"What did I just say?"

Cambria paused. "I'm sorry."

"What's going on? You okay?"

Cambria faltered, and that was her tell.

Mara leaned forward. "What's going on?"

"It's nothing. Just a stupid fight I had with Lawson."

"What happened?"

"Nothing. He just…" Cambria paused. "He has a bit of a temper."

"Tell me."

"He goes from zero to one hundred in a matter of seconds. I try to reason with him, but it's like he has tunnel vision, and nothing I do or say can bring him out of it."

"Does this happen often?"

"Not often. But… enough."

"Get him a punching bag," she took another sip of her drink. "My dad had one in our garage growing up. Said it helped him blow off steam after a long day." She sat back in her seat. "Men aren't like us. They have testosterone, and rage. They just want to destroy things. Wasn't it Freud who said man has two drives? Sex drive and kill drive?"

"Yes."

"Yeah, exactly. That's all they do—kill and fuck; that's simply how they operate. But that's why we need to calm them down and mellow them out. Women are nurturers by nature. We're drawn to the damage. It's our job to fix them."

"But that shouldn't be my job," Cambria said. "I wasn't put on this earth to save a man who can't even save himself."

Mara tilted her head, squinted her eyes. "I'm going to give you one piece of advice, hon. Learn to deal with his rage and help him get it under control, or it's going to be you he takes it out on."

Too late for that, Cambria thought to herself.

They spent the next hour going over Lawson's entire life, from childhood to adulthood, trying to pinpoint exactly where the rage stemmed from.

Right off the bat was his parent's divorce. It didn't take a psychology degree to understand this had royally fucked him up. And it had only been a year earlier that Lawson walked in on his mother screwing another man.

His father had been away for the weekend. Lawson, who was nine at the time, ventured downstairs around midnight to get a glass of milk after having yet another nightmare. He'd been getting them since he was five, when his father started beating him.

He was sworn to secrecy by his mother, who told him that if his father ever found out, he'd come home and shoot her in the head. Then he would kill Lawson next, because he never really liked him in the first place. Then he would light their house on fire, killing his sister in the fallout.

His mother didn't seem to care about either of her children, but her daughter she preferred over Lawson.

After the divorce, she took everything and then some. She jetted off across the world with the man from the kitchen, who she married a year later, popping in and out of Lawson's life whenever she felt like it, which meant he was left with his father.

His father could barely afford the meager farmhouse he was forced to move into after the divorce. He'd been fired for drinking at work and therefore was constantly between jobs. Lawson had nowhere to go, forced to watch his father drink himself to sedation. Lawson would silently tiptoe across the room, turn off the television, and cover his father with a blanket before creeping up the stairs and finding solace in his bedroom, where he could finally be alone with his thoughts.

But even that wasn't much better.

He was bullied at school. Kids told him he was ugly and poor, which he was. The irony was not lost on him that his mother was living a luxurious life in the south of France while her son was wearing the same clothes for the third day in a row, barely scraping by with enough food to survive. Plus, he was giving whatever leftover food he had to his sister. That was how he began stealing money—first, from his father's pockets. He would go through his clothing and dump out the change, collecting it in his hands. Then he'd check the sofa. Then the bedrooms and under the beds. Next, he began doing it at school, going into other kid's bags, looking through the teacher's belongings.

He began taking other things too. Things he knew had value that he could sell. He'd split the cash and give half to his sister. Then he'd stash whatever remained in a tiny box beneath his bed, hoping one day he'd have enough for a plane ticket.

Of course, his dreams were futile, and a plane ticket was never acquired. He was never able to escape. He remained living under his father's reign until the age of eighteen, when he finally had enough money saved from selling drugs that he was able to move out for college.

He never looked back.

He still visited with his mother from time to time. She had a habit of disappearing from his life then re-emerging when it was convenient for her. She'd bring him shopping for new clothes, take him for a haircut, get him a new pair of golf clubs. (He didn't even golf) The only useful thing that woman ever did for him was buy his very first truck.

The truck became his escape. He suddenly had the liberty of going wherever he wanted, whenever he wanted, and was never forced to stay anywhere he didn't want to. It was the freedom he had so desperately needed.

Then there was college, where he fell in with the wrong crowd. They sold drugs, they did drugs. They harassed girls, hosted parties. They had the run of the place. Everyone feared them. And that was what Lawson had always wanted: for people to fear him.

And then he met Cambria, and suddenly all of that changed. There was something different about her. She was special and unique, and he wanted to possess her. He began envisioning a future with her. He wanted to make her his wife and give her a child.

Just like all his exes before her.

When Cambria really thought about it, she had to empathize with Lawson. She had never experienced half the shit he had gone through. It would be unfair of her to judge. And at the end of the day, he treated her right and gave her more love than anyone else ever had.

Was she really in a position to complain?

The next morning, he showed up unannounced to take her out for breakfast, acting like everything was normal, as if he hadn't just hit her across the face the day before

She obliged, grudgingly, and used the drive to the restaurant to formulate her response.

As they sat at the table, Lawson across from her cutting into his bacon, she studied his facial features, watching how his eyes focused narrowly on the plate in front of him. He was gorgeous, with his emerald eyes and perfect jaw line. She wondered how it was possible, this duality that existed within him, as if he were two different people simultaneously.

"We need to talk about yesterday," she said, breaking the silence.

"What about?" he continued cutting into his food, stuffing a piece of egg into his mouth. "You hit me, Lawson."

He stopped, as if only just now remembering. "Fuck. I am so sorry."

"Why would you do that?"

"I didn't mean to. I just…" he paused. "Something came over me. I'm not sure what. My vision went black, like I was blind with rage. You know I would never hurt you."

"But you did hurt me."

He looked down, then after a moment, returned his eyes to her. "Are you okay?"

"I'm fine. I just don't understand how you could do that to me."

"It was an accident."

"You don't *accidentally* hit someone you claim to love."

"I *do* love you. More than anything. I've never felt this way with anyone before. You know all about my past. You know everything there is to know about me. I've never shared this much with anyone. But I feel close to you, I feel… different with you. You understand me. And you love me regardless of everything else. I don't want to screw this up. I can't lose you. Please, you can't leave me."

"I'm not going to leave you. But that can't happen again."

"I promise it won't."

"You really need to work on your anger. I understand you've had a difficult life, but there's things you can do to manage the rage."

"I know, I'm sorry. I promise I will."

"Are you trying to turn into your dad?"

She instantly regretted saying it, seeing the look on his face. "I am nothing like my father."

"Well then don't act like him."

The weeks that followed were blissful and flawless. March faded into April, and Cambria soon forgot about the incident altogether. His behavior was exemplary, never raising his voice even a decibel. He showed up on time. He picked her up and took her out, made her breakfasts and dinners. He took her shopping, buying her anything she desired. He even surprised her with a necklace.

No one had ever bought her jewelry before.

"I would do anything for you," he said to her. "I would die for you. I would kill for you."

As the weather got nicer, they'd venture down to the beach, a blanket and picnic basket packed with their favorite snacks. But as she sat there with Lawson watching the waves crash into the shore, she couldn't help but think about one person in particular.

That was *their* spot, after all.

She hadn't seen Jackson since that night at the bowling alley. They'd spoken a few times since then, but their correspondence dwindled significantly as she spent more time with Lawson. She knew Jackson didn't like that she had gotten a boyfriend, and that angered her, because he was a hypocrite. But at the same time, he was her best friend, and she couldn't deny that she missed him.

She called him the very next day.

"Hey, stranger," he said. "Long time no talk."

"How have you been?"

"I'm good. Things are… good. How are you?"

"I'm good," she replied.

"Busy with the boyfriend?"

"I guess you could say that. How's Natalia?"

"She just bought a motorcycle."

"A motorcycle? I didn't know she was a biker."

"She's not. Don't ask."

Cambria laughed. "I miss you."

"Yeah I'm sure you do."

"Don't you miss me too?"

"Sometimes." It was quiet for a moment. "My family's been asking about you."

"Really?"

"Yeah, wondering where the hell you disappeared to. I told them you've been preoccupied with your new relationship."

"Don't say it like that."

"It's true."

"Are you mad at me?"

"No. Are you mad at me?"

"No. I want to see you."

"Oh. Okay. When?"

"Thursday? After work?"

"Coffee, or drinks?"

"You know I'm inclined to say drinks, but maybe we should do coffee."

"That's fair. Okay, it's a date. See you then."

On Wednesday night, she and Lawson sat in her kitchen eating dinner. She had made his favorite (fettuccini alfredo) in hopes to cheer him up since work had been rough for him that week. "You should take a bath," Cambria suggested. "I'll give you a massage afterwards."

"You're a doll. Thanks, babe."

"I have Epsom salt."

"What the hell is that?"

"How do you not know what Epsom salt is? It's good for sore muscles."

"Oh."

"Yeah."

He stretched his arms above his head. "Do you want to go see a movie?" he asked.

"Tonight?"

"No. Tomorrow."

"I can't tomorrow."

"Why?"

"I have plans."

"With who? Mara?"

"No," she hesitated. "Jackson."

"Jackson?"

"Yeah, you remember my friend Jackson?"

"I'm not an imbecile, Cambria. I remember him. I also remember that he's in love with you."

"Oh my God, he is not."

"Why do girls always do this—act all innocent and dumb about it?"

"Can you stop? He's my best friend and I haven't seen him in a while. I thought it'd be nice to get coffee and catch up."

"So this was *your* idea?"

"Is that a problem?"

"*Coffee?*"

"Why are you saying it like that? It's just coffee, Lawson."

"Coffee. On a Thursday night. Seems a bit conspicuous, no?"

She actually had to laugh at that. "Are you serious right now? What, you think I'm going to go fuck him at Starbucks?"

"Are you?"

"You're actually insane."

"I'm insane? *You're* insane. You're the one who thinks this is okay."

"HE'S MY BEST FRIEND. I'VE KNOWN HIM LONGER THAN I'VE KNOWN YOU."

"I don't want you being friends with him."

"That's not up to you."

He stood abruptly, the chair shoved backwards in his wake. "I suggest you reconsider what you just said to me."

She stared at him, challenging him. "Go fuck yourself."

At that, he grabbed hold of the kitchen table and threw it to the side, all its contents crashing to the floor. He grabbed her and heaved her up, shoving her against the wall, his grip tight.

He held her there for a moment, their faces mere inches apart. Cambria stared back, not daring to move a muscle. She did not blink.

Then, he spit in her face and released his grip on her. She slid to the floor. He picked her up again and tossed her to the side. She skidded across the floor, over the broken plates, landing on her shoulder. She winced in pain as something cut into her. He grabbed her again and threw her in the other direction, and this time, she hit the fridge. She knocked her head off the corner and fell forwards, landing on her face.

She did not move. She could feel him hovering over her. He waited a moment, then used his foot to push her over so that she was on her back, facing him. "Let's try this again," he said as he stared down at her, his face unwavering. "You're not seeing Jackson for coffee tomorrow. Understand?"

She breathed in once. Then again. And again and again and again. She lay there, holding his gaze, counting her breaths. Then she opened her mouth and said, "fuck you."

His face contorted into something she'd never seen before. That was the last thing she saw before his foot came down on her face, and everything went black.

EIGHTEEN

With nowhere else to go, she went to the only place that made sense—her safe haven.

Jackson was taken aback at the sight of her. "What happened?"

"I fell."

"It looks like you got in a fight."

"You should see the other guy."

He gave her a peculiar look. "Are you okay?"

"I'm fine. Can you get me some ice?"

They diverged in the foyer; he went to the kitchen, and she went upstairs to his bedroom, grateful his family wasn't around to ask questions.

Cambria flopped onto his bed and grabbed a pillow to hug. She thought about Lawson and her heart clenched. Jackson walked in just as she began to cry.

He looked at her, then closed the door behind him and sat on the bed next to her. "Are you going to tell me what happened now?" he said as he handed her the icepack.

"I'm fine, it's fine."

"You're clearly not fine. You look like shit."

She sniffled and wiped her eyes. "Thanks."

"Did someone do this to you? Did *he* do this to you?"

She didn't respond.

He stood, "I'm calling the police."

"No!" She grabbed his arm.

"Why not?"

"Please, Jackson. Please don't."

He hesitated a moment, then sat down again. "Tell me what happened."

She told him everything. When she was done, he said, "has this happened before?"

She hesitated. "Well, no."

"That's a lie."

"Not like this. This was… something else entirely. Last time it was just a slap across the face. But that was a month ago, and it never happened again."

"Real men don't hit women."

"I know."

"Do you, though? Because it doesn't seem like you're holding him accountable right now."

"I just don't know what to say."

"I tried to tell you from the beginning. I warned you."

"Don't. Not now, Jackson."

There was so much more he could've said, but he didn't. "We'll talk more in the morning."

"Am I staying here?"

"Obviously."

"What about Natalia?"

"What about her?"

"Won't she be mad?"

"She doesn't need to know." He held her gaze for a moment, then stood. "I'll get you something to sleep in." He went to his closet and grabbed a pair of trackpants and a Metallica t-shirt, then went downstairs to get her water.

When he returned, she was curled up in his bed. He turned off the light, then crawled into bed next to her, pulling the covers over them both. He gave her an extra pillow to hold.

She lay on her back, staring up at the ceiling, counting her breaths. Her face stung. Her shoulder hurt. And most of all, her heart ached, which was worse than any physical pain.

She listened to Jackson's breathing and matched her own breaths to his. She was restless, her mind erratic. She knew she'd never find sleep. Not like this. "Jackson," she said through the silence of the dark.

"Cambri."

"Can we smoke weed? I don't think I'll be able to sleep."

"Sure." He sat up and turned on his bedside lamp. Then he got up and went to his dresser, grabbing the weed and pipe. He opened the window, and she sat up and crawled over to him. He packed it for her and lit it.

Once they had both taken a few hits and she was decently high, they crawled back into bed.

He turned off the light, and she closed her eyes. Minutes passed. Her body was itching to touch him. She turned onto her side and moved closer to him. He lifted his arm instinctively and she snuggled into him, laying her head on his chest. And it is there that she finally found sleep.

The next morning, she awoke to Jackson's alarm blaring. Her head was still on his chest—neither of them had moved in the night.

At the sound of the alarm, they both startled awake. He reached over and turned it off. It was seven-thirty. They both had work at nine.

She extricated herself from him and moved back to her pillow. He looked over at her, eyes sleepy. "You okay?"

She nodded.

Jackson got up and got dressed for work. He disappeared for a few minutes, then returned with a pair of dress pants and a blouse from his sister's closet. He handed them to Cambria, and she went to the bathroom to change.

While in there, she scoured the drawers, looking for Victoria's makeup. Once she located some concealer and foundation, she caked her face until the bruises were barely visible.

When they were both dressed and presentable, they made their way down to the kitchen. His parents, thankfully, were already gone for the day. Jackson put on a pot of coffee and popped two bagels into the toaster. Cambria slid into the chair and bit at her fingernails.

"You clean up well," he remarked.

"We can thank your sister's makeup for that."

"How do you feel?"

She shrugged. "I've been better."

"You should go to the police."

"I'm not going to the police."

"Then you're an idiot."

She furrowed her eyebrows.

"Sorry but it's true."

"Alright."

He stared at her. "Are we going to talk about it?"

"No. Not now. Not… with you."

"Why?"

"Because you won't understand. You'll never understand."

"Yeah, you're right, I don't understand. Explain it to me. Make it make sense."

"I'm not doing this."

He shook his head. "You're delusional."

"Maybe." She looked down, picking at her fingers. "I appreciate everything you've done for me. I don't know what I'd do without you."

At that, he snorted. "You're going to go back to him, aren't you?"

She didn't respond.

"He's just going to keep doing it, you know that, right?"

As badly as she wanted to convince herself otherwise, she knew Jackson was right. And despite how wrong Lawson was for her, she also knew this wasn't the end for them.

Not by a long shot.

Because at the end of the day, what it really came down to was how being with Lawson made her feel. No one else could do that for her. And what Cambria feared more than anything—more than Lawson himself—was being alone. His words reverberated through her mind: *Go ahead, leave me, try and find someone else.*

For the first time she wondered at which point she began to lose herself completely and become someone unrecognizable.

NINETEEN

As Rita Mae Brown once said, insanity is doing the same thing over and over again and expecting a different result. If that was the case, then perhaps Cambria really was insane.

Enthralled by the violence, she thought there could be no greater love. Trapped in a paradoxical cycle of fighting and forgiving, screaming and then sex. Happiness, and heartache. It was a mercurial high, and she was addicted.

She took the good days as they came and relished the euphoric feeling that Lawson's presence brought. She anticipated their next fight, where he'd pin her against the wall, arms above her head. And then his mouth would be on hers, hot and violent.

He was a drug, and her tolerance kept going up and up, constantly needing more just to feel something.

Over time, her subservience weaned, and she became someone else entirely: she turned into something resembling him.

When he'd yell at her, she'd yell louder. When he'd slap her across the face, she'd slap him back twice as hard. Anything he did to her, she reciprocated, wanting to give him a taste of his own medicine.

By doing this, she felt she had garnered his respect. And while that may have been true, he still needed control, and Cambria's relentless endurance only made him angrier, her blatant disregard for conceding ultimately making things worse.

On the last Friday in April, he took her out to dinner. She finished getting ready in the upstairs bathroom while Lawson waited for her in the kitchen. She put in her earrings, adjusted her dress, and made her way downstairs.

Upon entering the kitchen, Lawson's eyes trailed the length of her body. His face tightened. "You're not leaving the house in that."

"Why not? I thought I looked nice."

"You do. But I don't want to have to kill anyone tonight."

This pleased her.

"You're so fucking hot," he said.

She walked towards him, slow and methodical. "How bad do you want to fuck me right now?"

"So fucking bad."

"Then fuck me."

In one quick motion, he turned her around and bent her over the kitchen table, pulling up her dress. She wasn't wearing underwear. "Jesus, are you trying to get me arrested?" He unbuckled his jeans and pushed inside her. He shoved her face against the table and fucked her rigorously.

Once he came, he pulled out and zipped up his jeans, handing her a few tissues. She tugged her dress back down her thighs, then re-applied her lipstick.

At the restaurant, they sat in a corner booth at the back, away from everyone else, just as Lawson preferred. He hated being around other people. Hated conversing. Hated her socializing with anyone that wasn't him.

They ordered appetizers and beers, and each got a shot of tequila. Cambria was only on her second drink by the time Lawson was on his fifth. "We should go away somewhere," he said, stars in his eyes.

"Like where?"

"Cabo. Hawaii. I'd go anywhere with you."

"I'd love to go to Asia."

"Fuck Asia."

The waiter appeared to collect their plates, and Lawson looked up at him. "Can I get another rum and coke?"

"I'll take another as well," Cambria chimed in.

"Uh, she's good, actually. She'll just have water."

She looked at him. "I don't want water."

"I think you've had enough to drink." The waiter stood there uncomfortably, unsure of how to proceed. "She'll take a water," Lawson reaffirmed. The waiter looked to Cambria. "Don't look at her, look at me."

"Lawson!" At that, the waiter disappeared. "What the fuck is your problem? I've only had two drinks."

"Alright, Cambria," he laughed dismissively, like she was some dumb teenager who couldn't handle her alcohol.

As Cambria frowned, two men walked by their booth and her eyes flickered in their direction.

Upon seeing this, Lawson snapped. "Did you just look at her?"

The two men stopped once they realized he was speaking to them. "Uh, no, buddy, we're just going to the restroom."

"Together? Faggots."

"*Lawson*!"

"Keep your eyes off my fucking girlfriend."

The men continued walking, thankfully, and Cambria's face flushed with heat. "You're embarrassing me."

"Oh, I'm embarrassing you, am I? You're fucking embarrassing me. You're trashed off two drinks."

"I'm not even drunk! I'm fucking sober."

"Alright, that's enough," he abruptly stood. "We're going home."

"We haven't even finished eating yet."

"I'm no longer hungry." He took out his wallet, threw down a few bills, then grabbed her, yanking her up.

"You're causing a scene," she growled as he dragged her through the restaurant, eyes trailing after them.

They walked outside in a haste. Lawson pulled out his keys as they approached his truck, heading straight for the driver's side.

Cambria intercepted him, grabbing his keys and blocking the door.

"What are you doing?" he said.

"You can't drive, you're plastered."

"Are you fucked? Give me the keys." He tried to grab them from her, but she pulled away, causing him to lose his balance.

She laughed. "See?"

"Give me the keys."

"You're not driving."

"I smoked my first cigarette at the age of ten—you really think you can tell me what to do?"

"I'm not seeing the relevance *or* the correlation."

"Give me the fucking keys."

She did not relent.

He lunged forward and shoved her head back against the truck. She dropped the keys reflexively. He bent down and grabbed them before she had the chance. "Get in the fucking truck."

Hand pressed to her head, she conceded, walking around to the passenger side and getting in. He stuck the keys in the ignition.

As he reversed out of the spot, she made a silent prayer that they would crash. Maybe then he'd die. Maybe they both would.

By some miracle they made it home unscathed. Cambria did not believe in God, but that night she did. He parked the truck in the driveway, and they went into the house.

She went straight to the kitchen and filled a glass of water. He came up behind her and she handed it to him. He drained the whole thing in three seconds.

"Are you still hungry?" he asked.

"No."

"You look beautiful."

"You're fucking insane."

"I would kill for you."

She rolled her eyes. "I'm aware."

"Do you believe me?"

"Honestly? Yeah. And that scares me."

"You shouldn't be scared. Opposite of scared. You should feel safe and protected."

"Yet somehow, I don't."

He took her by the hand and led her upstairs to the bedroom, where slowly, inch by inch, he kissed her entire body before removing her dress.

As she lay back on the bed, he crawled on top of her, kissing her neck, her mouth, and she let him, because this was her favorite part, after all.

His kiss deepened, and she melted into him. He took off his pants and flipped her over so that she was on her stomach. She arched her back, bracing for him to enter her. And once he did, a searing pain ripped through her body. She cried out, pushing him off her.

"What? What happened?"

"It hurts." She turned around and looked up at him.

"Why?"

"What do you mean *why*? We've had sex four times today."

This seemed to perplex him. "I'll be gentle."

Reluctantly, she turned over, and they tried again. He pushed in slower this time, as if that would make a difference.

She gasped out in pain. "Stop."

He pulled out and collapsed onto the bed next to her, looking up at the ceiling.

She rolled onto her side to face him. "Lawson?"

He didn't respond.

"I can't help it that I'm sore," she said. "That's *your* fault, not mine."

"Yes, it's my fault. Everything is always my fault."

"Well it *is* your fault. This is *your* doing."

"Are you really that disgusted by me? You can't even look at me or have sex with me."

"What the fuck are you talking about? I'm in pain. You fucking hurt me."

"If you don't want to have sex with me just say it. You don't need to make up bullshit excuses."

"I'm not making this up."

"I know you don't love me. I can see it in your face. You're repulsed by me. You don't want to be with me anymore. You're going to leave me, just like everyone else."

"You know that's not true."

He turned over on his side, away from her.

"Lawson," she reached out and touched his shoulder. "I love you."

"Do you?"

"Yes, you know I do. More than anything, or anyone."

Slowly, he turned around. Once they were face to face, they stared into each other's eyes. "I'm nothing without you," she continued. "I need you."

"Tell me you love me."

"I love you." Then she kissed him. It was slow at first, tentative, but quickly gained momentum. He pulled her on top of him, and she moved her hips, grinding her body into him.

He kissed her harder, deeper. Then he lifted her hips, just slightly, and brought her back down slowly until he was inside of her again. She nearly screamed out in pain, but his mouth engulfed hers, silencing her cries. It felt like she was being ripped apart from the inside as he thrusted into her.

The burning pain seemed to lessen the longer it went on. She was tuned out mentally, and the less she focused on it, the less she could feel it.

Finally, just when she couldn't take it any longer, he finished, and Cambria pulled herself off him, turning to the side as she lay there and caught her breath.

Lawson stood abruptly and went into the bathroom. She heard the shower start.

He didn't come back.

TWENTY

On the fourteenth of May, Cambria turned twenty-three.

It had been exactly one year since she woke up in her childhood bedroom on the other side of the country, the realization dawning on her. One year since she made the decision that would change the course of her life.

Her parents called to wish her a happy birthday. She spoke with them for over an hour before Lawson interrupted with breakfast in bed. Bacon, eggs, and orange juice. She smiled and thanked him as he slid into bed next to her, kissing her cheek. "I have the entire day planned for you," he told her.

"You're sweet," she smiled. "I feel old."

"You are far from old."

"I've always wondered what age I'd live to," she confessed. "I remember being a kid, learning what death was. And ever since then, I've had this weird fascination with it. More curiosity than fear. There's so much uncertainty surrounding it."

"Not really. I mean, that's life. You live and you die. There's not much more to it."

"But what if there is? That's the thing, we don't know. It's the ambiguity that gets to me."

"Do you think you're going to die or something?"

"No. I don't know. But when I do, I want to make sure I lived a good life."

He kissed her on the nose. "You have nothing to worry about. You're young and vivacious." He gave her a look. *That* look. "I'll give you something to live for." He lifted the sheets and went down on her.

Despite Lawson's grandiose plans, Cambria had only one request for her birthday, and that was to go to the waterfront. That was her happy place.

Prior to that, they drove around in his truck, picked up milkshakes, played tennis. She thought about home and wondered when she would visit next. Perhaps her parents could come out here, see the life she'd created for herself, meet Lawson.

On second thought, maybe it was best they didn't meet Lawson.

After a couple hours at the beach, Lawson took her out to an expensive restaurant for dinner. She wore a red dress and heels that he did his very best not to rip off her.

As she sat across from him at the table, watching as he cut into his food, she felt a strange feeling erupt inside of her. She loved him, she really did. It was true that no one had ever made her feel the way that Lawson did. He adored her, worshipped her, and treated her like gold. Except for the times he didn't. Obviously there was the violence, the anger, the aggression. He was two different people existing in one. But she didn't see the two as mutually exclusive. She couldn't have one without the other. She knew she both loved and hated him. And so, she learned to take the good with the bad, cherishing whatever moments they were able to have together. But sitting there across from him, it suddenly dawned on her how different her day would've been if it had been Jackson there instead.

They would've started the day with chocolate chip banana pancakes, their favorite. They'd take their bikes around town and end up getting pizza from Gina's. They'd go to the beach, jump off the pier. Maybe have a picnic, split a bottle of rosé. They'd drive around in his car, blasting music, singing at the top of their lungs. They'd have cake with his parents, and smoke weed in his backyard before going in the hot tub, where they'd gaze at the stars and talk about the universe. Then they'd end their night by the fire, cuddled up with a blanket and a few beers.

After all, it was his birthday too. And that, for them, would constitute the perfect day. She'd fall asleep in his bed beside him, happy and content, not a worry in the world.

But instead, her day was hijacked by Lawson, who projected his idealized version of what a perfect birthday for her should be. She didn't even want bacon and eggs for breakfast, nor did she want to dress up in high heels just to eat a meal.

He thought he knew her so well, but in reality, he did not know her at all. He simply enjoyed creating a version of her that he preferred, and she, stupidly, had let him.

She didn't even know who she was anymore. She had only come to know the version of herself that Lawson wanted her to be.

Since she was unable to spend their actual birthday together, the very next day Cambria came up with an excuse as to why she couldn't see Lawson and covertly made her way to Jackson's house. She had spent hours the night before making him a mixtape of his favorite songs.

They sat at his kitchen table eating leftover birthday cake. He told her about his day, and she did the same. Then, because she couldn't wait any longer, she pulled out the mixtape, which was wrapped in a red bow, and handed it to him.

He turned it over in his hands, staring at it. She watched his face, waiting for him to break out in a smile, or look at her, tell her thank you—anything. But he remained placid, his face unwavering.

"Do you know what it is?" she asked.

"Of course I know what it is."

"Do you hate it or something?"

He pursed his lips together, then grinned from ear to ear, yet still did not say anything.

"What?" she asked. "Why aren't you saying anything?"

"Stay here." He left the room, disappearing down the hall, the mixtape still in his hand. When he returned a moment later, he handed her a present. "Open it," he said. "Now."

Baffled, she tore into the wrapping paper. It was a mixtape. "No way."

It was only then that he started laughing, and so did she.

"Should we go test them out?" he said.

"What are we waiting for?" She stood, and just like that, they were out the door, down the driveway, and in his car.

They played the mixtape he had given her first. Jackson rolled down the windows, and they sang *Highway to Hell*, wind whipping her hair violently in every direction. *Pour Some Sugar on Me* by Def Leppard, *I Remember You* by Skid Row. She was giddy. The tape ended with Scorpions' *No One Like You*, which was one of *their* songs.

Every song on the tape was one of *their songs.*

After that, they switched it over to the tape she had given him. *Hey Jude, Thunderstruck, Master of Puppets,* and finally ending with Queen's *You're My Best Friend.*

Jackson turned down the music and said, "You're my best friend."

This warmed her soul. "You're *my* best friend."

"You know, I can't act like this with anyone else."

"Why not?"

"Everyone's judgmental. Natalia's always telling me to grow up."

"That's rude."

He shrugged. "She thinks it's immature."

"We're not immature. We're just having fun."

"That's what I said."

"She needs to fuck off."

At this, Jackson laughed. Then he looked at her somberly. "I like that I can be myself around you. You don't judge me. You accept me. It's not like that with anyone else."

"Not even your parents?"

"My parents expect a lot from me. It's hard to explain."

"And what about Natalia? Who are you supposed to be when you're around her?"

"Her boyfriend."

"Yeah, but who is that?"

He thought about it. "I'm not sure I know."

She remained quiet as she watched the road pass before them. How had it never occurred to her that what Jackson was describing was exactly how she felt about him? She didn't see it before, but she saw it now; how she was always slipping into different skins depending on who she was with. How she was constantly shapeshifting into whatever version people expected of her. But not with Jackson. Jackson was the only person she could be her true, genuine self with—no fear of judgment, no repercussions. She could let her guard down. She didn't have to hide anything. She had always felt like no one understood her. But Jackson did. And that was because he was the same.

This was the real Cambria. And it was with him, and only with him, that she truly felt like she belonged.

TWENTY-ONE

Once she was back in Jackson's orbit, it was like she'd never left. And she realized she'd do just about anything to keep it that way.

Knowing that Lawson would never approve of their friendship, she decided to keep it a secret.

Turns out it was easier than she thought.

As the summer months approached, Lawson became busier at work. Long days turned into long nights, and it felt like the universe was working in her favor. The timing couldn't have been better. During the last five months, she and Lawson had been nearly inseparable. And now, all of a sudden, he was not as available as he'd once been. Cambria had all the time in the world to herself.

Jackson, of course, was still with Natalia, a fact that baffled Cambria entirely. It seemed nothing had changed in their relationship. They still fought and bickered and argued constantly. He complained about her all the time. Most of the complaints centered on Natalia's perpetual trust issues which stemmed from the fact that her last two boyfriends had cheated on her. Regardless of Jackson's good intentions, on top of his proven track record of being faithful and loyal, she remained skeptical of his love for her. Hence why she hated Cambria and did not want

Jackson being friends with her, convinced they were having an affair. It didn't help that nearly everyone in Pine Hills had mistaken Cambria for Jackson's girlfriend.

But the trust issues didn't end with Cambria. Natalia was wary of every person Jackson encountered. Anytime he went out with his friends, she was convinced he was cheating. Girls were viewed as The Enemy: potential competition, attempting to steal Jackson. It also didn't help that Jackson had slept with half the town. Cambria and Jackson couldn't go to the mall without running into a one-night stand from the past. Cambria found this hilarious. Natalia, not so much.

That's not to say Jackson didn't have his fair share of issues. He was domineering and controlling. He didn't want her talking to other guys. She couldn't even go out with her friends without Jackson throwing a fit. He did not trust her, convinced she would cheat on him solely to spite him. (She probably would.)

Natalia would deliberately flirt with other men in front of him, just to piss him off. Then, she'd drink enough to black out and pick a fight in front of their friends.

She brought out the worst in him.

He told Cambria there wasn't a single thing they could agree on. Didn't matter what they were talking about, it would somehow lead to an argument.

"Then why are you with her?" Cambria asked.

"Because I love her. And I know she loves me."

"That doesn't sound like love."

"You're one to talk."

She couldn't argue there.

Cambria didn't like discussing her relationship with Jackson. Since fleeing to his house that night, she'd kept her mouth shut.

That's not to say Jackson didn't push, because he did. And sometimes he could be relentless. "You're actually an idiot," he said to her. "An idiot with half a brain. Actually—no brain at all. Even a person with half a brain would leave."

"Fuck off."

They were both hypocrites.

Cambria had drawn her own conclusions as to why he stayed with Natalia, and she was pretty certain Jackson feared being alone just as much as she did.

On a Saturday evening at the end of June, Cambria let herself into Lawson's house with the spare key he had given her. She wanted to cook him an elaborate meal. He was working long hours now that it was summer, so she didn't know exactly when he'd be home, but she had a good enough guess.

Sure enough, just after seven o'clock, the door opened, and Lawson came stumbling into the house. The table was set. Cambria sat there drinking a glass of merlot. "Are you drunk?" she said upon seeing him.

"What? No. Are *you* drunk?"

"I've had two sips."

He scoffed. "Smells like something's burning."

"Nothing's burning, Lawson."

"Well it smells like there is."

"Maybe you're having a stroke."

Maybe that wouldn't be the worst thing.

He dropped his things onto the floor and walked into the kitchen, pulled open the fridge, and grabbed a beer.

"I made your favorite," she told him.

He opened the beer, chugged it back.

"Oh my God, you *are* drunk."

"Fuck off."

"What the fuck, Lawson? Were you drunk at work?"

"Lay off, would ya? I've had a long day."

"Didn't your father get fired for drinking on the job?"

He whipped the bottle across the room, and it smashed into the wall, shattering into pieces.

She remained placid. "You're a spaz, you know that?"

"Go fuck yourself."

"Are you hungry?"

He pulled out the chair and took a seat, then grabbed his fork and started into the food.

She waited until he had taken several bites and had his mouth stuffed with food. Then she said, "we need to talk."

He continued eating, not acknowledging her.

"Did you hear me?"

He swallowed. "I'm not fucking deaf, Cambria. I heard you. Can I at least finish a meal before you start lecturing me?"

"Actually, now's the perfect time for me to speak. Maybe you'll actually listen for once instead of interrupting me every five seconds."

He rolled his eyes. "Go on, then."

She had another sip of wine, then cleared her throat. "As you're probably aware, there are many issues that exist between me and you. Issues that started early on in this relationship and have continued ever since. We've been together for six months now, and when you really think about it, that's not a long time at all. Yet somehow, it feels longer than that. We've experienced a lot more together than most couples do. Wouldn't you agree?"

"Are you proposing?

She rolled her eyes. "I love you. So much. Don't ever think that I don't. I want to be with you, more than anything. But with the way things are going, I just don't see how this will work."

He stopped. "Are you breaking up with me?"

"I just want to have a conversation with you. We need to discuss these things in order to fix them."

He sat back in his chair contemptuously. "As if you're so fucking perfect. You have issues too, you know."

"I'm aware. I never claimed to be perfect. I can admit my flaws and acknowledge what needs to be done to fix them. To fix *us.* And I'd like for you to do the same."

"Alright," he said. "Tell me, then. Tell me everything I do wrong."

She held his gaze for a moment. Then she said, "the anger, above all else. This is your number one issue. You have so much rage inside you. I'm not sure whether that stems from childhood, or young adulthood, or perhaps it's from all the drugs you're constantly doing. Which brings me to the next issue, which is the drugs. I confided in you and told you about my brother. You promised me you'd stop. But you didn't. You continued doing it behind my back for months, and when I found out and called you out on it, you gaslit me and tried to make it seem like it was *my* fault."

"BECAUSE IT *IS* YOUR FAULT!"

"You doing drugs has nothing to do with me and everything to do with yourself."

"Why the fuck do you think I do drugs in the first place? Because you're constantly on my back, bitching and complaining about every little thing I do. And this right here is a perfect example. I can't even come home from a long day at work without you bitching at me. I can't be *perfect* for you, Cambria."

"I'm not asking you to be perfect. Is it really too much to ask that you not snort cocaine around my colleagues at a work function?"

"Oh, fuck off."

"How can you not see that you have a problem? You're an addict, Lawson. You should be in NA."

"Addicts can't stop. I can stop. Anytime I want."

She had to laugh at that. "Then why haven't you?"

"BECAUSE YOU DRIVE ME FUCKING MENTAL!"

"I'm willing to work with you. Because I love you, and I care for you. We can get you the help you need. I've looked into some programs. And as for the anger management, I've found some great psychotherapists you can talk to."

"Are you fucked? I'm not talking to a shrink. If you think I have so many anger issues then maybe you should stop fueling the fucking fire and beating me when I'm down. Ever think of that? Or are you too fucking dumb to realize that maybe *you're* the problem?"

"I'm only trying to help you."

"Oh, so your idea of help is yelling at me? Controlling me? Telling me what I can and can't do?"

"The only times I ever yell is when you yell first. And you're louder than me. You constantly interrupt me and talk over me. I can't get a word in. And if you consider my attempts at helping you as *controlling*, then I'm really not sure what to tell you. I only want the best for you. I've only ever wanted the best for you. But you fight me every step of the way."

"Because you try to tell me what to do like I'm a fucking child. If I wanted to be bossed around, I'd go see my mother."

"Don't compare me to your mother, that is *not* the same thing."

"You bitch at me all the same. What's the difference?"

"The difference is I actually love you."

"And you think you know what's best for me?"

"Yeah, I do. More than your mom does."

"My mom doesn't even like you."

"SHE DOESN'T LIKE YOU EITHER."

"At least I *have* parents. Where are yours?"

That one had her speechless. "Are you delusional? There is something seriously wrong with you. There's no arguing with you because you don't use logic. It's impossible. I'm trying to discuss *actual* issues with you so that we can make this relationship work, and you're acting insane."

"Sorry that I have a lot of shit going on in my life. I wouldn't expect you to understand, given that you've lived a silver-spoon life since you were born. You've never known poverty. You've never known abuse."

"Are you fucking kidding me? YOU ABUSE ME ALL THE TIME!"

"That's different. I'm talking about from a parent."

"Oh, so when you do it to me, it's okay?"

"Stop bringing this shit up. I've lost my temper *a few times* and things have gotten out of hand. But you're no angel either, or have you forgotten that? And guess what? At the end of the day, you stay. You choose to stay knowing everything. So, you can sit here and complain, calling me abusive, but you're every bit responsible as I am. Take accountability for once in your damn life."

She sat there staring at him, completely and utterly flabbergasted at his lack of ability to comprehend the situation for what it was, the lack of self-awareness, and lack of ability to, as he put it, take accountability.

He was manipulative. He was abusive. He was narcissistic. He was a pathological liar. He felt no remorse or empathy. He used emotions as a tool to get his way. And he was unstoppable.

Enough was enough.

Any further efforts to argue with him and prove her point were futile. He would never learn, never change, never understand. How did she ever think this would work? He could not be reasoned with.

Slowly but surely, she felt the fight leaving her body, dissipating through her, a coldness washing over her with relief. She smiled at him. "You really are fucking insane." She stood.

"Says the psychopath smiling right now."

"You just don't get it, do you? You never will. Your brain is so warped and demented that you lack the ability to grasp the situation. Maybe your mother fell when she was pregnant with you. Maybe it's from fetal alcohol poisoning. You've only made it worse with the copious amount of drugs you've filled your body with since you were eleven. There's no hope left for you. There's no hope left for us."

He stood abruptly. "What are you insinuating? That you're leaving me? You said this was just a conversation."

"Yeah, well, I tried. And failed. This *conversation* has been very enlightening, to say the least."

She turned to walk away but he grabbed her arm. They stared at each other. "You won't do it. You won't leave."

"Oh yeah? Watch me."

She went upstairs and collected all her belongings she'd accumulated at his house these past six months. Her makeup, her toothbrush, her clothes. Her bras, her books, all the jewelry he had bought her. She threw everything into a bag, then trotted back down the stairs.

He was standing there, arms crossed, watching her. "You won't actually do it. You can't. You're nothing without me. You said it yourself—you can't survive without me."

She slipped on her shoes, reached for the door handle, and looked back at him. "Yeah, I think I was wrong about that."

For an hour she drove, trying to clear her head. Six months of memories circled through her mind. She wasn't even focusing on the road. She really shouldn't have been driving, but the last thing she wanted to do was go home to an empty apartment.

From the moment she'd walked out that door, the adrenaline had been pumping—a rush of endorphins and serotonin fueling her as she rode the high, feeling triumphant for doing what she should have done long ago.

She was invincible.

But that feeling was fleeting. And then came the crash.

The realization hit her like a ton of bricks. She had done it. She had left him. But what did that mean for her? Now she was alone. And she didn't know if she was ready for that.

She went to the only place—the only person—you'd expect her to at a time like this. Only problem was, Jackson wasn't alone—he had Grayson and Ian over.

"What's up?" Jackson asked upon seeing her. "You never show up unannounced anymore."

"I was in the neighborhood. And wanted to drop by."

"Bullshit."

"I just wanted to hang out with you."

"Okay, well, come on in, we're out back. You want a drink?"

"I want several drinks."

"Roger that. You staying over?"

She hesitated. "No, I'll go home."

"You can stay here."

"I know."

"Okay. Drink limit, then."

She followed him to the backyard where Grayson and Ian sat around the fire under the gazebo. "M'lady!" Grayson said as they approached. "What do we owe the pleasure?"

"I wanted to see you guys!"

"Us? No way, I don't believe you."

"You know I love hanging out with you guys."

Grayson pulled her onto his lap. "And we love hanging out with you."

"I'm going to grab some more drinks," Jackson told them.

Cambria pushed herself up from Grayson. "I'll come with you."

She followed him into the house and down the stairs to the basement. "You want a beer?" he asked as he walked around the bar to the fridge.

"Sure."

"Or do you want something stronger?" He poked his head out and looked at her.

"Hmm, I think I need something stronger."

"What would you like?"

"What do you have?"

"I can make you a dirty martini."

"Okay."

He pulled out the olives, then grabbed the gin and vermouth. She sat at the bar with her chin in her palm, watching him.

"Are you okay?" he glanced up at her.

"Give me an olive."

He picked one out of the jar and stuck it in her mouth.

She chewed it and swallowed. "Lawson and I broke up."

Jackson, who was about to shake up her drink, stopped midair. "For real?"

She nodded.

He began vigorously shaking the shaker while holding her gaze steadily. He stopped and poured it into the glass, sliding it over to her, but not before stabbing three olives onto the stick and setting it in her glass.

She took a sip and scrunched her face. "Delicious."

"What the fuck happened?"

"I'm done," she said. "I can't do it anymore."

"How do you feel?"

"I feel like I need a drink."

"Perfect. Grab that and let's go. There will be plenty more where that came from."

They headed back outside and sat by the fire with Grayson and Ian. Conversations were had, drinks were shared, and Cambria soon felt herself getting lost in the moment, feeling free and unencumbered.

Grayson and Ian sat on the one sofa sharing a joint while Jackson and Cambria sat on the sofa across from them, a blanket draped over their laps. Cambria was on her third drink. All she wanted was for Grayson and Ian to leave so she could be alone with Jackson.

As if reading her mind—or perhaps by the grace of some divine intervention—Grayson stood and said, "who wants to go in the hot tub?"

"I'm in," Ian said.

Cambria didn't say anything. Neither did Jackson.

Grayson looked at them. "No hot tub?"

"I'll join you in a few minutes," Jackson told him. "You guys go ahead."

Grayson saluted, and the two went into the house to change. Cambria and Jackson remained as they were, staring into the fire.

Jackson reached for his drink and took a sip. "How do you feel now?" he asked her.

"Numb."

"In a bad way?"

"Do people feel numb in a good way?"

"Well, when they're drinking, yeah. Or on drugs."

"Okay, well, I feel numb in a bad way."

"Why? I thought you said you were fine."

"I never said I was fine. When did I say I was fine?"

"Uh, I don't know, I just thought you were fine. You seemed fine."

"Well I'm not fine."

"Okay… but, why? He's a piece of shit."

She looked at him like he had two heads. "I love him."

"You'll be fine."

"Why are you like this?" She crossed her arms and sat back.

"Like what?"

"So bad at empathizing."

"I'm not," he said. "Why would you say that?"

"Because I'm upset, for a very good reason, and you can't just be there for me."

"I thought I *was* being there for you."

"You're disregarding my feelings."

"Okay… what do you want me to say?"

"I don't want you to say anything, you should just know what to say."

"You want me to say something? Okay, I'll say this. I've been telling you since January that he's not a good guy. And that night you came to my house, after he hurt you—I thought it was over. But then you went back to him. You willingly chose to stay with someone who did that you. And I couldn't understand that. I still don't. You're kind of fucked up, Cambria."

"You're fucked up too, Jackson, let's not forget that. You're in a toxic relationship that you'll never admit is toxic, and we both know you're not a good boyfriend to Nat."

"You're so obsessed with someone who doesn't care about you."

"You think I don't hate him? I do. I hate him so much. I know he doesn't love me the same. He loves the idea of me. He loves possessing me. He uses me to fill the void inside himself. He can't be alone. I guess we're the same in that sense. And you're like that too, which is why you're still with Natalia."

"I know I complain about her, but our relationship isn't always what I make it out to be. We have our good moments, it's not all bad."

"Which is what I've been trying to tell you, you hypocrite."

"Okay, but it's not the same. He's worse."

It was quiet for a moment. "I'm scared," she said, "of being alone."

"Is being alone really the worst thing?"

"To me it is."

"Worse than being hit?"

She didn't respond.

"Promise me you won't go back to him."

She looked at him, and they locked eyes, his brown eyes mirroring her own. Then she stuck her pinky out, and he did the same. "I promise."

It had been a long night. The liquor was dulling her senses, and she was exhausted. Resting her head on the arm of the sofa, she stretched her feet across Jackson's lap. He readjusted the blanket over her. They both stared at the fire, their faces warm from the flames.

His hands rested atop her legs, tapping rhythmically. Then eventually, he slipped them beneath the blanket, onto her bare skin. They remained there, his fingertips touching her skin.

She closed her eyes.

Ever so gently, his hands drifted across her legs, down her thighs, then back up again towards her waist. They went to her hipbone, underneath the hem of her shirt, across her stomach. She wasn't sure what he was doing, but she didn't want it to stop.

At his touch she was electrified. An overwhelming sensation came over her, making it hard to breathe. Goosebumps covered her skin.

She was on the verge of imploding.

He stopped moving his hands and kept them resting beneath her shirt, on her bare stomach. Eyes closed, he hung his head forward, as though he were resting, or sleeping. He looked peaceful.

Cambria didn't dare move. She didn't know what to do. Surely they had crossed multiple lines, but for the life of her, she couldn't put a stop to it.

Ever so hesitantly, and trembling with trepidation, she brought her hand to his head and slowly ran her fingers through his hair. Such an innocuous act, yet it contained so much intimacy.

Realizing she may be taking it too far, she retracted her hand and brought it to her chest. He opened his eyes and looked at her. She knew what that look meant—he didn't want her to stop. Again, she ran her fingers through his hair, and he closed his eyes and relaxed.

Her heart was beating through her chest. For the longest time, they'd been mounting towards something monumental, and now it was finally happening.

She was on fire, ignited by him, and nothing could put it out. This was like nothing she'd experienced. She was enraptured. All she wanted was to pull him to her. And she knew, without a doubt, that he was feeling the same.

The restraint was killing him just as much as it was killing her.

"Jackson!" Grayson called from the hot tub. "Get your ass in here!"

She looked at him, and he held her gaze. Then he said, "want another piggyback?"

That night changed everything. All this time, she'd been suppressing it without even realizing. She questioned, once again, whether she had feelings for Jackson. And now, for the first time, whether he had feelings for her.

The answer may seem obvious to you, dear reader. But that is because we observe from a distance, equipped with hindsight and reason. What is clear to us was not clear to Cambria. She really didn't know.

Rewind to December, after Jackson accused Cambria of having feelings for him. She concluded that the only way to discern whether she truly had feelings for him was to fall in love with someone else. If she did and these feelings for Jackson dissipated, she would know she had just been confused, mistaking loneliness for something else. But if she fell in love with someone else and these feelings for Jackson persisted, then she'd finally have her answer.

What transpired between them that night was no platonic misunderstanding. It couldn't be justified as anything else. Between them existed a thousand quiet moments, each significant on its own, now converging into something undeniable. His hands on her torso, her fingers in his hair. The feeling of elation, and beneath it, a deep, aching sadness—to be so close, yet still so far. Wanting more, longing for it, craving it, yet doing nothing.

It was tragic. It was tantalizing. It was consuming. It was heartbreaking.

And lo and behold the date: it was June 30, 1990. Exactly one year since the night they met.

The night that changed her life forever.

Some might call that… fate.

December 1990

TWENTY-TWO

Christmas was in the air, but it didn't feel like it—not exactly. The days were warm enough that you could still roll down your car windows, and the air smelled more of salt than it did snow. In every shop window, lights were tangled around surfboards, and fake snow dusted the glass.

It just wasn't the same as it was back home.

But this holiday season, Cambria would not be returning to Linden Falls—she was staying put, right where she was. Because, despite everything she had gone through, she was content with her new living situation. In fact, it was probably the only good thing she had going for her. Well, besides her new job.

She walked home from work with a candy cane latte in hand, mentally running through her to-do list. When she walked through the front door, Hailey was already in the kitchen cooking dinner. "You're home early," Cambria remarked as she set her purse on the counter.

"Yeah," Hailey said. "Surprisingly."

"What are you making?"

"Risotto."

"Why?" Cambria asked.

"What do you mean *why*? Because it's good."

"Ew."

"You're having some."

"Is Mara home?"

"Nope."

"You almost done in the kitchen?"

"Yep, just finishing up."

"K, I'm going to shower. I'll be down shortly." Cambria grabbed a granola bar from the cupboard and headed upstairs, despite Hailey telling her she'd spoil her appetite.

She went straight to the bathroom and closed the door, then turned on the shower and stripped off her clothes. It had been a long day. Every day was a long day nowadays.

As the room began to fill with steam, Cambria stood in front of the mirror and studied her reflection. Her hair was now chocolate brown. She was still adjusting to it, but she liked it. It was different—a much-needed change. She wanted her appearance to align with the internal metamorphosis she'd been experiencing lately. And trust me when I say there was a lot that had changed.

For starters, it had been five months since she'd spoken to Jackson. Five months since that fateful night in his backyard. And while five months may not seem like that long in the grand scheme of things, it felt like an eternity to Cambria, whose life would never be the same without him. Not a day went by that she didn't think of him. He was once the very air she breathed. Now, she struggled to get through life knowing she no longer had him.

On the outside, she appeared fine, but inside, she was dying. She had perfected the art of dissociation, suppressing any and all thoughts of him. It had to be like he didn't exist. Otherwise, it was too painful. The thought alone made her heart ache, and she didn't know how she was supposed to survive without him.

And it was all because of that night; most notably, what happened afterwards.

Let's go back there, shall we?

Something had shifted between them. Boundaries and lines were crossed. Cambria was besieged by a flood of emotions she had never allowed in before, and for the first time, required confronting. She couldn't simply go back to how things were before, tiptoeing around the truth, pretending they didn't feel what they felt. No longer did she want to pretend.

That night changed everything. Yet after that night, nothing changed.

She had expected something big—a eucatastrophic explosion of revelations. But that's not what happened. You want to know what happened?

Nothing.

Yes, you heard me—nothing.

Two days after *that night,* Jackson called, telling her to get her bathing suit and come over.

She was tentative, unsure of what to expect. When she arrived, his whole family was in the backyard, and his parents were barbequing. Kyle handed her a beer. Victoria asked if she had plans for the fourth of July. And then there was Jackson, lounging on a pool floatie, beer in hand, waving to her.

Confounded, she got in the pool and made her way over to where he was floating, hoping they were far enough out of earshot from his family.

"Hey, loser," he clinked his beer against hers.

"Hi."

"I hope you're hungry, dad's cooking steak."

"I see that."

"How was work?"

"Work was fine," she stared at him. "You?"

"Busy. But TJ let me leave an hour early."

"Lucky you."

"Did they already ask you about Wednesday? We're having a party."

"Victoria mentioned it."

"You coming? We're getting a keg."

She stared at him, completely and utterly perplexed. She wasn't following—couldn't grasp the strange normalcy unfolding before her; could not fathom how they could surpass several forcefields yet remain as they'd been before. How he could trace his fingers across her skin and stare into her eyes with such longing and desire and not say a single word about it.

And that was how things continued— like it never happened, just like their kiss the year before. That seemed to be their unspoken rule. Sweep it under the rug, ignore its existence. It was infuriating—*he* was infuriating. But if Jackson wasn't going to acknowledge it, then she sure as hell wouldn't either. She refused to open herself up like that, to bleed in front of him only to be rejected for feeling. And if it wasn't reciprocated like she thought, the last thing she wanted was a repeat of last Christmas—being accused of having feelings for him and risk losing him as a friend because Natalia thought she was trying to steal him.

So, despite everything inside that was screaming for her to say something, alas, she did not. If he was going to play that game, then so could she.

She spent the entirety of the fourth of July party watching him, waiting for him to get drunk and slip up; kiss her like he did before, tell her that he hadn't stopped thinking about that night.

But he didn't. He carried on pretending that night never happened.

She questioned whether she hated him for that.

It was a recipe for disaster, the perfect storm that would subsequently lead her down the same path she had gone down all those times before. If only Jackson had said something, acknowledged it, confirmed what she was so convinced of.

But he didn't. And she could blame him all she wanted, but ultimately it was her own fault what happened next.

Five days—that was all it took. In those five days, Cambria had never felt lonelier. There was an ocean between them, even though he was right there. Vulnerability bred susceptibility, and that was exactly how she ended up back in Lawson's arms—mending her wounds with the same hands that caused them. She couldn't see how fragile she'd become, and how easy she was to manipulate. It was like some twisted version of Stockholm syndrome; no matter how badly Lawson treated her, being with him was better than being alone. If Jackson was never going to acknowledge what was going on between them, then what else was she supposed to do? Being with Lawson—even with all the detriment—was better than having no one at all.

Cambria told Jackson that Lawson had apologized, and she was going to give him another chance. Jackson wasn't thrilled, to say the least. "You're joking, right?" he said to her.

She didn't respond.

"You promised you wouldn't go back."

"Yeah, well, I guess we all make promises we can't keep."

This response did not appease him. "You're a liar."

"I know. I'm a liar. I'm a hypocrite. You don't need to tell me twice."

"Do you not care? It's just going to get worse, you know."

"Maybe. But maybe not."

"If you actually believe that then I think you really have lost your mind."

"I don't expect you to understand."

"Do you know how dumb you sound? You're one of the smartest people I know, but you're also so fucking stupid."

"Give me a reason."

"A reason? You think I need to give you that? It should be obvious."

She held his gaze, waiting for him to say something—anything. Now was his chance. All he had to do was say the words and she'd be his.

But he didn't say anything. And that was all the answer she needed.

"I don't want to see you anymore," he told her.

"I don't want to see you either."

And so that was how they ended, Cambria and Jackson. It was the last thing she wanted, but at the same time, she couldn't continue with how things were, this game of pretending, suppressing her true feelings—it was killing her.

She was losing him either way.

Jackson's absence left a gaping hole in her chest—a hole she believed would never mend. And the only person there to fill that void, was Lawson.

The devil had never looked more appealing.

Contrary to what Cambria had initially thought, breaking up with Lawson was, in fact, not the end—it was only the beginning.

The months that followed were even more tumultuous than before. Cambria desperately clung to the good moments, deluding herself into thinking he could actually change. She had tunnel vision, only seeing the Lawson she chose, the Lawson that was doting and loving. But that was a façade. And like clockwork, the mask would slip and reveal the true Lawson that had been there all along.

Cambria believed she was in love, and while it's one thing to believe something, it's another thing entirely to know. We cannot blame her for not knowing. To her, it really was love in the highest form (I'm sure future Cambria would love to give her old self a smack). But it was not real for Lawson. Everything was a game, a test, a trial. She was simply a prop in his life, and despite his insistence on not needing her, he needed her. He needed her to control. He needed her to dominate. He needed her to make him feel better about himself. He needed her to use, and manipulate, and spit out once he was finished.

They were doomed from the start, and she knew that, but it didn't change anything. It only made her try harder. She had put so much time and energy into this relationship. To give up and throw it all away would mean that had all been for nothing. And since she no longer had Jackson, she clung to this relationship with everything she had left.

She missed Jackson vehemently. The void she had been trying so hard to fill was only getting bigger, and being with Lawson wasn't helping in the way she had hoped. She felt it deep within her, this pain that seemed to reverberate through her entire being, which was, in truth, worse than anything Lawson had ever done to her. But there was nothing she could do. Jackson wanted nothing to do with her. She had blown it by choosing Lawson, by choosing so-called requited love.

What it always came down to was that reliance—one that overpowered all logic and morality—to have someone, to belong to someone, to not be alone. To accept love in any form, even if it was perilous. She never felt good enough, or deserving enough, to leave him and be on her own. She did not yet possess the self-assurance or confidence required to exist independently of him.

That was, until she decided to cheat on him.

It wasn't like she'd *planned* on cheating on him (is it ever that premediated?)— it sort of just happened in a spur of the moment; a series of events that coincided perfectly.

The last weekend of October, Lawson was out of town visiting family. Cambria wasn't invited. She was never invited. Instead, she and Mara decided to go out for Halloween. They dressed as an angel and devil, Mara wearing a red dress and horns, Cambria wearing a white dress with a halo.

It happened organically, as these things often do. She was outside getting some air while Mara stayed behind at the bar. "Do you have a cigarette?" someone asked her.

She turned and observed the stranger before her. He had brown hair, brown eyes, and a baby face. He kind of looked like Jackson. She replied, "do I look like I have a cigarette?"

"Damn," he said, impressed by her attitude. "Sassy, I love it. And I should've known—angels don't smoke."

That was all it took. A conversation was sparked, and she was immediately captivated by this stranger who was showing interest in her.

It was somehow decided that they were going back to his place. She didn't even feel remorse or hesitation in the cab ride over. Was that wrong? Maybe. But she no longer had it in her to care.

She confessed that she had a boyfriend only after they'd had sex. And then she broke down crying and told him all the painful details of her relationship with Lawson Wolf.

He dried her tears with sympathy and comfort, and then they had sex again. He ordered pizza and she lay on his chest and cuddled with him until four in the morning; the most connected she'd felt to someone since June 30.

The next day, she felt strange and unfamiliar with herself. She didn't feel guilt, and maybe that surprised her. She felt surprisingly calm, a wave of tranquility washing over her. As she stood in the shower, water streaming onto her face, the stark reality hit her, what she had done, and the realization sunk in. She didn't feel bad—she felt liberated. She knew what she needed to do.

"I slept with someone," she said to Lawson later that day. Why she decided to do this at his house was a mystery. Surely she should've known it wouldn't end well.

At first, he didn't believe her. He thought she was joking or trying to get a rise out of him. But once he realized she wasn't, anger took control, and next thing Cambria knew, she was falling backwards down the stairs.

She woke up in the hospital, hooked up to different machines, Lawson by her side. No broken bones, fortunately. Just a sprained wrist and a fractured rib. She had the doctor call security and Lawson was removed from the premises.

She filed a police report and pressed charges. She got a restraining order. Yet still, he tried to come after her with everything he could. He threatened her with lawsuits and injunctions, flashing his mother's money and her husband's district attorney status as though that would do anything.

That was when she decided it was time to move. Together, she and Mara put an ad in the classifieds looking for a third roommate. The process was effortless, and they soon found themselves loading up a U-Haul and moving all their small belongings to a house in Bay Ridge with their new housemate, Hailey.

Bay Ridge was a suburban neighborhood on the other side of Pine Hills, right near the water. And coincidentally, closer to Jackson's house. The area wasn't drastically different from where Cambria lived before, yet still, she felt an immense change in the air, as though she were somewhere new entirely.

The idea of starting over appealed to her immensely. As much as she loved the independence of living on her own, she loved sharing a house with Mara and Hailey even more. She would always cherish the memories she made in that apartment. It was the first place she called home after leaving the east coast and landing in Pine Hills. But if there was one thing Cambria had learned, it was that all good things must come to an end eventually; to make room for bigger and better things, new chapters, new lives.

This was her new chapter.

After the move, she got a new job. She'd been feeling stagnant at H&S and wanted to grow. When the supervisor of the marketing department told her he knew a doctor that was looking to hire someone for a clerical position within her practice, Cambria was on it, asking if she could get a recommendation. She met with Dr. Francesca Wilde and got the job.

It helped that she had a year and a half experience working at Hargrove & Swanson. Cambria found it ironic yet comical that this was her *second* job in the medical field when she had a degree in English and Linguistics.

Her official title was Medical Office Assistant. The job was pretty straight forward. She was responsible for scheduling appointments, processing payments, bookkeeping, answering the phone, and all correspondence. She had a good rapport with Dr. Wilde, which made coming to the clinic each day easier.

Unlike Hargrove & Swanson, the clinic was small. No longer was she taking elevators up to the third and fourth floor, traversing through hallways, venturing down to the cafeteria for lunch. Everything she needed was in one place. There was a significantly smaller staff (only eight of them that worked in the building), and most of them had years on Cambria. Initially, she felt insignificant and out of place. Her newness flashed like a strobe light, and she almost regretted accepting the position without having had accumulated more knowledge. But as the novelty wore off, so did her fears and apprehensions, and before long, she was well adjusted, happy and comfortable in her new environment.

Born an introvert, Cambria loved her alone time. She didn't need to be around people—she was content in her solitude. In fact, she often got sick of people and could only stand to be around others for so long. There was, however, an exception to that, and that was Jackson. He was the only person she did not get sick of. She could spend her entire life with him and never complain.

Cambria worried about getting sick of Mara and Hailey, but the opposite happened: she *loved* spending time with them. The three of them made sense; they just clicked. She had always struggled with fitting in, but with them, she felt like she belonged. And with Jackson no longer in her life, she had all the time in the world with them. Jackson's absence allowed them to get close and strengthen their bond.

Everything was easy and effortless with them. They'd cook meals together, have movie marathons on Sundays, braid each other's hair, steal each other's clothes. They'd go out on weeknights, and drink wine on Wednesdays.

They didn't like being apart from each other. Mara always kept her door open. Cambria would wait in the living room for them to get home from work so they could hang out.

It was like having sisters, if this was what having sisters was like.

To complete the transition to her new life, she decided to change her hair, dying it from her natural dirty blond to a dark chocolate brown. She wanted to be unrecognizable, no traces of Lawson lingering, no traces of her old self remaining,.

The exception to that, of course, was Jackson—he was the only thing from her old life that she still wanted.

She wiped the mirror, which had fogged up from the steam, and got in the shower.

Once she was done, she got dressed and headed downstairs. She stopped mid stride when she saw Jackson seated on the couch in the living room, her heart jumping out of her chest. Instantly, she was overcome with emotions, her body ablaze.

As she gripped the railing and walked down the stairs, she began to tremble. She got to the bottom and saw Hailey standing there. "Hey, sorry," she said, "you were in the shower. He wanted to see you."

"That's okay."

"Good luck," she whispered, then left them.

Cambria slowly turned to face Jackson. Her heart was beating uncontrollably; she thought it was going to explode in her chest. "How did you find me?"

"Mara," he said. "I ran into her at the grocery store a few weeks ago—now that you guys are so close."

"That was not intentional."

He grinned. "I'm sure it wasn't."

She approached with caution and took a seat beside him. "Hi," she said.

"Hi," he replied, his face so close to hers. "Your hair is brown."

"Good observation."

"Mental breakdown?"

"The opposite actually. I'm reinventing myself."

"I heard. Your new job included in that?"

"Is there anything Mara *didn't* tell you?"

"She told me you broke up with Lawson."

Cambria gaped. "She never even told me she saw you."

"Are you actually done for good this time?"

"It's been almost two months now," Cambria said. "And I have a restraining order."

"Damn, okay. Mara told me he pushed you down the stairs."

"Yeah, he's insane."

"Clearly."

"But I did cheat on him."

"*Did you?*"

"Yes!" she laughed. "And he deserved it."

"He definitely deserved it."

"Should we kill him?"

"Yes."

"Mara and Hailey can help us dispose of the body."

"Hailey—that's her name. How'd you con her into living with you?"

"She broke up with her boyfriend and had nowhere to live. I love her, she's great."

"My family's been asking about you."

"Really?"

"Yeah. They're like, *where's Cambria these days?*"

"Wait, did you not tell them we stopped being friends?"

"No."

"Why???"

He shrugged. "I don't know."

"I thought surely you would've told them what an insane idiot I am."

"Nope. I never told them anything."

This surprised her, yet placated her.

"So…" he said, "will they be seeing you any time soon?"

"I would like that."

He smiled. "I've missed you."

"I've missed you more than you know. Life without you sucks."

"I know, I'm just the best, aren't I?"

"Shut up," she smirked. "I thought you hated me."

"I did, kind of. But I missed hanging out with you."

"Me too. Why didn't you ever reach out?"

"I don't know. Why didn't you?"

"I didn't think you'd want to hear from me."

"Well, I do now."

"I'm sorry for being an idiot. I've finally learned my lesson."

"It felt like you were choosing him over me."

"I guess in a way I was. I just didn't want to be alone."

"So what are you going to do now? Are you going to be okay being alone?"

"I think so," she said. "I feel so much better. Like a weight has been lifted off my shoulders. I can finally breathe again, finally be myself again. I haven't been that in a long time.

"My mom asked me why I stayed so long with someone like that. And you know what I said? *We take what we can get.* That's the only explanation I have. We take what we can get, even if it's far from what we deserve.

"I loved him. And I thought he loved me too. But he didn't. And I was so scared of being alone, convincing myself that if I didn't have him, I'd be alone forever. It sounds so stupid now, in hindsight. But that's what I believed. But I'd much rather be happy on my own than miserable with him."

Amen to that.

TWENTY-THREE

Briskly they slipped back into friendship as if no time at all had passed. Jackson spent every evening that week at Cambria's house. They drank each other's presence and never wanted to part, Jackson often staying until one in the morning. No longer would she spend her nights awake, wondering what he was doing, if he was thinking about her as she was thinking about him. Now, she knew.

They had a lot of catching up to do, albeit not that much had changed. Jackson was still with Natalia, astonishingly. Cambria was certain they would've broken up by now.

The subject of Jackson and Natalia's relationship was one she could not spend too long thinking about, as she knew it was something she'd never grasp. It remained the biggest enigma of their friendship.

The good news was that Natalia was going back to school to get her Masters, which meant they'd be spending a lot less time together, and Cambria could have Jackson all to herself.

That was, until her degree was finished.

Cambria wondered what she would do if Jackson proposed to Natalia.

Probably die, she surmised.

Their relationship was a mystery to not just Cambria—others noticed it too. "Are you sure you have a girlfriend?" Mara pestered Jackson as they all sat in the living room casually drinking champagne.

"I'm sure," Jackson replied.

"You never seem to be with her," Mara pushed. "You're always with Cambria."

"Not for the last six months I wasn't."

"Touché," Mara replied. "Making up for lost time."

"It's been five," Cambria said.

"Five and a half," Jackson countered.

"How did you two meet?" Hailey asked.

"At a bar," they said in unison.

"Thanks to me," Mara gloated.

"That's true," Cambria said. "I never would have left my house that night otherwise."

"And how did you and your girlfriend meet?" Hailey asked Jackson.

He and Cambria exchanged a glance, then he said, "at the same place, the same night."

Hailey's eyes widened. "Oh, Jesus Christ."

Jackson laughed.

"How many people think Cambria is your girlfriend?" she continued.

"A lot," Jackson replied.

"Do you want her to be?"

"Okayyyyy," Cambria interjected. "Stop interrogating him. We get it."

Hailey smirked.

"I'm interested in hearing more about Hailey," Jackson leaned forward. "Why did you and your boyfriend break up?"

"I think I fell out of love with him," she said.

"Ouch."

"Yeah. We were kind of like roommates. There was no passion."

"That sucks. So are you looking for a relationship, or you want to stay single?"

"I don't know. I don't really think I want to be single."

"You guys can all be single together!" Jackson exclaimed. "Maybe get a few cats."

Mara scowled at him. "I'm not single, you dipshit."

"Mara has a boyfriend," Cambria told him.

"Since when?"

"For like, over a year?"

"Well how was I supposed to know that?"

"You've met him."

"When? Where?"

"I don't know, somewhere."

"What's his name?"

"Hayden."

"Hayden. Sounds like a stand-up guy. I'm sure I'd like him."

"I'm pretty sure you guys played pool together at Cognito's," Mara said.

"Sounds like me. Was I drunk?"

"When are you not?" Cambria said.

"I'd be down to get a cat," Hailey said. "Or a dog."

"Cambria hates dogs," Jackson told her.

"You do?"

"Hate's a strong word," Cambria said. "I strongly dislike them."

"You prefer cats?"

"Yes."

"She's weird like that," Jackson said. "Who doesn't like dogs? Weirdos."

"At least I can remember when I meet someone," Cambria countered.

"I really don't think I've ever met this guy."

"You definitely did," said Mara. "Maybe you really are an alcoholic."

"I told you," Cambria said.

"Alright," Jackson continued. "Well at least I didn't date a sociopath for a year."

"Yes, fine, you win there."

"Not like your girlfriend's much better," Mara drank from her glass and averted her eyes.

"I don't really think you can compare my girlfriend to what Cambria dated."

"Fair."

"It wasn't even a year," Cambria said. "Ten months."

"Same shit," Jackson said. "Close enough."

"It's almost been a year since I met him," she said. "New Years."

"Barf. Don't remind me."

"Did I ever tell you I got my period that night?"

"Ew."

"While we were having sex."

"Nice. I didn't need to know that."

"It was funny, actually."

"Great. Anything else you'd like to share?"

And it was then, finally, that the gears started turning in her brain, counting backwards the weeks to when she would have gotten her period last. She realized, suddenly, that it must have been early October. Before the breakup. Before the hospital.

Over two months ago.

She stood. "We need to go to the pharmacy."

They looked at her, perplexed. "Right now? For what?"

"I need to buy a pregnancy test."

Together, the four of them got into Hailey's car and drove to the nearest CVS. Jackson and Hailey waited in the car while Mara and Cambria went inside and bought three pregnancy tests. Then they went back to the house and Cambria sat in the bathroom alone. Once she was done, she came out, and Mara set a timer.

It was the most grueling three minutes of her life.

She already knew what the result would be, despite how hard she prayed otherwise. But there was also a small part of her that still held out hope; that there was a perfectly reasonable explanation as to why her period was so late.

No one said a word, not even Jackson, who under normal circumstances, could not shut up.

Once the timer went off, Cambria braced herself and went into the bathroom to read the results. All three tests said positive.

At first, she was in shock. Her brain couldn't make the connection that the two parallel lines meant that she had a baby growing inside of her. She couldn't grasp that the situation was real and happening to her.

She broke down crying once it finally hit her.

Afterwards, the four of them sat in the living room. No one touched the champagne. Cambria lay with her head on Jackson's lap, a pile of tissues crumpled beside her. Mara said, "who's the father?"

Cambria lifted her head and looked at Mara. "What?"

"The guy from the bar," Mara said.

Jackson looked at her. "What guy from the bar?"

Cambria had nearly forgotten about that. "Oh, right. No, I don't think so."

"Did you use a condom?"

"Yeah."

"But wait—aren't you on a birth control?"

"I was. I'm not anymore."

"But at the time you were?"

"Yeah. But clearly it didn't work."

"Clearly."

"What guy from the bar?" Jackson asked again, looking to Mara.

"That's the guy she cheated on Lawson with."

"Oh."

"He's actually very sweet," Cambria said. "I'd see him again."

"Are you going to tell Lawson?" Hailey asked.

They looked at her and said in unison, "no."

"Do you know what you're going to do?"

The answer was obvious. She wasn't ready to be a mother—not even close. And she most certainly was not going to give birth to anything that came from Lawson. She would never delude herself into thinking she had such power to change genetics. He was a bad apple. And every bad apple came from a seed. She would not be the one responsible for bringing this seed to fruition. Plus, she'd be tethered to him for life.

She grabbed the champagne bottle from the coffee table and drank whatever remained.

"Fetal alcohol syndrome," Jackson remarked. "Love it."

"That's probably what happened to Lawson," she replied.

Shortly after that was when they all headed upstairs to bed. Jackson stayed the night with Cambria. She cried some more, then they smoked a joint out her bedroom window. "Do you remember what you told me," Jackson said, "that night we talked about kids?"

"Which part?"

"If you had a daughter, what you would name her."

"Yeah," she said. "Wynter."

"Keep it in your back pocket. For later."

"I will."

If she was going to have a baby, it was going to be on her own terms. With the right person, at the right time. And it would be created from love, not hatred.

TWENTY-FOUR

The next morning, she began calling clinics. The soonest available appointment was five days away, which was lucky, considering Christmas was on Tuesday.

There was nothing she could do until then but wait.

When Christmas day arrived, Mara and Hailey were both with their families. She couldn't even see Jackson because he, too, was with his family, and then Natalia. She spent the day alone and crying

In that moment, she regretted ever meeting Lawson. She had never once regretted her relationship, not even the worst parts, because she was a big believer in *everything happens for a reason*, and *what doesn't kill you makes you stronger*. But how was this going to make her stronger? All she wanted to do was die.

She decided to name it Darwin, because why not? She'd talk to it periodically throughout the day, narrating the things she was doing. She took a bubble bath and stared down at her flat stomach, wondering how she could be so unlucky. She even thought, *what if I kept it?* But couldn't picture herself as a mother. Then she smoked a joint and wondered if she'd ever find true love and happiness.

When the day finally arrived, she was much calmer than she thought she'd be. The waiting was the most grueling part, and now that that was over, she was almost at the finish line.

Mara took the day off to drive her, and they arrived at the clinic for ten. Cambria was anxious and overwhelmed and had no idea what to expect. She had been told when she made the appointment no eating or drinking beforehand, wear baggy clothes, and expect bleeding after. They sat in the waiting room and Cambria filled out the intake forms. Two hours passed before they called her name.

A nurse brought her into an office and sat at the desk across from her, asking questions about the pregnancy—whether it was planned, if she used protection, or was on birth control. She inquired if she had ever had an abortion before and whether she was sure of her decision. Afterward, the nurse carefully explained the entire procedure from start to finish and provided pills for anxiety and pain. Then, Cambria was taken to a changing room to change into a medical gown before sitting in a room with other girls waiting for the same thing.

She was in there for another half hour before she was called for bloodwork and an ultrasound. They took her blood pressure, then pricked the tip of her finger to get a blood sample. Next came the ultrasound, which was when Cambria discovered how far along she was.

Ten weeks.

She had no idea she'd been pregnant when Lawson pushed her down the stairs.

After this, they brought her to the surgical room, which was white, sterile, and nothing like she had imagined. She lay in the center of the room as doctors and nurses busily worked around her, barely acknowledging her presence. They slipped her feet into stirrups and spread her knees. A pulse oximeter was placed on her index finger to monitor her heart rate, and an IV needle was inserted. Immediately, she felt the drugs taking affect—dizziness and light-headedness that she welcomed. She relaxed, closed her eyes, and tried not to think about being awake and fully aware during the procedure.

The procedure itself was quick—only about five minutes to remove the cluster of cells inside her uterus that, without intervention, would have developed into a baby. The pain was unlike anything she had ever felt before. At first, a slight discomfort, a sense of something being pushed deep inside her. Then came the sharp, unrelenting sensation—the vacuum sound accompanied by the suctioning of every last bit. She felt it moving violently within, tearing at her insides. She squeezed her eyes shut and clenched her fists, but the pain didn't ease. Overwhelmed, she struggled, and the nurses held onto her to keep her still.

And then just like that, it was over. The noise ceased and the room went silent. She felt exhausted, drained, defeated.

The nurses slid cloth underwear with a pad inside onto her, then helped her sit up and escorted her to the recovery room filled with other girls. There, they lay her on a bed and placed a heat pack on her stomach to ease the cramping. She was given apple juice and crackers to help regain her strength.

She sobbed silently, hoping no one would notice.

After twenty minutes, a nurse came to check on her. As she went over the after care, Cambria zoned out, missing the entire spiel. The nurse told her she was good to go and helped her up.

She was escorted to the dressing room, where she changed back into her clothes. After that, she exited through the double doors and was back in the waiting room, where Mara sat reading a magazine.

Once she saw Cambria, she stood and made her way over. "You okay?"

Cambria nodded but couldn't speak or she'd burst out in tears.

Mara looped her arm through Cambria's and helped her out to the car. "You hungry?"

"I'm starving." Cambria hadn't eaten since the night before, so they stopped at McDonald's before going home.

Mara helped her up the stairs to her bedroom, then tucked her into bed and kissed her forehead. "Just holler if you need me," she told her. "I'm just down the hall." Then she closed the door and left, leaving Cambria to be truly alone.

She cried until there was nothing left.

TWENTY-FIVE

At the end of January, Cambria's grandmother died. They hadn't been close, but the loss gutted her, nonetheless. The funeral was to take place the following week.

Jackson and Cambria sat on her couch one evening, calling airlines to find flights to Connecticut. They'd been spending a lot more time together now that Natalia was back in school, talking on the phone every night before bed, often falling asleep while still on the line. As much as she enjoyed hanging out with her housemates, they simply couldn't compete with Jackson. Plus, Hailey had started seeing someone from work. So much for being single together.

"Come with me," she said to him.

"I can't."

"Why not?"

"Natalia would kill me."

This displeased her. "I don't care."

Jackson contemplated it. "You're putting me in a really tough position."

"You've never been to the East Coast. It'll be a good opportunity to travel."

"Your grandma just died."

"You can come to the funeral."

"Will your parents care?"

"My parents love you. Please?"

"Ugghhh."

"Jacksonnnnn."

"Okay. Fine."

"Actually!?"

"If I die for this…"

"I'll throw you the best funeral."

Two days later, they landed at Bradley International. Cambria's parents picked them up and were absolutely delighted to finally meet Jackson after hearing so much about him over the last couple years. She gave him a tour of her hometown, just as he did when she first arrived in Pine Hills. The funeral was the next day.

Cambria's parents had the reception at their house afterward. There were friends and relatives there that she hadn't seen in years. Talking to people was exhausting. Once her social battery had run out, she grabbed Jackson and snuck away to her childhood bedroom, crawling out the window to the roof.

Times like these made Cambria forget that Natalia even existed. It was as if Jackson lived two completely separate lives—one with Natalia and one with Cambria—and neither was privy to the other. She had no insight into the inner workings of his relationship with Natalia, just as Natalia knew little of what Jackson did when he was with Cambria. Compartmentalizing was something he had long mastered, but it still bothered her. She wished he would have only one life—the one with her.

Jackson sat next to her eating coffee cake off a paper plate. She leaned over and took a bite off his fork, then chased it down with wine. "Today was a lot," she said, looking out over the skyline.

"Yeah. And a lot of people."

"I want to go home."

"You are home."

"No. Pine Hills."

"Oh."

"Yeah."

Silence.

"I feel neglected," she said.

"By whom?"

"You."

He looked at her peculiarly. "How?"

"When you're with Natalia, it's like I don't even exist."

"You do know she hates you, right?"

Cambria didn't respond.

"What do you expect me to do?" he said, "call you every hour?"

"No."

"Then what?"

"I don't know."

"I think you're overreacting. And being unrealistic."

"Is it so wrong of me to feel hurt by something?"

"I'm here, aren't I?"

"Yeah. But it's like whenever we're together, we're living on borrowed time. I don't know. Even this feels like it's going to run out soon. It always does."

He didn't know how to respond to that. "I don't know what you want from me."

"Neither do I."

There was a moment before the funeral when Cambria was in the bathroom getting ready. She needed Jackson's help zipping up the back of her dress. After that, she handed him the necklace she was to wear, which belonged to her grandmother.

He took it from her hands as she turned around, lifting her hair from the back of her neck. She could feel him behind her, his body so close to hers, the pendant falling softly onto her chest. A moment passed as he struggled with the clasp. She held her breath.

Then, just like that, the moment was over. He stepped away, and she let her hair fall, turning to face herself in the mirror.

On their final night in Linden Falls, Cambria and Jackson sat in the dining room eating dinner with her parents. "I have something I want you to read," her mother said. She got up from the table, disappeared into the other room, and returned a moment later with a book, handing it to her.

"What is it?" Cambria asked as she turned it over in her hands.

"It's called *Love at First Sight: A Study on Human Intimacy.*"

"Why do you want me to read it?" Cambria asked, skeptical.

"Well, because it's fascinating," her mother replied. "And I think you could benefit it from it."

Cambria made a face. "I'm perfectly fine being single, thank you very much."

"Just read the damn book."

Once they finished eating, Cambria and Jackson grabbed some cake and a bottle of wine and headed up to her old bedroom.

The book explored the psychology of love, along with methods to develop deep emotional connection between people. The first exercise focused on human intimacy and attachment, seeking to accelerate the process through a guided set of personal prompts. They called it the Empathetic Disclosure Sequence.

Cambria sat cross-legged on the bed, flipping through the pages. "Sounds interesting. Should we do it?"

"Sure." He sat next to her and peered over as she read. She was honestly surprised he didn't reject the notion.

She went through the introductory pages, then skipped ahead to where the prompts started. "Okay, first one," she said. "Identify three similarities between you and your partner."

"Am I supposed to go first?" he asked.

"Sure. And then I'll go."

He took a drink of wine as he inspected her. "We have brown hair. We're twenty-three." He had to think about the last one. "And we're both pretty fucked up."

"True," she agreed. "Basic, but true."

"What do you mean *basic*?"

"I mean exactly that—those are basic comparisons."

"I'd like to see you do better."

"Okay." She grabbed the wine from him and took a sip. "We have the same birthday. We enjoy late night drives. And we love the ocean. *And* we find things funny that most people don't."

"That's four."

"*And*," she said again, handing him the wine, "we're both alcoholics."

"*You're* an alcoholic," he countered.

"Yeah, because of you." She rolled her eyes and looked down at the next question. "Given the choice, would you rather be rich, or famous?"

"Both," he replied.

"I think you're supposed to choose one."

"Hmmmm. Well if I'm famous, that means I'm rich by default, right?"

"Not necessarily."

"I think I'd be both."

"Jesus Christ, you're bad at this."

"Fine. I choose fame."

"Really?"

"Yeah. Is that surprising?"

"Not really. I could see it."

"Me being famous?"

"Yeah."

"Me too," he smirked.

"You have the personality for it," she said. "The *charisma*. I hate you for it."

"Would you want to be famous?"

"Hell no. I don't like people looking at me."

"Weirdo."

"I'll take wealth over fame any day," she said proudly. "Okay, next one: *In order to get to know someone, you must first understand who they respect and admire. Name one person you idolize and explain why.*"

"Karl Benz," was his answer.

"Who's that, and why?"

"He's known as the father of the automobile," he explained. "He designed and built the Benz Patent-Motorwagen, which is considered the first practical automobile designed specifically as a gasoline-powered vehicle for road use. It was the first automobile to combine engine, chassis, and wheels in a functional vehicle that was commercially viable and fueled by gasoline."

"Wow, look at you, car nerd."

"I know some things," he flashed a smug smile. "Your turn."

"Hmmm," she thought about it. "I'd probably pick Margaret Hamilton. I don't expect you to know who that is," she teased. "She's the scientist responsible for getting humans to the moon. I respect the hell out of her. She joined the Apollo project at MIT and became director of the software engineering division. It was because of her and her team that the Apollo 11 landing was saved when their computer overloaded right before touchdown."

"*Boring*."

"Are you fucking kidding me? What's wrong with you?"

"I'm joking, relax. She sounds cool."

"Uh, she's more than cool. She's brilliant."

"Alright," he said. "Next question."

She looked down at the page. "*What is one thing you're grateful for?*"

"My parents," he said promptly. "My family."

"Me too. I'm very grateful for them, and for how they raised me."

"Your parents are pretty cool."

"So are yours. I love them." She read the next question. "*If you could choose one superpower to have, what would it be?*"

"Time travel," he said.

"Ou, that's a good one. Can I steal it?"

"No, get your own."

She brought her hand to her mouth, pondering. "A photographic memory."

"Nice. That's so you."

"Thanks. I know." She cleared her throat. "*Imagine you are with a fortune teller. What is the one thing you would ask?*"

"When I'm going to die," he said without hesitation.

"Seriously?"

"Yeah. Wouldn't you want to know?"

"Er, not really."

"There's plenty I'd like to know," Jackson continued. "When I get married, who my soulmate is, if I have kids, and how many."

"You believe in soulmates?"

"Yeah, don't you?"

"No. I've told you this."

"So you don't think we're soulmates?" he winked.

She rolled her eyes. "I think I'm complete on my own, thank you very much."

"Shut the fuck up and stop being pretentious for two seconds." He turned so that his body was facing her. "Have you lost all hope when it comes to love? Are you all cynical now that you don't have Lawson?"

"No—I've never believed in soulmates. I think people find people and there's nothing more to it."

"That's bullshit. You believe in the inner workings of the universe and all that crap."

"Yeah, so?"

"So, how can you believe in that, but not in soulmates? Isn't that like, the whole point?"

She held his gaze. "I don't know, okay? But back to you—you just said you'd like to know who your soulmate is, which implies you haven't found yours yet. You don't think Natalia is your soulmate?"

He cackled. "No."

"Then why are you with her?"

"Just because we're not soulmates doesn't mean we shouldn't be together right now."

"So, what, you're just… biding your time?"

"I guess." He took another drink.

"Until something better comes along?"

"Yeah," he winked. "Until my soulmate comes along."

She squinted at him through slitted eyes.

"You still haven't answered the question," he reminded her.

"Oh—what was it again?" She looked down and read it. "Oh, right. I wouldn't want to know anything. I think life should be a surprise as it comes; not knowing your cards until they're dealt."

"You're saying there's nothing—absolutely nothing—you would like to know?"

She shook her head and smiled smugly. "Nope." She grabbed the wine from him and took another sip.

"Strange."

"*What is a long-held dream you've had, and what's stopping you from doing it?*"

They both sat in silence.

"I don't know," he finally said.

"Me neither. There's nothing really that I've dreamed of doing."

"I guess I've wanted to pursue music but never have."

"Why haven't you?"

"I don't know. I'm not good enough."

"But what if you are?"

"But what if I'm not?"

"Well… don't think like that."

"Read the next question."

"*Name the most important quality you look for in a friendship.*"

"Trust," he said. "You?"

She looked at him. "I hope you can trust *me.*"

"I do. You're probably the only person I do trust."

"I trust you, too." She looked down at the page again. "What I value most in a friendship is the ability to be myself. And with you, I can," she looked at him again. "It's not like that with anyone else."

"Same here." He held her gaze.

She could've stayed like that forever, simply staring into his eyes, the ones that matched hers so perfectly. But instead, she broke away and read the next question. "*In terms of friendship, what is one thing you want your partner to know about you*?" She looked at him again. "I think, for the sake of this exercise, we're supposed to pretend that we're strangers. So, answering it hypothetically, I would want you to know that I'm a good friend, through and through. Once you have me, you have me, and nothing will change that. And if you mean the world to me, I'll probably do anything for you."

His eyes held hers for a moment. Then he said, "I'd want you to know that I can be a bit of an asshole, and sometimes I neglect the people I care about. But that doesn't mean I don't care about them. I'm just bad at expressing myself."

"I know you are."

"You're not supposed to know," he teased. "We're strangers, remember?."

"Right. But… I definitely think you should go to therapy—to fix your personality."

"And you should go to a plastic surgeon, to fix your face."

"Ha ha ha, you're so funny."

"How many do we have left?" He reached over and grabbed the book from her. "Oh, we're almost done."

"You can read the rest." She exchanged the book for the glass of wine.

"Okay," he started. "*What is something that should never be joked about?*"

In unison, they said, "nothing."

"Glad we're on the same page," he said. "*Reveal to your partner your most embarrassing moment.*"

With exaggerated innocence, she said, "I can't think of a single thing."

"Bullshit."

"What can I say—I'm perfect!" she smirked. "You go. I'm dying to hear this."

"I don't have any embarrassing moments. *I'm* perfect."

"Oh, fuck off. I'll ask your mom when we get home."

"Ya and I'll ask yours."

"Good idea."

"*Point out one thing you genuinely admire about your partner, and don't hold back.*"

She thought about it. "I like your—"

"Everything, I know."

"Well, yes, obviously. But… I like your sense of humor. You're funny and you make me laugh. And I like how we get along so well—we're on the same wavelength."

"Same wavelength. I like that."

"And what do *you* like about *me*?"

"Nothing."

"Thanks. Try again."

"Everything!"

"I know! But be more specific."

"This is hard."

"It's really not that hard to tell someone what you like about them."

He sighed. "I like that we get along. And that I can tell you anything. And that I trust you."

She smiled. "I'm glad you feel that way."

"Okay, last one," he said. "If today was your last day alive, what is the one thing you'd most regret not telling someone? And why haven't you told them?"

They were both quiet for a moment. "That's a hard one," she said.

"It's dumb."

"How is that dumb?"

"It just is."

"Well you have to think of something."

"I can't. You go."

She took the book from him and read the question again. "If I were to die tonight, I'd most regret not telling someone…" she paused. "How I feel about them. And why haven't I told them? Well, because it's not that easy."

She looked up, and he was staring at her. "Are you insinuating something?" he asked.

"I'm not insinuating anything."

It was quiet between them. She closed the book and slid it across the bed. "Well, that's it. Game's over. Wasn't that fun?"

"Not really."

"Don't lie. You enjoyed it."

He flopped backwards on the bed. "Sure. It was fun. Is that what you want to hear?"

"Why is it so difficult for you to just admit things sometimes?"

He laughed audibly at that. "You should ask yourself the same thing."

TWENTY-SIX

Cambria and Jackson were once again inseparable. She'd spend the entire evening at his house, often staying until midnight or later, and then as soon as she got home, he'd be calling her.

They couldn't get enough of each other.

As we all know, Cambria had a tendency of getting bored of people. If she spent too much time with someone, she needed a break. She valued her alone time, and under normal circumstances, would never spend this much time with another person. But like most things, Jackson was the exception. She could spend her entire life with him and never get bored. Even when they weren't doing anything at all, she was content. He was the only person she wanted to do nothing with.

Nothing else mattered when Cambria was with Jackson. The world could be ending and she wouldn't even notice, probably wouldn't even care.

"How's Hailey's new boy toy?" he asked before taking another bite of pizza.

Cambria sat cross-legged on his couch, plate in hand. "Which one?"

"What do you mean *which one*? There's more than one?"

"Oh, yeah, she's also seeing Brandon now."

"Who's Brandon?"

"She met him at Cognito's."

"Is he cool?"

"Yeah, he's nice."

"And what about Jeremy?"

"Jeremy's also nice."

"Can you come up with a better adjective besides nice?"

"Hot."

Jackson rolled his eyes. "And what about you, Miss Single?" He dipped his pizza into the sauce and took a bite.

"What about me?"

"Are you going to start dating again?" he asked with his mouth full.

"God, no. I think I need to stay single for a very long time."

He swallowed. "You're probably right."

"I just don't think I'm ready. And besides, I'm too scared to talk to boys anyway."

"Why would you be scared?"

"Uh, because it's scary?"

"How?"

"What if they don't like me?"

"Why wouldn't they like you?"

"Because I'm ugly."

He gave her a look. "You're not ugly. I think you know that."

"No, I really don't."

"Didn't Lawson ever compliment you?"

"He did," she said, "all the time. But do you think I believed him? I've felt this way my entire life—believing that no one could possibly love me or want to be with me. That's why I stayed with him for as long as I did. He was the lifeline I was so desperately clinging to."

"Do you still feel that way?"

"No," she said. "Maybe. I don't know. It's not that black and white."

"I understand."

"I feel like you don't—but I don't expect you to."

"What do you mean?"

"You exude confidence. A little too much, actually—you cocky fuck."

He laughed and set his plate aside. "I know my worth."

"I wish I could be more like you in that regard."

"You can."

"Yeah, with alcohol, maybe."

"Well, there you go, problem solved," he winked. "Can you give me a massage? My shoulders are sore from yesterday."

"Sure."

"Actually—let's go in the hot tub first, relax the muscles."

"Good idea."

They both stood. Jackson went through his drawers to find their bathing suits. Cambria had started leaving hers here since it was the only place she ever used it.

"It's not in here," he told her.

"Then where is it?"

"No clue. Where'd you leave it?"

"Hanging in the bathroom."

"Go check."

She left and checked the bathroom, returning a moment later. "It's not there."

"Are you sure you left it here?"

"I always leave it here."

"Maybe you took it home."

"I think I'd remember if I took it home."

"Well it's not here."

"Okay, well I guess I'm not going in the hot tub then."

"Just wear something of mine." He opened another drawer and pulled out a pair of swim shorts and a t-shirt. He tossed them to her, then left the room so she could change.

Once she was done, she wandered downstairs and found him in the kitchen, stealing fruit from the cutting board where his mother was. "What's the hot tub at?" he asked her as he sucked on a slice of orange.

"101," Leanne replied. She looked up and saw Cambria. "Oh, you're probably looking for your swimsuit."

"It's here?"

"It's in my bedroom."

Jackson gave her a look. "Why?"

"Natalia was coming over, and it was hanging in the bathroom."

"Oh."

"I'll go get it." She set the knife down and left the kitchen.

"Well that's awkward," Cambria said.

"Who cares?"

They stayed in the hot tub until their fingers were pruney. After drying off and wrapping themselves in towels, they went back inside, snagging glasses of the sangria Leanne had just made before heading back up to Jackson's room.

Jackson chugged half, picking out the fruit chunks with his fingers and popping them into his mouth. He set the glass on the coffee table. "Okay, massage now."

"You're so lucky to have such a good best friend who offers to massage you when you're sore."

"Oh, yes, I'm so lucky!"

"*And* I give *good* massages, not just thirty second massages. That's what Lawson would do. He'd massage me for one minute and then complain that his hands were sore."

"That's what Natalia does."

"So annoying. Like, I actually need help sometimes."

"Same." Jackson jettisoned his towel on the floor and lay face first on his bed.

Cambria tightened the towel around herself then straddled him. "Do you have lotion?"

"Top drawer."

She reached over to his nightstand and grabbed the body lotion, squirting some onto his back. "That's cold!" he yelped.

She pressed her hands into his muscles, kneading deeply as she worked the tension away.

Once she was done, she hopped off and threw her towel to the floor. "My turn."

They switched positions, Jackson getting on top of her. He moved her hair to the side and began kneading the muscles in her shoulders, his hands slowly moving down her back.

Her skin erupted in goosebumps.

"Are you cold?" he asked her.

She hesitated. "No."

It was astonishing how when her own fingers touched her skin, it felt so mundane. But when *his* fingers touched her skin, her entire body was ignited.

This could go on forever and she'd never complain. She'd wreck every muscle in her body, just to have him touch her like that again.

When he was finished, he rolled off and lay beside her on the bed. She turned her head to face him, and they stared at each other in silence.

Jackson closed his eyes, so she did the same. It was getting late, and she was tired. She wanted to crawl into her own bed and go to sleep.

They remained like that for five and a half minutes, eyes closed, breaths synchronized. She peeked open one eye to steal a glance at him—only to find he was already doing the same.

He had been watching her.

Soon enough the clock would strike midnight and her carriage would turn into a pumpkin, so she lifted herself from the bed and told him that she needed to get going. He wanted her to stay longer, as he always did when it was time for her to go home. "What would we even do?" she asked. "Just lay here doing nothing?"

"Yes."

She laughed. "What would you be doing right now if I wasn't here?"

"I'd be calling you."

She put her clothes on over top of her bathing suit and grabbed her bag. Just as she was doing this, Jackson pulled her in for a hug. She was caught off guard and froze in his arms, then instantly relaxed, resting her head on his shoulder.

He held her tight, as he always seemed to do whenever they hugged. In that moment, there was so much being said, though they didn't say a word. It was in the air, in the lingering touches, in the stolen glances. Cambria decided if she died right then and there, she would be okay with it—as long as she was with him.

But instead, she went home and went to sleep, thinking of all the things they'd never be.

TWENTY-SEVEN

Cambria hadn't heard from Jackson for over a week.

She called every day but never heard back. The longer she went without hearing from him, the more neurotic she became. She envisioned wild scenarios in which Jackson was somehow incapacitated as to not be able to call her back. No—he was ignoring her. And for a reason. She just didn't know what that reason was. And because she was an overthinker, her mind went wild with possibilities.

He was mad at her, she concluded. But for what reason…?

She found herself unable to do anything productive. All her thoughts were of Jackson. She couldn't focus, couldn't concentrate. She didn't want to hang out with anyone, didn't want to leave the house. She was angry and sad and upset, as she should be. And then finally, after eight agonizing days of torture, Hailey knocked on her bedroom door to let her know that Jackson was downstairs.

Cambria was so enraged at this point that she didn't even want to see him. Well, she did want to see him. But she was hurt. And she wanted him to feel the same hurt he had caused her. And the only thing she could think of to hurt him in the same way that he had hurt her was to do the same thing back to him that he had done to her. Logic, right?

"Tell him I don't want to see him."

"Are you sure?"

"Yes."

Hailey closed the door and left. Cambria flopped back onto her bed.

A moment later, the door opened again. But this time it wasn't Hailey. It was Jackson. He entered the room and closed the door behind him.

Cambria sat up and glared at him. "I don't want to see you."

"Why?"

"You don't say a single fucking word to me for over a week. Then you waltz back in here expecting everything to be fine. Fuck you."

"Can I explain?"

"No."

He sat at the edge of her bed. "Nat finished her first semester of school, so we've been busy."

"Busy. For eight fucking days. You couldn't pick up the phone just *once* to let me know that? A heads up would've been nice."

"I'm sorry."

"No, you're not. You clearly don't care. And I don't want to see you."

"Cambria."

"No."

"You're being unreasonable. She's my girlfriend."

That hurt even more. "Get out."

He held her gaze and did not move.

"Jackson, get out."

"Are you being serious?"

"Yes I'm being serious. I don't want to see you."

He frowned, then stood. "You're actually ridiculous. I'm trying here. I came to see you."

"Yeah, well, too late."

He held her gaze for another moment, waiting to see if she'd change her mind, giving her one last chance to say something.

But she never did.

"Alright," he said. "That's really fucked up."

"Does it look like I give a fuck? Get out of my house."

And so, another week went by that they did not speak to each other. Except this time, not only was she mad at him, but now he was mad at her.

They were exhausting.

Cambria had never encountered someone who was just as stubborn as she was. However, Jackson was worse. And while she didn't want to be the first one to break, she knew he wouldn't, and therefore, they would never speak again. Cambria, at least, could put her pride and ego aside, if it meant being good again. Plus, their birthday was next week, and she just wanted things back to normal.

"Stop being mad at me," she said after barging into his bedroom unannounced.

He was sitting on the couch with his guitar, stunned to see her. "What are you doing here?"

"Let's just stop this, okay?" She walked toward him. "I can't take it any longer."

He smirked and lowered his guitar. "Miss me?"

"Fuck you. Want to get drunk?"

"Yes. But not here, my parents are having friends over."

"Okay. My place?"

"Let's go."

Cambria waited in the kitchen and made small talk with Leanne while Jackson packed a bag. "You're more than welcome to join us," Leanne told her as she cut up cheese. "We're having a Euchre tournament."

Cambria couldn't play cards if her life depended on it. "As tempting as that sounds, I think we have other plans in mind."

"I'm glad you two are talking again. Jackson's been miserable without you."

"Has he?"

Leanne gave her a look. "What do you think?"

"I didn't realize. I didn't think he cared."

"Of course he cares. But he's Jackson. He's been cursed with the inability to express his emotions."

"Sounds about right."

Jackson appeared, and they drove the three minutes it took to get to Cambria's house. "Where are Hailey and Mara?" he asked once they were inside.

"Hailey's back home with her family for the weekend, and Mara's at Hayden's."

"House to ourselves."

"Yeah, but don't get too wild."

They went to the kitchen and Cambria grabbed a bottle of wine. Jackson opened his bag and began unloading bottles of liquor.

"Jesus Christ, how much did you bring?"

"Enough." With him he brought rum, whiskey, gin, and beer.

"Enough to sedate a horse," she remarked.

"Lucky us," he replied.

She grabbed the wine, and he grabbed the rum, and they went into the living room to watch TV. By six o'clock they were decently drunk, and famished, so they ordered Chinese.

Once they finished eating, and she was feeling a bit sobered up, she asked him, "why didn't you call?"

He pushed their takeout containers to the side. "I told you; we were busy."

"Doing what?"

He leaned back into the couch. "I thought you didn't want to talk about that."

"Well I'm asking, aren't I?"

He hesitated, then took a drink of his beer. "We did all sorts of things. The zoo, restaurants, picnics, horseback riding."

This unsettled Cambria. "Horseback riding!? That's so random."

"She used to have a horse."

"Okay… and picnics? Did you go to our spot?"

He didn't respond. Which meant, yes, he brought her to their spot.

For some reason, this angered her greatly.

"It was pretty exhausting, if I'm being honest," he said.

She poured another shot and took it. "I'm sure."

"And what did you do?" he looked at her. "These last eight days. Besides miss me." He smirked.

She glared at him. "Nothing."

"Nothing at all?"

"Nope."

"What a loser. You couldn't have hung out with your roommates?"

She looked away from him. "Maybe I didn't want to. Maybe I'd rather hang out with you."

"Well I know that. Obviously."

She looked at him. "Everyone else is irrelevant compared to you."

He didn't know what to say to that, so instead, he poured them each another shot, and they took it back.

"Do you want to do ecstasy?" he asked immediately after.

She stared at him, bewildered. "Like, right now?"

"Yes."

"Umm. Hmmmmmm."

"You said you wanted to."

"I know. But I'm scared."

"There's nothing to be scared of. It's fun."

She contemplated it. She *did* say she wanted to try it. And if she was going to do it with someone, it would be Jackson. And no one was here; they had the house to themselves. It was a Saturday. They were in a calm, safe, controlled environment. "Okay. Sure. But what happens if I'm not okay?"

"Nothing will happen. You'll be fine."

"Promise?"

"Have I ever let anything bad happen to you?"

She held his gaze but didn't respond.

He stuck out his pinky and shook hers. "I promise."

He went to the kitchen, grabbed his backpack, and produced a small baggy containing tiny crystal rocks. "Were you planning for this?" she asked him.

"No, I brought it just in case."

"So you *were* planning it."

He rolled his eyes.

She watched as he dumped the tiny rocks onto the coffee table and crushed them into a fine powder, like how Lawson used to do with cocaine. Cambria was fascinated. He pinched some between his fingers and dropped it into his own glass, and then hers.

"We just drink it like that?" she asked.

"Yeah."

She picked up her glass, inspecting the inside, then downed it all at once. He watched her in astonishment, then followed suit. "Now we just… wait?" she asked.

"Yeah. We just relax."

They continued watching TV. Within ten minutes, Cambria started to feel funny. "I think I feel it."

"Too early."

"But I feel weird."

"You're fine." Jackson grabbed the remote and turned off the TV. "We need music."

Cambria jumped up and put a CD in. Jackson poured them another shot. "Here," he handed it to her.

"I'm not thirsty."

"No, drink it."

She took the glass from him, clinked it against his, and shot it back.

Cambria continued to feel weirder and weirder, and then after another ten minutes had passed, she flopped back onto the couch, staring up at the ceiling. "I think it hit."

It was a peculiar feeling—like nothing she'd ever experienced before, but in the best way. Her hands were cold but warm at the same time. Her heart was racing, her vision erratic. Everything was moving at hyper speed. Her stomach was doing a million summersaults, and she felt like she might puke (but in a good way). "Do you feel it?" she asked him.

He came over and stood above her. "Yeah."

She sat up. "I want to do everything." Then she stood and began walking around the room. Everything was fascinating. She looked down at her hands and held them out away from her body. *Mesmerizing.* Her heart was beating out of her chest. All she wanted to do was run, bolt, jump around, dance. She turned up the music. "I feel amazingggggg," she said, smiling ear to ear. "I feel so so so good."

He stood there observing her. "I told you."

She turned and looked at him. "Why haven't I tried this sooner? This is the best feeling in the entire world."

"I know."

"How many times have you done it? Does it always feel this good?"

He laughed. "You're talking really fast."

"Am I? I can't help it. Everything's moving so fast. My heart's going so fast. My brain's going so fast. Brrrrrrr. I want to run."

"Don't run."

She bolted out of the living room and ran up the stairs. He followed after her.

First, they went into Mara's room to explore and look at her things. Then they did the same to Hailey's. Then they turned off every light in the house and used flashlights. "It feels better in the dark," she told him.

"Come look at your pupils." He brought her to the bathroom and they both leaned forward, inspecting themselves in the mirror. Their pupils were massive.

Cambria giggled uncontrollably.

"Are you glad you did it?" he asked her.

"Yes!" She stood back and looked at him. "This is amazing."

"No regrets?"

"Definitely not."

He was grinning cunningly. "I have to tell you something."

"What?"

"I put some in your drink."

"I know," she said.

"No, before."

"Before what?"

"Before we ate."

"What? Actually?"

"Yeah. That's why you started feeling it so fast."

"Jackson!"

He laughed.

She laughed too. "What if I had said no?"

"I knew you wouldn't."

"You're lucky I'm me," she smirked. "Because that's bad."

They continued wandering around the house, shining their flashlights and inspecting everything. Then they went to her bedroom, where she lay on her bed staring up at the ceiling. Jackson put on some music.

Listening to music on ecstasy was an entirely different experience. The sound entered her eardrums, then spread like ripples through her bloodstream, reaching each fingertip. It pulsed inside her—a river of rhythm flowing beneath her skin. Every touch was electric, every surface alive. She traced slow circles along her arms, delighting in the warmth and softness, savoring the simple pleasure of her own skin. The music wasn't just heard; it was felt, lived, and breathed from within.

Time seemed to pass at a different speed. Hours felt like minutes, and before she knew it, it was almost midnight. "I don't want to sleep," she said. "I don't feel tired at all."

"Yeah. That's the point."

"I want to go on an adventure."

They grabbed their sweaters and went out the front door.

This was the most alive she'd ever felt. Her senses had been locked away, but now they danced wildly, awakening every fiber of her being. It was transcendent. She didn't know what to do with herself, it was all too much.

She wanted to encapsulate this feeling and keep it forever.

They went to the park and sat on the swings, kicking their legs as they went higher and higher. She felt like she might spontaneously combust (in a good way). Then they took their flashlights and went exploring through the forest, wandering down to the river.

"Let's go home," Jackson said.

"I don't want to go home."

"Cambri," he gave her a look. "It's late. Let's go."

"Fine," she acquiesced, then jumped on his back.

He carried her the rest of the way home.

Once they got back, Jackson filled a glass of water and they went back upstairs, deciding to once again go into Mara's room. They sat on her bed taking intermittent sips as they passed it back and forth.

Cambria went to the bathroom to pee. When she returned, Jackson was lying on the bed staring up at the ceiling. *Stairway to Heaven* was playing. She lay next to him and looked up.

Her hands were cold, so she placed them under Jackson's back. His body was always much warmer than hers. She felt calmer than she did earlier and assumed the drugs were wearing off. She didn't want it to end. It had been the best night of her life.

Still feeling cold, she turned onto her side and snuggled into Jackson. He lifted his arm and put it around her. She closed her eyes, feeling tranquility wash over her, though, she knew she'd never sleep—her body was buzzing.

She placed her head on his chest and listened to the beat of his heart. She matched her breathing to his. Then, she brought two fingers to his neck and felt his pulse.

He put his fingers to her neck and did the same.

Close wasn't close enough—she wanted to be closer. To melt into him, combine atoms, become one.

She couldn't stay still, and neither could he, running his fingertips down the length of her arm. Goosebumps erupted across her skin. She closed her eyes and pressed her forehead to his chest, breathing steady. It felt good but it wasn't enough.

She, too, traced her fingers across his skin. Down his chest, across his torso, up his face. It felt just as good to touch as it did to be touched. His fingers charged with electricity; she jolted every time he touched her.

Looking up at him, she discovered that he was already looking down at her, as if waiting. That was always the thing with them; it didn't matter where they were, anytime their eyes wandered across a room, they'd find each other.

They held each other's gaze, as they did, communicating without words, which were not necessary for them. His eyes possessed a sadness that Cambria recognized in herself.

Then, he kissed her. And it didn't feel strange and unfamiliar—it felt just right, like this was how it was supposed to be. He started slow and tentative, but within seconds, became starved for her. Rolling her onto her back, he kissed her deeper. She parted her legs and pulled him closer, her fingers digging into his back.

Without hesitation, she pulled his shirt over his head and tossed it to the side. He lifted her torso, peeling off her top with slow, deliberate movements. His lips trailed kisses along her neck, her breasts, her stomach, savoring every inch of her skin. Then, with gentle urgency, he slid her pants down and lowered himself between her legs.

Cambria needed him, now, desperately and vehemently. She pulled him up so that his mouth was on hers again, then tugged off his jeans and tossed them to the side.

There was a moment of pause as he hovered above her, their faces inches apart. He stared at her, and she stared back. Not hesitation—

longing. And then just like that, he was inside her, and it was everything she'd imagined it would be.

Pure ecstasy.

TWENTY-EIGHT

"What the fuck are you doing in my bed?"

Cambria jolted awake, panic spreading through her as Mara stood before her.

"And why are you naked?"

Cambria's eyes darted around the room—there was no sign of Jackson. For a brief moment she wondered if she had dreamt the entire thing. "I passed out," she said.

"Who did you fuck in my bed?"

Cambria stared at her blankly, deer in the headlights.

"Cambria Annabelle Nickson."

"I don't know."

"You don't know?"

Cambria shook her head.

"What, you brought some stranger back here?"

Cambria nodded.

Mara rolled her eyes. "And you couldn't have done that in your own bed?"

"I was drunk."

"You're crazy." Mara dropped her bag and flopped down onto the bed next to her. "How was it? Did you come?"

Cambria rubbed her eyes. "What time is it?"

"It's one o'clock in the afternoon, you freak."

"Oh—whoops. Can you get me a robe? I'm going to shower."

In the shower, she stared vacantly at the wall as the scalding water ran down her body, the night before playing in her mind on a loop, complete with Jackson's body on hers.

Fuck. This was bad. So so bad. Jackson was her best friend. Her best friend who had a *girlfriend.*

After twenty minutes of not moving, she finally turned off the water and got out, wrapping a towel around herself.

She had no appetite whatsoever—couldn't eat if someone paid her. Jackson had warned her about this. He said she may experience a comedown. She had no idea whether this was from the drugs or from everything else she was feeling. Her heart was racing with anxiety. She wanted to die.

Looking like a drowned rat, she got dressed and made her way down to the kitchen. Mara, who was in the living room reading a book, peered up at her through slit eyes. "You left this place a disaster."

"I'm sorry. I'll clean."

"I don't mind, it's just funny. You must've had a good night."

Cambria moved deliberately to the coffee machine, her body weighted. "I don't remember."

"You blacked out?"

"Yes." She grabbed a coffee mug from the cupboard.

"How much did you drink?"

"Too much."

"Clearly." She continued staring at her, studying her, and Cambria wished she'd stop. "Are you okay?"

"I'm fine."

"You don't seem fine."

"I feel sick."

"Hmm. Drink pickle juice, it has electrolytes."

She spent the remainder of the day in bed, feeling anxious and shameful. But something else too; satisfaction.

Try as she might, she could not get that image out of her head: Jackson above her, inside her. And she realized that, despite how wrong it was, she liked it.

She was utterly exhausted, drained of all energy. She could sleep for a week and it wouldn't be enough. Most of her day was spent in bed, tormented by her own thoughts. She only got up to use the bathroom and get water. As the hours passed, and the phone remained silent, her anticipation only grew more.

Cambria was terrified for how their next conversation would go. She knew they'd always tread close to the line but never crossed it—well except that one time. But now… now the line had *really* been crossed. And there was no going back from that.

She waited and waited, but the phone did not ring. Sunday turned to Monday. Monday to Tuesday.

Two days passed without hearing from him. He was avoiding her, she knew. So, on Tuesday during her lunch break, she ambushed him at work, knowing he'd have no option than to face her.

She picked up two coffees and went to Ford, where the receptionist directed her to Jackson's office. Walking down the hallway, she peeked her head through the open door. There he sat, at his desk, sorting through paperwork. He looked up when she walked in, clearly aghast. "What are you doing here?"

She handed him the coffee. "I come bearing gifts."

He eyed her. "Thanks."

"Hi," she said.

"Hi."

"Everything good?"

"Yeah, why?"

"I haven't heard from you."

He sat back in his chair, moved some papers around. "I've been busy."

"Doing what?"

"Just stuff."

"Alright. What are we doing for Thursday?"

He didn't look at her. "I have plans."

"What do you mean *you have plans*? That's *our* day."

His eyes met hers. "Can you close the door?"

She turned around and closed it, then faced him again, waiting.

"We never made plans," he said.

"I didn't think we had to. I thought it was a given."

"I don't know what to tell you."

"Why are you being like this?"

"Being like what?"

"An asshole."

"I'm an asshole because I have plans for my birthday?"

She didn't know how to respond. "Are we going to talk about it?"

"Talk about what?"

"Are you fucking serious right now?"

"I have a girlfriend."

She wanted to scream. She was actually going to scream. "So we're just going to act like it never happened?"

"Do you have feelings for me?"

There it was again; the question that haunted her from beyond the grave. She faltered, "No. Do you have feelings for me?"

"No."

"Alright. Well, have fun on your birthday with your *girlfriend* who you claim to love so much yet didn't hesitate to cheat on." She turned around and opened the door, turned back around and grabbed his coffee, then left, throwing them both in the trash.

Days passed. She spent her birthday alone and miserable. Hailey and Mara surprised her with a cake that she didn't even eat. She wanted to get into her car and drive off a cliff.

She hated him. She actually hated him. No, the opposite. But he infuriated her more than anyone ever had. She wanted to strangle him. Kiss him. Slap him across the face. Push him down the stairs.

She wanted him to show up at her door and profess his love for her, then kiss her like he had that night. She hadn't stopped thinking about it—it was quite literally all she thought about. All week she replayed that scene in her mind, over and over again.

She wanted to scream. Or kill someone. Preferably him.

Finally, when she could take it no more, she broke down and confessed everything to Mara and Hailey, who weren't all that surprised.

"I've always thought he was in love you," Mara said. "Obviously."

"I agree," Hailey added. "Definitely in love with you."

"He is *not* in love with me. Trust me."

"No offence, but you don't know what you're talking about."

"No, *you* guys don't know what you're talking about. You don't know us. We're best friends."

"Best friends don't have sex with each other."

She covered her face with a pillow and screamed.

"It's okay to admit you have feelings for him."

"I hate him. I actually think I hate him."

"Soooo," Mara raised an eyebrow. "That's who you fucked in my bed."

Cambria winced. "Please don't."

"Was it good?"

She sighed. "It was the best sex of my life."

After two weeks in solitary confinement, Cambria finally caved and reached out to Jackson, asking him to come pick her up.

What jarred her the most about her friendship with Jackson Harding was how eerily normal he seemed after any sort of conflict or mishap. If she hadn't known any different, she would've thought everything was completely fine. It was a talent, really. A skill not just anyone could master. And he, was a master. A master of compartmentalization.

They made small talk, which she loathed. She didn't dare ask about his birthday—she didn't even want to know. The thought of Natalia made her want to vomit. If he uttered her name she was prepared to jump out of the car.

Cambria was careful not to bring up *that night*, or the fallout, or anything else she knew would drive him away. She needed to navigate carefully from now on.

After that, he allowed her back in, but at a distance. Nothing was the same. Their interactions were forced and awkward. She felt a dissonance between them that had never existed before. And there was nothing she could do about it. She knew it'd be futile attempting to talk to him, because he was Jackson, and he was impossible.

He was pushing her further and further away.

Then, one Sunday night, as they had plans to go to the movies, Jackson called and canceled at the last minute. Cambria, rightfully, was furious. "What reason could you possibly have for bailing on me?"

"They're showing Phantom of the Opera tonight at Costa Mesa and Nat wants me to take her."

"Please tell me you're joking."

He didn't respond.

"You're bailing on plans with me to see a fucking musical? YOU HATE MUSICALS."

"I already said yes."

"What the fuck is your problem?"

"I don't have a problem."

"Oh, believe me, you have plenty."

"Don't be bitter just because you're not getting your way. You can't always get what you want."

"Fuck you."

"I don't know why you're so mad. We're just friends."

She hung up on him.

No matter how hard she tried to see it from his point of view, she couldn't. None of it made sense to her. Jackson had always been her home, her happy place. She knew that no matter what, at the end of the day, she had him. And he had her.

But not anymore.

It dawned on her, suddenly, how alone she was. Jackson was the only person she really cared about, the only thing that mattered. The truth was, Cambria did not care if anyone in her life left. It would not phase her even the slightest. But Jackson was a different story. She could not live without him. She would have done anything for him, anything to make him happy. She'd have followed him off a cliff if he asked her to.

It was difficult to endure. More difficult, she'd argue, than any of the hardships she'd faced with Lawson. This was probably because she never really cared for Lawson as much as she liked the idea of being with him. But Jackson was different. Jackson was the air in her lungs, the blood in her veins. It was impossible to go a day without thinking about him. She had become so accustomed to everyday life with him, talking on the phone each night before bed, anticipating the next time they'd see each other. And then just like that, all of it gone, ripped away from her. All because of one night.

They had finally reached a pinnacle, only to hit a standstill once again, pretending like it never happened.

But, she knew, if she had a time machine and could go back and change the past, she wouldn't do it. Because one night with him was somehow worth all the turmoil that followed. Even though she lost a part of him that she wasn't sure she could get back, she *still* wouldn't take it back.

She wouldn't trade it for anything.

TWENTY-NINE

She was wrong—she *could* get him back. And she did.

Albeit it wasn't identical to how things were before, but things were a lot better than they had been. Jackson split his time between Cambria and Natalia. Cambria really couldn't complain—she would take whatever she could get. She used her free time as an attempt to better herself. She started going to the gym, meal prepping, riding her bike again. But no matter what she did, it felt like something was missing.

In July, she went on a date. He talked constantly and didn't ask her a single question about herself. Then, when it was over, he tried to kiss her—unsolicited. She dodged it, said she had to go, then left.

She cried herself to sleep.

As summer progressed, she and Jackson began spending more time together. Something was healing between them. Or perhaps enough time had passed since *the incident* that it was pretty much forgotten. Either way, Cambria wouldn't complain—she just enjoyed being in his presence. She wanted to be anywhere he was.

But every time she looked at him, her mind went back to that night; his hands on her body, his lips on hers. She knew it was wrong, but she couldn't help it.

There was something unnerving about listening to a phone conversation between Jackson and Natalia. It made Cambria want to crawl out of her skin. She tried not to pay attention and make herself invisible, even if she didn't feel invisible.

Once Jackson hung up, he went to the open window and lit a cigarette. He turned around to look at Cambria, and she stood, as if on command, and went to him.

"Everything okay?" she said.

He exhaled. "Yeah."

"She knows I'm here?"

He brought the cigarette away from his mouth and looked at her. "You seem surprised."

Over the course of their friendship, it had simply become a secret that Jackson and Cambria still spent time together. Natalia was none the wiser, believing they'd stopped being friends long ago. *It's just easier that way*, Jackson had said.

"Well obviously I'm surprised—she hates me," Cambria said. "What did she say? Is she okay with it?"

"She doesn't really have much of a choice."

"But she's not mad?"

"She's not mad."

Cambria was utterly flabbergasted. "This is crazy! We're making progress!"

"Settle down," he said. "She's still not a fan of you."

"But she's fine with us hanging out?"

"She'll tolerate it."

Cambria was smug. "That's a win in my book."

CAMBRIA

August turned into September, and Natalia returned to school. Suddenly all of Jackson's evenings were free, just as they'd been before Natalia's summer break. And just like that, they became inseparable again. As if nothing had ever changed between them. They reverted to how they were before summer, before May, before the night that changed everything.

"If you were me," she said to Mara one night, "would you tell her?"

"Who, Natalia?"

"Yeah. About what happened."

"Uh, definitely not."

"Why?"

"Well, one, she'd probably murder you. And two… well, maybe this should be one—it's not your place."

"It's not?"

"No," Mara said. "Is it fucked up? Yes. Do I think you're a bad person? Meh, debatable. But do you have a responsibility to tell her something like that? No, that's up to Jackson. And if he's not going to tell her, then neither should you."

"But what we did was wrong."

"Don't act like you're on some high-horse-holier-than-thou shit. Guilt is not your incentive for wanting to tell her—you just want them to break up."

"No…"

"Yes. I know you, Cambria. You're insane."

"I am not."

"Do you love him?"

The question caught her off guard. "As a friend, yeah."

"Bullshit."

"What, you think I'm in love with him or something?"

"Are you?"

"No! He's like a brother."

Mara laughed. Then she laughed even harder. "I didn't know you were into incest."

"Fuck off."

"I think it's time you stop lying to yourself. Everyone can see it. Everyone but you."

"I think I'd know if I was in love with him."

"Love makes people do crazy things. Just remember that."

The end of September arrived once again, and with it came Grayson Welch's annual end of summer party. Jackson and Cambria had been spending every single day together. He complained about Natalia constantly and told Cambria he didn't want her coming to Grayson's party. "I told her to just sit this one out," he said. "She can come to the next one."

That meant Jackson and Cambria were going together, and any outing she could attend with him would be cherished, as this was not a regular occurrence for them.

All week Cambria anticipated the party. And then, on the night of, just as she was getting ready to head over to Jackson's, he called and told her Natalia was coming.

"I thought you didn't want her there," Cambria said, perplexed.

"Yeah, well, I changed my mind."

"So you're bailing on me?"

"I'm not *bailing on you.* We're going to the same party, we'll see each other there."

"It's not the same. We were supposed to go *together.*"

"What difference does it make? What's the big deal?"

"The big deal is that you said you didn't want her there! You've just spent the past week complaining about her and saying how you don't want her there. What changed?"

"It doesn't matter. At the end of the day, she wants to come. I'll just see you there."

"This is so unfair."

"Why are you making such a big deal out of this? It's just a party."

But it wasn't just a party to her. It was one of the only opportunities she'd have to spend the night with him like that.

She brought Mara and Hailey instead, and from the moment she walked through the doors, had a vendetta. Hell hath no fury like a woman scorned. They went straight to the kitchen, Cambria sorting through the bottles of liquor. "Want to do shots?"

"Easy killer," Mara said. "We just got here."

"I'm thirsty."

Grayson appeared and ducked his head into their circle. "Ladies, good evening."

"Hi, Gray." Cambria hugged him.

"There's appetizers in the living room," he told them. "And pizza will be on it's way shortly."

"Thank you, darling," Mara said. "Host of the year, as always."

"It's my pleasure."

"Where's Meredith?"

"Oh, you didn't hear? We broke up."

Cambria's jaw dropped. "What? No fucking way. When?"

"A couple weeks ago. Jackson didn't tell you?"

"Jackson neglects to tell me anything of remote importance," Cambria rolled her eyes. "What happened? I thought you guys were endgame."

"I did too. She kind of just ended it out of the blue. Said we were going different directions."

"I'm sorry. Are you alright?"

"No. Not even close," he laughed. "But that's what alcohol is for."

Cambria grabbed four shot glasses and filled them with tequila. "To new beginnings," she said as they clinked them together.

They took the shot and set the empty glasses on the counter. "Is Jackson here yet?" Cambria asked Grayson.

"Yeah, they arrived a few minutes ago. I'm surprised you and Nat can be in the same room."

"She can tolerate me now, apparently."

"Apparently. Well, you should go say hi. I think they're with Fendi."

"I think I'm good," she grabbed another bottle and began filling her cup.

"Cambria's angry, if you couldn't tell," Mara told him.

"Oh no, dare I ask?"

"Who do you think," Mara quipped.

"Ah, Jackson, yet again. What'd he do this time?"

"Jackson can go fuck himself," Cambria said. "I don't want to see him."

"*And* that's my cue to leave," he gave her a kiss on the cheek and left.

Cambria touched her face where his lips had just been, turning to watch him as he left. "What do you guys think of Grayson?" she asked as he disappeared from sight.

"He's very nice," Hailey replied.

"Grayson's Grayson," was Mara's response.

"Hmm." She looked around the counter for more alcohol.

The more she drank, the better she felt. Her lips were numb and her head was light. She floated through the rooms, conversing with people just for the sake of it, despite her contempt for socializing. Very unlike her. But that was the alcohol talking.

She spotted Jackson from across the room, and he was alone. She made a beeline over. "Can we talk?"

He met her gaze unwillingly. "About what?"

"Please, Jackson?"

The person standing before her was unrecognizable. His eyes were distant and his tone was cold. "There's nothing to talk about."

And at that, something in her snapped. "You're going to regret saying that to me," she said, and stormed off.

She went straight to the pool, stripping down to just her bra and underwear. Without hesitating, she jumped in headfirst and joined a group of people who were throwing a beach ball around.

After doing that for a few minutes, she got bored and needed something else. That was when she spotted Grayson, alone in the hot tub. She climbed out of the pool and made her way over.

When she would look back on this moment, she wouldn't have a clue as to what she said. Her memory was a bit of a blur, and so was she. But what she remembered was this: She got in the hot tub and moved her body on top of his, straddling him. His hands gravitated to her hips naturally. And then she kissed him.

Jackson watched from his vantage point on the balcony, where he had gone to keep an eye on her.

Once she was finished sticking her tongue down Grayson's throat, she got out and marched back into the house, on a rampage. She was feeling good. Charged. Vengeful. Nothing could stop her. Nothing would get in her way.

She grabbed a random towel and wrapped it around herself. Then she searched the house until she found Natalia, who was conversing with the other girls. "Can I talk to you?" she said over the music. They were suddenly face to face. The room was spinning. She looked like a madman.

Natalia was caught off guard. "Is everything okay?"

"We need to talk."

"About what?"

"Your boyfriend."

Natalia took a step back. "What about him?"

Cambria didn't even hesitate. "There's something you should know—"

Before she could continue, Jackson was there, materializing from thin air, yanking her away from everyone. He did not let go until they reached the bathroom, where he pushed her inside and closed the door behind them. "What the fuck do you think you're doing?"

Cambria hiccupped. "Fuck you, Jackson. Go fuck yourself."

"What is *wrong* with you?"

"I'm pissed off, that's what's wrong with me! You piss me off!"

"Why, because I didn't come to the party with you? Boo hoo, get over it."

"Why are you such a fucking asshole to me?"

"You're insane. What you were about to do right there, is insane. And don't think I don't know about you throwing yourself on Grayson. How embarrassing."

"This is because of you! You did this!"

"I didn't do anything," he held her gaze. "We are not together."

Tears filled her eyes. "You're supposed to be my best friend. Why are you treating me like this?"

"Best friends? Yeah, not anymore. You're fucking delusional." Without another word, he left, slamming the door behind him.

She woke up the next morning on her bathroom floor. Her clothes were off, and there was vomit in the toilet. Her purse was upside next to her, all its contents dumped out. Beside that was half a joint, stubbed out on the floor. She rubbed her eyes, which were thick with makeup. Her head was pounding and the room was spinning. She leaned over the toilet and vomited again.

When she opened the door, Mara was waiting by the banister. "Hey, dumbass."

Cambria closed one eye and squinted at her through the other.

"You're alive," Mara remarked.

Cambria ran her fingers through her hair. "Barely."

"You look like shit."

"I'm aware."

"What do you remember?"

Cambria shifted on her leg. "Everything, for the most part."

"Hmm." Mara came towards her. "Jackson called."

At this, she came alive. "When?"

"This morning."

"What did he say?"

Mara looked down, avoiding eye contact.

"Mara."

She looked up at her. "Well, he's not too happy about last night."

"Okay…and…"

She held her gaze. "And… he told me to tell you…" She paused, knowing how painful the words would be. "He's done with you. For good. And he said don't ever contact him again."

April 1992

THIRTY

The first few days of April felt like a glimpse of what was to come; the rain had managed to cease, and the sky was blue again. Normally, spring represented new beginnings and the arrival of the vernal equinox. It was a time for hope, and delight.

But not for Cambria.

She slid on some jeans, threw her hair into a messy ponytail, and left the house. It was Saturday afternoon, and she had spent most of her day reading. When she had gone to the kitchen to make coffee, she realized they were out hence her sudden decision to leave the house. She didn't feel happy, and she didn't feel sad either, and that was because she was on Xanax, which left her devoid of emotion.

That was how it had to be. Because when she wasn't on Xanax, she felt everything, always, all at once. Her emotions were overwhelming, and they often got the best of her.

She'd been struggling a lot lately. Well, let's be honest—she'd been struggling for the last six months, since she destroyed her friendship with Jackson. It hadn't gotten any better—the pain was ubiquitous.

In the beginning, she thought about that night constantly. And still, to this day, she thought about it, just not as much. What she mostly thought about was Jackson. And how empty she was without him.

She knew that what she did was wrong. She knew her anger that night was an overreaction, as well as misplacement. She knew she was crazy. And she also knew that no matter what she did, Jackson would never forgive her.

But now there was something else she knew.

It all made sense, why she did what she did. The answer had been right in front of her for quite some time. When Mara had asked if she was in love with Jackson, Cambria thought the notion was preposterous and denied it vehemently. But she had been wrong, which was difficult to admit. She'd been in denial, lying to herself for so long, trying to convince everyone of something that she was so desperately trying to convince herself. All it took was losing him for her to finally realize the truth: she was in love with him.

How she hadn't realized sooner was astonishing, albeit understandable. Sometimes we don't see the most obvious things, even when they're right in front of us, flashing on a neon sign. And in Cambria's case, that sign said: I'M IN LOVE WITH JACKSON.

She loved Jackson. She had always loved Jackson. Blinded by excuses, buried beneath the naivety of their friendship, hidden behind little white lies and clandestine crossing of lines. What constituted love? What distinguished love from friendship? It happened so naturally, without any effort. They were destined, from the moment they met, the stars aligning. She'd felt an inexplicable familiarity with him, forming an instant kinship. Late nights on the phone that would normally be spent alone. His presence taking all the air from her lungs. Teaching her things about herself that she never would've known otherwise. They had their own language that only the two of them understood. She saw no one but him. All this time she thought it was friendship, but it had always been so much more.

The last six months had passed agonizingly slow. They had been the most difficult six months of her life—much harder than the previous time they stopped talking. Because the last time, it had been a mutual decision. Plus, she had Lawson to fall back on. But this time was different. Jackson had finally reached his breaking point with her. There was no fixing the damage she had caused. He was gone for good.

Each day without Jackson was like living without air. In her chest was a gaping hole where her heart had once been. His memory left her gutted each time it surfaced. An infinite injury; the wound that would never mend. She was perpetually bleeding, and it could not be controlled. She didn't know how long she could go on living like this.

Getting through each day required effort she didn't have. She lost all motivation to leave the house. When she was home, she barely left her bedroom. She stopped eating, stopped spending time with Mara and Hailey. Everything that once brought her joy was gone.

It was an insurmountable loss—one from which she would never recover. She knew, deep down, that she would never move on or be okay again. She had destroyed the best thing that ever happened to her; she'd never find anything close to what she had with Jackson.

This, she was certain.

And then, on this fateful day in April, all of that changed.

It was as she was walking down the street, hands in her pockets, numb from the Xanax, that she stumbled into a coffee shop on the corner of Main Street. She had been there a few times before and always enjoyed their lattes. The Grind had a casual and cozy atmosphere that attracted a wide array of people. She stood in line, staring blankly at the exposed brick wall, the cafe bustling around her. When it was her turn to order, she got a French vanilla latte with a double shot of espresso, then waited off to the side.

The barista called her name, and she grabbed her latte and sat at a table in the corner. Gazing out the window, she watched as the cars drove by, thinking of nothing. Only that she was lonely. And that she missed Jackson.

She wasn't trying to eavesdrop, but she could hear the conversation behind her between a man and a woman discussing their parent's thirty-fifth anniversary party, which was on the twenty-third of April.

"Do you know what you're getting them?" the woman asked her brother.

"I have an idea in mind."

"Okay, share."

"I'd like to replace dad's wedding ring. I know how much it gutted him to lose it. Mom pretended like it was fine, but I know she was sad too."

"Aw, that's sweet. What a good idea, Finn—they'll love that."

Cambria, who recognized the date, turned around instantly, no reservations or hesitations. That was because of the Xanax—it made her apathetic to everything. "When did your dad lose his ring?" she asked.

They looked at her, matching blue eyes that were the color of the sea. The woman's hair was blond, tied back in a ponytail, and the man's was brown, cut short. They had the same face. "It must've been three years ago," he said.

"1989," she replied hastily.

"Yeah."

Suddenly, everything clicked into place. The sky opened, and a beam of light shone down on him.

"I know this is going to sound crazy," Cambria said, "but I think I have your dad's ring."

They left the coffee shop immediately, Finn and Cambria. His sister needed to go, but she was expecting updates once Finn saw the ring.

Cambria's house was a ten-minute walk from The Grind. Mara and Hailey were both away for the weekend and she had the place to herself. Was it risky bringing a complete stranger home with her? Probably, but she'd done worse.

She unlocked the front door and they stepped inside. "Wait here," she told him. Then she hurried up the stairs to her bedroom, going through her things until she found the ring. She rushed back down the stairs to where Finn waited eagerly.

Once she handed it to him, he held it up, inspecting it for himself, incredulous. "I don't believe it," he said, completely awestruck. "This is it. This is my father's wedding ring." He looked at her. "How on Earth did you come to be in possession of it?"

"I found it walking home one morning," she told him. "Three years ago, in June. I had just moved here from the East Coast. I didn't want to leave it there, so I took it with me, in hopes that I could eventually find the owner. I used to keep it in my purse, just in case. But I never did. Obviously."

He looked at it again. "This is unbelievable. Truly remarkable."

"I can't believe it myself," she said. "I had completely forgotten about it."

He met her eyes. "How can I repay you?"

"Oh, you don't need to do that."

"I insist. To show my gratitude. Are you doing anything right now?"

"I'm not doing anything at all."

"Can I take you to dinner?"

She was in a baggy t-shirt and jeans, her hair thrown into a messy ponytail. She wasn't even wearing makeup. "Sure."

"I don't even know your name."

"It's Cambria," she said. "I'm Cambria."

"Cambria," he said, and there was something about the way it sounded in his mouth. "I think I was supposed to find you."

Half an hour later, they sat at a table at Red Lobster, drinking white wine, completely engrossed with each other. They'd just ordered their food and could now focus. "What are the chances?" he said to her.

She leaned forward on the table and rested her chin in her palm, gazing at him in awe. "Slim to none."

"My parents will be over the moon. And wait until they hear how I found it."

"How'd he lose it?"

"Oh, that was me."

"*You* lost it? How?"

"Well, he gave it to me. I'd never worn a ring before, and it was irritating my finger, so I had it in my pocket. It must have fallen out."

"Was he mad?"

"He was understanding. He knew it was an accident. But I know how much he loved that ring."

"Have you always lived in Pine Hills?"

"No, I'm from Meadowvale, but I've been living in Pine Hills for five years now. You said you moved here from the East Coast?"

"Yeah, Connecticut, Linden Falls. Small-ish town."

"What caused the move?"

"Um, I think I needed to for my own growth. I was stagnant, and I needed to escape. So, I came here. And it was the best decision of my life." She thought back to the plane ride over here, moving into her apartment, meeting Jackson.

"This is just so crazy, for you to have come all this way. We've probably passed right by each other."

"Probably," she smiled. "What a small town and what a small world."

"So, tell me," he took a sip of wine. "What do you do for work?"

"I work the front desk doing admin support at a private practice. Nothing too exciting."

"Do you enjoy it?"

"Yeah, it's fine, I can't complain. My boss is great. I don't dread being there. So, yeah, it's good, I guess. What do *you* do for work?"

"I'm an attorney."

She widened her eyes. "Wow, impressive," she took a drink. "What kind of attorney?"

"Employment and Labor Law."

"Do *you* enjoy it?"

He laughed. "I do."

"Good for you. I'm sure you make *real* good money," she winked. "And what do you do when you're not working?"

"I'm always working," he laughed. "But in the bit of free time I have, I go to the gym, as well as for runs and hikes. I love the outdoors. Fishing and camping too. I enjoy spending time with my family, seeing my niece and nephew. I like cooking. And just hanging out, relaxing."

"That sounds nice," she said. "I've never been fishing. Or camping."

"It's never too late to start."

"Can you drive a boat?"

He laughed at this. "I can."

"How many hours are you working each week?"

He laughed again. "Don't ask me that."

"Oh, God—are you a workaholic?"

"I'm not a workaholic, but I *am* an attorney. I don't pick the hours, the hours pick me."

"Fair enough," she took a sip of wine. "So, you're always busy."

"I'm not *always* busy. I can manage my time well. But what about you, what do you do for fun?"

"Honestly, not much these days. I love to sleep—can't get enough of that. Umm, I like to read. I've always enjoyed photography. I have two housemates. They're like my sisters. I like cooking, but I'm not good at it, so maybe you can teach me," she smirked. "I'm not terrible at baking though. And I like going for walks on the beach, and watching the sunset, and being near the sea. That pretty much sums it up."

"I can definitely teach you how to cook," he said. "I would actually love that."

She smiled. "Me too."

"What do you like to read?"

"Anything, really, I'm not picky. But I love Sci-Fi."

"My mom likes Sci-Fi. She says it's the best genre for learning."

"She's probably right."

He fiddled with his glass. "I take it you prefer summer over winter?"

"How did you know?"

"Sunsets, beach, the sea."

She laughed. "Yep, guilty."

"I take it that was factored into your move here?"

"Well it definitely wasn't a deterrent."

"You came here alone?"

"Yes."

"Your family's back in Connecticut?"

"Yep."

"That must be tough," he said. "Do you miss them?"

"Um, I mean, yeah, I always miss them. But you kind of just get used to it. And we talk on the phone all the time." She sat back. "Tell me about your family."

"Well, my father is also an attorney. My mother's a nurse. I have an older brother, Derek, and you met Erin earlier, she's the youngest."

"And who has the kids?"

"Erin. A boy and a girl, Nick and Katie."

"Cute. Do you want kids?"

"I do, yes. Do you?"

"I haven't decided yet."

"That's alright. Do you have any siblings?"

She hesitated, unsure if she should go there. But something about him felt safe; like she could open up and tell him anything. "I did," she said. "He died when I was sixteen."

"I'm so sorry."

She shrugged. "It was a long time ago."

"You don't have to talk about it if you don't want to."

"It's okay, I want to." She gave him a reassuring smile, then continued. "He killed himself. Overdose. He had a lot of problems, and I guess no one could help him."

"That's horrible."

"Yeah, well…"

"I'm sorry that happened to you."

"Like I said, it was a long time ago."

The waitress appeared then, setting their plates down in front of them.

"This looks amazing," Cambria said, gawking at the food.

When she looked up, he was staring at her. "I just want to thank you again," he said.

She laughed and shook her head. "You need to stop thanking me."

"I'm sorry—last time, I promise. But I really do appreciate it."

"It's fine, no problem," she blushed. "I was keeping it safe for you."

He held her gaze, and the look in his eyes made her stomach flip. "You have beautiful eyes," he said. "What color are they?"

She looked away instinctively. "I think they're hazel," she met his eyes again. "They change from time to time."

He was looking at her so intensely. "What brought you to The Grind today?"

She wasn't expecting the question. "I ran out of coffee," she admitted.

"How unfortunate," he replied.

"I know right. How about you?"

"My sister picked it."

"What luck," Cambria said. But it wasn't luck.

It was fate.

THIRTY-ONE

After they finished eating, they ended up driving around in his car for two hours because they didn't want to stop talking to each other. Just when she thought they'd run out of things to discuss, something else would come up. Conversation with him was natural, and she didn't feel any of that awkward discomfort she normally did when meeting someone new. He was so intelligent and sure of himself. Cambria could've listened to him speak for hours, swept up in the cadence of his voice.

When he reached over and placed his hand atop hers, she was suddenly speechless, her brain no longer functioning. In that moment, her entire body was ignited, electrified.

Who was this man, who seemingly came out of nowhere, at the exact time she needed him? He couldn't have been more perfect. She had spent the last six months yearning for human connection, convinced she would never find it, thinking she'd be alone forever. But now, suddenly, there was hope.

She didn't want the night to end, but alas, it always did. He drove her home, then got out to open her door and walk her up the front steps.

They stood there staring at each other. Cambria contemplated how to end such a perfect, serendipitous encounter.

"When can I see you again?" he asked.

"Whenever you want."

He laughed, finding this amusing. "Don't say that, I might get carried away."

She wanted him to kiss her, but she also didn't. Not because she didn't want to be kissed, but because she feared it was too soon, and she wanted to wait. It'd be better that way, she concluded.

Perhaps he had been thinking the same thing, because rather than make any sort of move, he took a step back, like the gentleman he was, and thanked her again.

"You better hold onto that ring," she joked.

"I will guard it with my life."

She smiled contently. "Goodbye, Finn Whitaker."

His face mirrored hers. "Goodbye, Cambria Nickson."

She went inside, closed the door, then leaned against it and slid to the ground like they did in the movies. A grin spread wide across her face. Her cheeks ached from smiling. Her stomach was doing a million somersaults. She was on cloud nine. It had been so long since she felt like this. And not even just romantically—she couldn't remember the last time she'd laughed or smiled.

She thought back to that moment in the car when his hand touched hers. She'd never felt anything like that before—except for that one night in the gazebo with Jackson.

What did that mean? What was her body telling her?

Could this actually be the start of something?

She picked herself up from the floor and walked to the kitchen, to do what exactly, she didn't know. Her mind was running at full speed. She couldn't just sit down and read—she needed to expel some of this pent-up energy.

Perhaps she could go for a run. Or a bike ride, like old times.

If there was one thing she knew for certain, it was that this wasn't luck—there was no way. Fate must've had some intervention here, three years in the making. An invisible string, leading her straight to him.

She'd never experienced anything so cosmic. Well, except for Jackson. She couldn't explain why, but meeting him had also been cosmic in its own way. She always believed the stars had aligned the night they met. There was something written in their destinies that led them to each other.

But now fate was orchestrating something else, and she knew she needed to just sit back and let it happen.

Just as she was getting the vacuum out, the doorbell rang. She glanced at the clock. It was quarter to eight. Finn had only dropped her off thirty minutes ago. Perhaps he had a change of heart and wanted to kiss her after all.

She walked to the front door, quickly fixing her hair in the hallway mirror before opening the door once again.

But to her great surprise, it wasn't Finn who stood before her—it was Jackson.

It was like seeing a ghost.

"Hi," was the first thing he said.

An eternity had passed since their last encounter. No, just six months. But it felt like an eternity all the same. She stood there, speechless, staring at him.

"Are you going to invite me in or what?"

She found words, "what are you doing here?"

"I broke up with Natalia."

"Oh." This, she was not expecting. "When?"

"Last night."

"And your first thought was to come here?"

"Yes."

Cambria processed this for a second, then took a step backwards, allowing him into the house.

"Where is everyone?" he asked as they walked down the hall.

"Not here." She did not elaborate.

They reached the kitchen and stood there awkwardly, as if unsure what to do. Then Jackson pulled out a chair and took a seat at the table.

Cambria stood there watching him. "Do you want a drink?"

"Do you even need to ask?"

She walked over to the fridge and grabbed two beers, then placed them on the table and sat across from him. "I can't believe you're really here," she said, still in shock. "I didn't think I'd ever see you again."

"I think we both know that's not true," he twisted the cap off his beer. "We'll always see each other again."

"You sound so sure." She did the same with hers and took a drink.

He shrugged. "What can I say?"

"I thought you hated me."

"I did, kind of. But not really. If you had shown up at my house with a bottle of wine, all would've been forgiven."

She gaped at him. "Are you fucking kidding me? I've just spent the last six months in purgatory without you."

"*Oh, no,*" he mocked. "Your life's just not the same without me."

Now she was glaring at him. "You told Mara you never wanted to speak to me again."

"I was mad."

"Clearly," she rolled her eyes. "Maybe don't say things you don't mean." She couldn't believe they were having this conversation right now—that something so simple could've solved something so colossal. That the agony she experienced over last six months could've been prevented.

"I did mean it," he said. "At the time. But I might have overreacted."

"I'm the one who overreacted," she said. "I never should've done that. It was wrong of me. I was drunk and angry and I let my emotions get the best of me. And for that I am sorry."

"It's okay."

"If I had known I was going to lose you I never would've done it."

"I know. You were upset. I had been a dick to you for a while. So, I'm sorry too."

"Thank you for saying that. I was just so hurt. You were my best friend, but it always felt like I was coming in second."

"Well she was my girlfriend," he said in defence. "But that won't be a problem anymore."

"What happened?"

He took another drink. "I finally had enough. We'd been fighting a lot these last few months. And it felt like things were going downhill. Maybe I knew it was coming—it was inevitable. You were right."

"About what?"

"About everything. We were never going to work."

She didn't know what to say. "I'm sorry."

"You don't have to be sorry. It's for the best."

"So you're okay?"

"Oh, I'm fine. I'm more than fine. I'm great." He took another drink.

She watched as he drank his beer, an idea forming. "You want something stronger than that?"

He put his drink down and met her eyes. "Always. What do you have in mind?"

She left the table and came back with a bottle of tequila, salt, and limes. "Want to play a game?" she said.

"What kind of game?"

"Truth or drink."

"Sounds dangerous."

She poured two shot glasses and slid one over to him. "I ask you a question. You can either answer it, or drink. Got it?"

"Got it."

She placed the salt between them, divvied up slices of lime, then looked at him. "Did you miss me?"

"Is that the first question?"

"No."

"Yes, I've missed you. Did you miss me?"

"More than you know."

"Okay, what's your question?"

She waited a beat. "Why didn't you ever reach out?"

He thought about this but made no move for the shot. "I don't know," he fiddled with the glass between his hands. "I was kind of just doing my own thing, not really thinking about it. But then there would be times that I'd think about you, and I'd miss how things were."

"Did you ever plan on talking to me again?"

"My turn," he grinned slyly.

"Okay, fine. Go."

"Have you slept with anyone in the last six months?"

She was caught off guard but not at all surprised by the question. "No, I haven't."

"Are you lying?"

"No."

"I feel like you should take a shot anyways."

She raised an eyebrow. "Do you *want* me to be lying?"

"No, I just think the game would be more fun if we were drunk."

"Okay, well if I'm taking a shot, you're also taking a shot."

"Deal."

Within half an hour, they were both drunk. It was like no time had passed, which seemed to be the case every time they became friends again. She knew now, with great certainty, that nothing could keep them apart indefinitely. There was something in them both that brought them back together time and time again. A magnetic pull, stronger than gravity. Just as the sun would rise each morning, Jackson would always return to her.

He was her other half, her person, a mirror image of herself. Cut from the same cloth, two peas in a pod—her best friend. The world seemed to revolve around them. They were the center of their own universe.

Perhaps they really had known each other in a previous life, as Cambria had once speculated. Nothing about it made sense to anyone including themselves, yet somehow it made all the sense in the world.

"Do you remember the night we met?" she asked him.

"No."

"Me neither," she joked. "We've been best friends ever since."

"Well…"

"Aside from a few times. But I meant, we became so close so fast. I've never had that with anyone before. Within days you were picking me up for drives, and we were talking on the phone after work. Have you ever had that?"

"No. I've never even had any girl best friends before you."

"Aw, are you calling me your best friend?"

"You are. My best friend."

"I just never hear it from you. You never say it."

"I didn't think I had to."

"No… you would never admit that we were best friends. You'd always say, *Grayson's my best friend.* Or *Nat is my best friend.* You'd never admit it, never acknowledge it."

"I'm sorry."

"It's fine, it's whatever. I was just saying, it's nice to hear, that's all." She grabbed her beer and took another drink. "You remember our very first night, when you took me around Pine Hills?"

He was gazing at her so fondly. "Yes."

"You asked me if I'd ever had sex in a car, and when I said no, you said, *do you want to?*"

He broke out laughing.

"You're fucked," she laughed. "You also asked me if I'd want to have a threesome. With you."

He laughed even harder.

"Do you say that to all the girls you pick up?"

He composed himself and took another drink. "No, darling, just you."

She smirked. "Do you remember when you asked if you could kiss me? At the abandoned house?"

"Did I?"

"Uh, yes. Do you not remember?"

"Mmmmm."

"We were upstairs, at the window, looking at Polaris. And you said, *you probably already know what I'm going to say.* And I said, *no, I really don't.* But I did. I knew what you were going to ask. I could tell just by how you were looking at me. And then you said, *can I kiss you*?"

He stared at her, holding her gaze. "You remember all that?"

"I do. I remember everything."

"Impeccable memory."

"But you remember, don't you?"

He was quiet for a second. "I do."

"And you remember what I said?"

"*Theo.*"

"Mhm. I've always wondered what would've happened if I had said yes."

"But you didn't."

"I didn't."

He stared at her. "Did you want me to kiss you?"

She paused. "Yes."

"Then why'd you say no?"

"Because of Theo. We had such a good night together and I liked him. It felt wrong to kiss his best friend if I was going to see him again. But look how that turned out. Part of me always wondered, what if it were you instead of Theo that night? But I guess it doesn't even matter because you met Nat the very same night."

"Only after you left with Theo."

She stared at him. "What are you saying?"

"Nothing, it doesn't matter."

"It *does* matter. Tell me."

"No, it doesn't, because it's not changing anything now."

She didn't know what to say. "Okay."

He checked his watch. "It's late, I should probably go."

"Okay."

They both stood, and she walked him to the front door. He slipped on his shoes and put his hand on the doorknob. Then he paused, looking back at her. "What about now?" he said.

She was confused. "What?"

He took his hand off the doorknob and stepped back. "What would happen if I kissed you now?"

She held his gaze, unwavering, silently daring him to do it.

Longing, lust, sorrow.

And then he did, without hesitation.

They stumbled backwards against the wall, his mouth on hers. She brought her hands to his face. His hands moved across her body, around her waist, down her ass. He kissed her neck, and her head fell backwards as she ran her fingers through his hair.

Slipping off his shoes, he grabbed beneath her thighs and lifted her, holding her tightly as he walked up the stairs and into her bedroom.

This time was different. It wasn't an accident, and it wasn't a mistake. This time, it was intentional. They both knew what they were doing, and they both knew what they wanted. Six months of agonizing torture, believing she would never see him again. And here he was, in her arms, in her bed, once again.

For her, he would always come back. Fate, destiny, whatever you want to call it—just two people who couldn't stay away from each other.

She wanted to capture this moment forever in time. She wished they could exist solely in this perfect bubble, where nothing ever went wrong or got destroyed.

Six months she had spent longing for him, yearning for him. All her prayers had been answered. Maybe God really did exist.

She was enraptured. And when she looked into his eyes, she saw herself being reflected back at her.

Maybe, she thought, *just maybe… things could be different this time.*

Afterwards, they lay next to each other, their breathing synchronized. It was quiet for a very long time. So long, in fact, that Cambria wondered if he had fallen asleep.

"Jackson," she said his name through the silence of the dark. There was something she needed to say, something she needed to ask. It had been on her mind for so long, the question lingering, and it needed to come out, needed to become a real, tangible thing, no longer existing solely in her head. She knew as soon as she said the words aloud, it would change everything. But she needed to know. She couldn't continue going on this way, not knowing.

"Cambria."

She could hear her own heart beating in her chest. "Can I ask you a question?"

A beat passed. "Sure."

She hesitated. She could still back out, tell him *never mind.* Go to sleep. Move on. Forget it ever happened.

But she couldn't. Not anymore.

"Are you in love with me?" she said.

It was silent again. Perhaps he had already drifted to sleep.

But then he spoke, repeating the question. "*Am I in love with you*?" he said. More silence. Then, "Are *you* in love with *me*?"

She didn't respond.

Neither did he.

But that said everything, didn't it?

THIRTY-TWO

When she woke up the next morning, he was right there next to her, which surprised her. He hadn't run away. She silently watched the rise and fall of his chest as he breathed, thinking about his hands on her body.

She reached over and plugged his nose, blocking his airway until he opened his eyes.

"Hi," he said once he saw her. His voice was gruff and his eyes were heavy. He looked angelic, gazing at her the way he was. There was something so pure and innocent about it.

"Hi," she said back.

"Your bed is so comfy," he said as he stretched his arms over his head.

"That's what all the boys say," she smirked.

He rolled his eyes. "What do you have for breakfast?"

"Eggs. Bacon. Toast."

"Do you want to make pancakes?"

"Yes."

It took them another hour to actually get up (they were too comfortable to move) and head downstairs to the kitchen.

"When will the others be back?" Jackson asked once they finished eating. He was drinking tea out of Cambria's favorite mug and the sight was refreshing.

"Not sure. Probably later."

"You need to clean your kitchen."

"I *know*, you don't need to tell me," she said. "Why don't you do it?"

"I'm not your maid."

"Really? You kind of look like one."

"I need a shower."

"Yeah, me too."

They tidied up the kitchen and headed back upstairs. It was another beautiful day, the sun shining through the windows. Cambria grabbed two towels, then changed into her bathing suit.

Jackson got in first, wearing nothing but his briefs. Then Cambria got in, pulled the curtain closed, and turned on the shower.

They took turns under the shower head, which wasn't really taking turns at all considering Jackson would get two seconds before Cambria was pushing her way in, trying to stay under the water.

"Am I going to smell like a girl?" Jackson asked upon realizing he would need to use Cambria's body wash and shampoo.

"Yes."

He grabbed the shampoo nonetheless and lathered up. Under the warm cascade of the shower, she dipped her hands into the sudsy shampoo and began massaging it through his hair with slow, deliberate strokes. She then gathered the strands and pushed them upwards, creating a spike that stood defiantly on his head. He did the same thing back to her, both of them giggling at each other.

They spent the remainder of the day lounging in bed watching movies. Jackson napped for an hour while Cambria lay next to him staring at the ceiling, unable to sleep. Once he was awake, they lay on their side, staring into each other's eyes, not saying anything.

But then Jackson opened his mouth. She knew what he was going to say and silently pleaded with him not to. *Please don't say it. Please don't bring up what I asked you last night. Not now.* But then he closed it, as if changing his mind, and she was relieved. Only for him to open it again a second later and say, "you asked me a question last night."

Her heart reverberated in her chest. It was astonishing that he was even acknowledging it. Their unspoken rule was that they didn't talk about these things. And Jackson especially never liked to talk about *anything.* He preferred to sweep it under the rug. But not this time.

Cambria didn't want to acknowledge it. She had only asked him because she was drunk and wasn't thinking clearly. To talk about it *now*, while they were sober, when the sun was still out, was condemned.

She could have said, *what question*? But she didn't. Instead, she closed her eyes and placed her face on the mattress, choosing silence instead.

He continued, "I didn't answer because I was so out of it and was falling asleep."

That didn't necessarily warrant a response. She didn't need to say anything at all. She kept her eyes closed and hoped it would just go away.

A few minutes passed. She peeked her eye open and his were closed. She opened hers fully and sat up, pounding her fists into the mattress around him. "Wake up!" she sang.

He opened his eyes and tried to grab her. She evaded his reach, then dove on top of him, tackling him to the other side of the bed.

They played around and wrestled for a couple minutes. He ended up behind her, in the spooning position. He had his hand on her stomach, and she froze, afraid he was going to tickle her. But he didn't. Instead, he started moving his hands across her body, feeling her stomach, her breasts, her waist.

She was completely caught off guard. *What was he doing?* Anything that had ever transpired between them had always been done under the influence. But this? Sober? In broad daylight?

She liked it.

Slowly, he reached his hand down the front of her pants and fingered her. Instantly she was wet.

That lasted approximately 3.8 seconds before he tugged his pants down from behind her, pulled hers down, and then was inside her.

It was happening—they were having sex, in the middle of the day, while sober. Mindboggling. Cambria couldn't wrap her head around it. But now really wasn't the time, because he was inside her, bare, and it felt so good that she couldn't formulate any other thoughts.

The headboard was banging against the wall, her nails gripping his back. She had thought their sex was good because they were either intoxicated or on drugs. But now they were sober and she could've sworn it was even better than before. How was that possible—to keep getting better each time? You don't have that kind of sex with just anyone, let alone your best friend.

She was in love with him. So much. She loved him more than anything or anyone. And she was *pretty* sure he was in love with her too.

Afterwards, he came on her back, then got up to get some tissues to clean her, which she thought was sweet. He lay down next to her and pulled her towards him. She lay her head on his chest and closed her eyes, content and not at all confused.

They did not acknowledge it—just as they didn't acknowledge anything that ever happened between them—and chose instead to continue watching their movie.

Around five o'clock, once their stomachs were growling again, they ventured downstairs to make food. Cambria boiled water to make pasta while Jackson set the table and opened a bottle of wine.

In the midst of their dinner preparations, they got a bit carried away, and next thing you know, Cambria was running across the main floor squealing while Jackson chased after her with a cup of water. And it was at this exact moment that Mara walked in.

"What the hell is going on in here?" she said from her spot at the door.

Jackson and Cambria stopped dead in their tracks, the cup of water in Jackson's hand frozen midair. Then, without hesitation, he poured it over Cambria's head, soaking her.

"JACKSON!"

He didn't go home until ten o'clock, only after watching the game with them and tormenting Mara as much as he could. "Wow, I sure missed him," she said sardonically once he was gone.

"How did *that* happen?" Hailey asked, her hand in a bag of chips.

"Don't ask," was Cambria's response.

The following evening, once Cambria was home from work and settled in for the night, the doorbell rang. A moment later, Hailey was calling her downstairs.

She got up, thinking how cute it was that whenever they reconnected after not being friends, Jackson was like a puppy with a toy—he couldn't get enough. But as soon as she started coming down the stairs, she saw it was Finn in her foyer, not Jackson.

Talk about a mind twist.

She had nearly forgotten about him.

Hailey was standing off to the side giving her a look. "Who's *this*?" she said.

Cambria reached the bottom of the stairs and stood before him, grinning uncontrollably. "Hi," she said to Finn.

"Hi," he replied.

"*Hello*?" Hailey interrupted.

Cambria turned to face her. "Sorry, this is Finn."

"Yeah, I can see that. Who is he?"

Cambria cleared her throat. "We met the other day. Under… unusual circumstances."

Hailey made a face. "I don't know what that means, and I don't think I want to." She flashed her a quick smile before heading back to the kitchen, "best of luck!"

Cambria turned her attention back to Finn. "What are you doing here?"

"I tried to resist but I couldn't. I hope that's okay. I wanted to see you."

Her face broke out in a smile. "Of course that's okay—you're so sweet."

"Have you eaten?"

"No, I was just about to make dinner."

"Ah, my timing is impeccable. I'm here to take you out."

"No way. Actually?"

"Yes."

"Why are you so perfect?"

"Stop," he laughed modestly.

"Where are we going?"

He held her gaze steadily. "Wherever you want."

Cambria spent the evening completely enthralled with Finn. It was like the curtain had closed and she had done a one-eighty. Instead of brown eyes, she was staring into blue. Blue the color of the sea. Blue so deep she could get lost in. Correction, already *was* lost in. *How could this be possible? So* soon, she barely knew him, yet it felt like she did. There was something stronger at play here. There were signs, and she needed to listen to them. The signs she had seen with Lawson were red, and they weren't signs—they were flags. Giant red flags that flashed WARNING.

Cambria knew, with the beauty of hindsight, that she had been blissfully ignorant. She had purposely chosen to ignore those red flags because she was so desperate and starry-eyed at the prospect of love that she was willing to ignore just about anything of grave importance. Not the wisest choice, but she was young, what can you say? Now she was older, and more mature, and also more attuned to these sorts of things.

Finn wasn't a red flag—he was as green as they come. There was nothing wrong or impure about him—he was perfect.

And somehow, for two and a half hours, she completely forgot about Jackson, sad as it is to say. She didn't think it was possible, considering he was the only thing she ever thought about. But alas, poof—he was gone. Replaced by a blue-eyed attorney who graduated from Stanford and ran marathons in his spare time.

When he dropped her off at home, he walked her to the door, just as he had on Saturday. She hadn't wanted him to kiss her then because it felt too soon. But she didn't feel that way anymore—she *wanted* him to kiss her. He must've picked up on that, or perhaps wanted to kiss her just as bad, and when he did, she saw fireworks.

After Finn drove off, she went inside, grinning from ear to ear. But her satisfaction was fleeting, ending abruptly when she saw her two housemates sitting on the couch waiting for her.

"Cambria Nickson," Mara said. "Why don't you come have a seat?"

Cambria ducked her head silently and sat on the couch.

"What's going on?" Mara asked her.

"What do you mean?"

"Don't play dumb," Mara scolded her. "Finn and Jackson. You're double dipping."

"I am not."

"Jackson was here until ten o'clock last night. And then tonight you're getting picked up for a date by some tall, handsome stranger? How'd you meet this guy anyway?"

"It's actually a crazy story," Cambria said, on the edge of her seat. "Remember that ring I found when I first moved here? I'd keep it in my purse in case I ever found the owner. Well, I finally found him. At The Grind on Saturday. I don't even know how it's possible, but yeah, the ring belongs to his father. I gave it to Finn, and then he took me out to dinner to thank me. He's so nice. And attractive."

"He *is* attractive," Hailey added.

Cambria smirked, feeling smug.

Mara still meant business. "Yes, he is quite handsome, I think we can all agree on that. But you need to figure out what the hell is going on between you and Jackson."

"Ugghhh," Cambria rolled her eyes. "I don't know!"

"I know you don't know. That's why I said you need to figure it out."

"I haven't even heard from him. He probably won't even talk to me. That's what he does."

"You guys are exhausting," Mara said, shaking her head. "You can't keep doing that, you gotta figure your shit out. He's single now, no more Natalia! What if he wants to be with you?"

"He doesn't want to be with me."

"How can you say that? He showed up here at your door. And you guys had sex. Really hot, passionate sex." Cambria covered her face. "Aren't you in love with him?"

"NO!" Cambria said. Then, "Yes."

Cambria was, without a doubt, hopelessly and fervently head over heels for Jackson Harding. She had spent the last three years (unknowingly) loving him while he was in a relationship with someone else. And now, for the first time since she met him, he was single.

Now was her chance. This was what she'd been waiting for.

But then there was Finn, who was a breath of fresh air. She had been so lonely and broken after losing Jackson, convinced happiness would evade her forever. Then he came out of nowhere and swept her off her feet, so serendipitous, exactly when she had needed him. He was loving and patient and kind. He was smart and charming and endearing. He was everything a girl could hope for in a man—the perfect partner. And somehow, even this early, she could see a future with him.

Mara continued, "yeah, so, you need to figure that out. And you can't do that when you're going on dates with another guy."

"But Finn is so sweet!" she protested. "And he's such a good guy. I could actually see a future with him."

Mara gave her a look. "You've known him three days."

"I know, but this is different! I think it's fate or something. How else do you explain it?"

"What, the ring? I don't know. That's one hell of a coincidence."

"It's not a coincidence!" Cambria said, incensed. "There's no fucking way. This is fate. I was supposed to find him. And I think this was *exactly* when I was supposed to find him."

THIRTY-THREE

Just as Cambria suspected, Jackson had pulled another magic trick and disappeared, once again. She didn't hear from him Monday, which was good, since Finn had showed up unexpectedly. She was anticipating his arrival on her doorstep Tuesday evening. Or perhaps he'd call once he got home from work. But… nothing. Days passed without hearing from him, and Cambria wasn't going to be stupid enough to make the same mistakes she did in the past, chasing after someone who didn't want to be found. If he wanted to disappear, then perhaps she should let him.

This, if anything, made it easier to let things happen organically with Finn. The weeks progressed, as did their relationship. They would talk on the phone each night before bed, sometimes staying up until four in the morning. She got butterflies at the thought of him, feeling giddy and excited whenever she heard his name or saw his face. She could not have found a more gentle, wholesome man. Someone who prioritized his family, his health, and his future. Someone who had aspirations and wanted her to be apart of them. Suddenly it wasn't so intimidating to talk about the future anymore, and the idea of marriage didn't seem as farfetched as it once had.

The first time they had sex she could've sworn she was in love. Was it possible to fall in love that quickly? He was strong yet gentle, accommodating yet dominant. She wanted to spend every waking second with him and could never get enough. She dreaded Sunday evenings when she had to go home, already anticipating when she would see him next.

"You are exactly what I imagined my future wife would be like," he said to her. "Is that weird to say?"

"Not at all," she swooned. "You're every girl's dream guy."

"But what about *you*?" he said. "Am I *your* dream guy?"

She didn't know how to answer that. "Yes."

"You're my dream girl," he told her. "You're so caring, and kind, and nurturing. You take care of me."

She had never been called nurturing before and honestly didn't resonate with the word. "I like taking care of you," she said.

"I know, you're very sweet. You're always doing sweet things. I appreciate them."

She leaned in and kissed him. "I appreciate *you*."

She was falling for him—hard. Maybe this one could be different, she thought. Maybe this one could be *the one*.

They say *when you know, you know*. Cambia was pretty certain this was it. And she had a very strong inclination that he felt the same.

Every year on her birthday, Cambria thought about Jackson, who, somehow, of all 365 days, was born on the same one as her. She once thought they were twins separated at birth. But then they kissed, and she never entertained that thought again.

She still thought of him as a twin, in a sense. The twin to her soul. Her other half. And despite all the hurt and confusion she felt as of late, she didn't want to spend the day with anyone else.

On the eve of their birthday, she showed up to his house unannounced. It had been a month since they last saw each other.

Leanne answered the door and brought Cambria to the backyard where Jackson was barbequing.

He closed the lid and held her gaze.

"Hi," she said.

"Hi."

"Whatcha cookin?"

"Steak."

"My favorite."

He shifted on his leg. "What's up?"

"I wanted to see you," she said. "I miss you. And I don't like spending our birthday apart."

"Me neither."

What she *wanted* to say was, *why haven't you called?* But she refrained. Talking about these things would cause him to shutdown, and she didn't want that. She just wanted things to go back to normal.

"Did you take the day off?" she asked.

"I did. Did you?"

She smirked. "Always."

"Okay," he said. "Well, it looks like we start celebrating tonight then."

She stayed for dinner, and they opened a bottle of wine. It was a mystery how they could slip back into regularity so easily. But she couldn't complain—the last thing she wanted was an uncomfortable conversation about where they stood and what this all meant. She just wanted her best friend back, at least for the day, doing what they do best.

After they finished eating, they sat around the kitchen table playing Euchre with his parents, another bottle of wine opened, chatting harmoniously as if no time had passed. Perhaps now was the opportune time to mention that she was seeing someone. But for some reason, she couldn't.

Cambria never held back when it came to Jackson—she told him anything and everything, potentially more than she should. There were no secrets between them. But when she thought about the prospect of sharing this new development with him, she worried what the consequence would be. You see, when Cambria started dating Lawson, Jackson made it abundantly clear that he was not happy about it. He didn't like that Cambria was spending time with someone who wasn't him. He'd never admit it, especially while dating Natalia, but Cambria knew. She didn't need confirmation.

Now, she feared that history would repeat itself. And what happened the last time Cambria started dating someone? He pulled back and stopped talking to her. She couldn't risk that happening again. She had *just* gotten him back.

And so, it was decided she would keep this small piece of information to herself, for now. She would tell him when the time was right.

Wednesday night turned into Thursday morning, and suddenly they were twenty-five—a quarter of a century. They went to the golf course in the morning; Jackson golfed while Cambria watched from the cart. Then they went back to Jackson's and made a big breakfast. Jackson wanted to go to the casino, so they did that. As long as they ended up at the beach, Cambria didn't care what they did. They were together, and that was all that mattered.

After the beach, and long after dinner, they sat in Jackson's backyard by the fire, drinking vodka martinis. The day had been more than a success—it was perfect. Cambria was pleasantly drunk and more-than-content to be in Jackson's presence. He elated her.

When Jackson came back out from getting a refill, he said, "something's wrong."

She sat up. "What do you mean?"

He set the drinks on the table and sat down. "Minnie just collapsed in the kitchen. My parents are taking her to the vet."

"What happened? Is she okay?"

"I don't know, that's all they said."

"Okay… has she seemed off at all?"

"Maybe? I don't know, it's hard to tell with her sometimes."

"Okay," she moved closer to him and put her hand on his back, rubbing it. "It's going to be okay. She's going to be okay."

Jackson finished his martini, then went back into the house. When he returned, he had two capsules of MDMA opened in his palm to show her.

"Right now?" she said.

"Yeah, why not?"

She could never say no to him. And she knew he needed to take his mind off things. Shrugging, she grabbed the capsule and dropped it into her mouth.

While waiting for that to kick in, they played a drinking game. The game was: whatever Cambria wanted it to be, and there were no right or wrong answers, only answers—but they had to come from her. *She* made the rules and decided the outcome. And for some reason, Jackson went along with this delusion, willingly, playing into her fantasies.

Around the forty-five-minute mark, they both started to feel it. Their pupils were huge, and they were grinning uncontrollably. Cambria could feel it in her fingertips, in her heart. She suddenly had the urge to bolt but resisted.

It was at this precise moment that Dave and Leanne returned from the vet. And suddenly everything changed, because Minnie was no longer with them.

Cambria and Jackson had to excuse themselves and go for a long walk. That was, hands down, the *worst* possible time for drugs to hit. They couldn't stop smiling from the rush of serotonin, meanwhile, the rest of the family was crying and grieving.

What a disaster.

By the time they returned, everyone had gone to bed, and the house was dark. It was two in the morning. Jackson and Cambria tiptoed through the house and up to Jackson's bedroom.

They lay on his bed wordlessly, the room dark except for the moonlight. Cambria didn't know what to say. She had never been good at dealing with death. Even after losing her brother, she didn't know how to cope. She hated the condolences people would give, never knew how to properly respond. "That was really fucked up," she said.

"I know," he replied, staring up at the ceiling. "Worst timing."

"Happy Birthday to us," she joked.

He didn't respond.

"Do you want to talk about it?" she asked.

"Not really."

She sighed. "I feel really fucking good right now."

"Me too."

"What should we do?"

Rather than answer, he ran his fingertips across her arm. Goosebumps covered her skin. It felt so good to be touched.

But then she thought of Finn.

She knew it was wrong, what she was doing. The line had already been crossed. They crossed it the moment they took MDMA. And now especially, lying in his bed after dark, energy coursing through her body. It was wrong, and she shouldn't have been doing it. Yet still, try as she might, she could not put a stop to it.

It was habitual, and there was comfort in it. And so, despite everything she was feeling inside—the trepidation, the hesitation, the longing for restraint—she let it happen.

The only one to blame was herself.

He kissed her soft and slow like he always did, and it felt so good, so right. She brought her hands to his face, felt the scruff on his cheeks. He moved on top of her, his body fitting hers just right, moving slowly, methodically. All the doubt she'd been having for the last four weeks was gone in an instant, and she knew with great certainty that she was in love with him. No amount of nights with Finn was going to change that, and suddenly she felt doomed.

She thought she could rid him from her system, but she was wrong.

He took off her clothes, and then his own. He looked at her in a way that was unique to only him. There was something about that look in his eyes, when they'd stare endlessly at each other, gazing into more than just eyes, but souls. That was how it looked to be completely seen, felt, and known entirely. She had never known someone who was every bit of her as she was them.

They were the same.

Her final thought before drifting off to sleep was of Finn. She knew then that she was a bad person, but she didn't plan on doing anything to change that.

CAMBRIA

THIRTY-FOUR

When she awoke the next morning, she felt a mixed array of emotions: contentment, guilt, confusion. The daylight was sobering, as was her reality now that the drugs had worn off—mostly. She felt sleepy and euphoric, an afterglow. Jackson lay next to her, sound asleep.

She shook him until his eyes opened.

"Hey," she said, a gentle smile on her face.

He gazed up at her. "Hi," he replied, his voice low and raspy. "How do you feel?"

"Amazing."

He chuckled. "Still feeling it?"

"Oh, yeah, for sure," she said. "I feel radiant."

His smile was fleeting. "Last night was fucked."

She looked down, suddenly somber. "I know. Are you okay?"

He shrugged, looking off to the side. She saw a tear form in the corner of his eye. At this, she threw her body on his, burying her face into his neck.

Only then did he allow himself to cry.

After that, they didn't talk about it.

The words were on the tip of her tongue, what she needed to say next. She couldn't hold it in any longer. She was dreading it but knew it was necessary. The time had arrived to acknowledge the elephant in the room and finally address everything that was happening between them. She wanted answers but knew it would come at a price—Jackson loathed conversations such as these.

But before she had the chance, Jackson began moving his hands across her body, feeling her, touching her. She let it continue, only momentarily, thinking she'd put a stop to it. In just a minute. But then he kissed her. And she was so pleasantly caught off guard by the whole thing that it never even occurred to her to stop it.

He moved on top of her, kissing her so gently, so passionately, that she seemed to forget everything else; his dead dog, the conversation she intended on having. And as he took off her clothes and moved inside of her, she couldn't help but think how right it all felt.

Afterwards, he collapsed next to her, out of breath. She looked down and saw there was blood. "Oh, fuck," she said.

He looked over. "Bad timing."

She hastily threw on his t-shirt and rushed to the bathroom to clean herself and find a tampon. Once she was done, she brought Lysol and paper towel back to the room to clean. But by then Jackson had already gotten rid of the stain.

She climbed back into his bed, overwhelmed. Something came over her, and she began to cry.

Looking over at Jackson, she said, "maybe we shouldn't be friends."

He was stunned. "What are you talking about?"

"I just don't know what to do anymore," she cried. "Everything's so messy and complicated."

"Where is this coming from?"

"What do you mean *where is this coming from*? Have you not been paying attention? To anything? At all?"

"I'm so confused right now."

"*You're* confused? *I'm* confused!"

"Is this because you got your period? Because I don't care about that, it's not a big deal."

"This isn't about my period, Jackson. It's about me and you. And everything going on between us."

"What's going on between us?"

"I don't know, you tell me."

He didn't respond.

"Why are you so bad at dealing with this stuff?" she snapped. "Why can't you just be a normal fucking human?"

"I don't know why you're so angry all of a sudden. Is it the PMS?"

"Holy fuck, if you bring up my period one more time…"

In silence they stared at each other.

"Do you have feelings for me?" she asked him point-blank, ripping off the band-aid. This was the moment of truth—time to confront it once and for all.

"*Do I have feelings for you*?" he repeated the question. He had a tendency of doing that—how annoying. "Do *you* have feelings for *me*?"

"I asked you first."

He was silent as he contemplated this. Then he said, "no, I don't have feelings for you."

And there it was. He would never admit it. Why was it impossible for him to confront his feelings? Why couldn't he just be honest and tell the truth? She hated him for it, for putting her in this position. And her anger was what propelled her next question. "Would you care if I got a boyfriend?" she asked.

"A boyfriend?" He pretended like he was thinking about it. At this point she already knew what his answer would be. So when he opened his mouth and said, "no," she wasn't even surprised.

She scoffed. "Figures."

"Why are you even asking me that?"

"Because I do," she snapped.

"You do *what*?"

"Have a boyfriend," she said. "I've met someone."

He stared at her in disbelief. "What?"

"Yeah. I have a boyfriend."

"Right now?"

"Yes, right now."

"Since when?"

She shrugged. "Not long."

He didn't respond, choosing instead to stare at the wall, fuming, as he processed this information.

"You said you wouldn't care," she reminded him.

"I don't."

At that she had to laugh. "You're impossible, you know that?"

"Is it serious?"

"I don't know, maybe."

"Why didn't you tell me?"

"Because I knew how you'd react."

"What's that supposed to mean?"

"Remember how you were when I started dating Lawson? You got distant and stopped talking to me. And I couldn't have that, not again."

"That wasn't because of Lawson."

"Yes, it was."

"I'm supposed to be your best friend, but you couldn't tell me that?"

"Are we?" she said. "Best friends?"

"I thought we were."

"And what about this?" she gestured between them. "What do you call this?"

He shrugged. "I don't know."

"Me neither."

He sat there confounded. "This whole time… you've been sleeping with him?"

She didn't respond.

"Nice," he said. "Classy."

She started to cry again, her body trembling as she sobbed.

He moved closer, bringing her to him. She dissolved in his arms, and he held her to his chest, stroking her hair, moving it out of her face which was wet from tears.

And then he kissed her. And despite how their conversation had just gone, she allowed it to continue; for it felt so good to be kissed by him.

He removed the tampon that she had just put in and replaced it with himself. She moaned as he moved inside her, biting into his shoulder, gripping his back. He fit her perfectly, like he was made for her. She had never experienced sex like this with anyone but him.

Afterwards, once they were done, she moved away from him, sliding further down the bed, pulling the sheets to her chin. She stared at the wall and remained silent.

"You asked me a question," he said, breaking the silence. "That night at your house."

She didn't respond.

"I'm going to ask you something," he continued. "And I don't want you to avoid it or beat around the bush. I just want you to answer honestly."

Of course she would. Why would she lie at this point? She'd been waiting for him to ask, and knew that when he finally did, she would answer. "Okay."

He held her gaze steadily. "Are you in love with me?"

She didn't hesitate. "Yes."

She couldn't maintain eye contact after that, breaking away, something she never did. But she couldn't do it, couldn't face him like this—not when she was this vulnerable, this exposed, and he was not.

"This is why you shouldn't be in a relationship," he said. "Because you're in love with me."

Enraged, she looked at him. "What the fuck do you expect me to do, be single forever?"

"Yes."

"You're insane."

"I asked you before if you had feelings for me, and you said no."

"That was two years ago! I didn't know it then!"

"So when *did* you know?"

"Once we stopped being friends, after that night at Grayson's. I didn't know it before, honestly. I think maybe it's been there all along, but I was in denial."

He remained silent.

She wanted to ask him the same question back but didn't out of fear of what the answer would be. She thought she was so sure, but now she was not. And she couldn't do it, couldn't ask him that, and risk the answer be no.

It would kill her.

"So you feel nothing towards me," she said instead. "Nothing at all?"

"I never said that."

"I'm confused."

"So am I, Cambria. It's been encoded in my brain that we're friends. Best friends. And now suddenly that changes?"

"I know, trust me. We have a perfect friendship—one I wouldn't trade for the world. I don't want to jeopardize that or ruin things—I can't lose you, not again. We've always worked so well as friends. But obviously there are feelings here. I don't expect anything from you, I want you to know that. Dating Finn is me showing you. It's me giving up on you, because I knew you'd never be with me."

"But you didn't even give me a chance."

"I want a shot at real love," she continued. "And with you, there's so much uncertainty. I need stability. Longevity. Someone who will love and care for me unconditionally—not leave when things get tough. Finn can give me that."

"And I can't?"

Curse him for asking her that. "I don't know, Jackson. I don't know."

THIRTY-FIVE

They had finally reached a pinnacle, Cambria and Jackson—only took them three years. Masters of compartmentalization, they were, keeping their feelings locked up and hidden. But now everything was coming out, and Cambria was overwhelmed, faced with an even bigger predicament.

Cambria had always known, almost for certain, that Jackson had feelings for her. Infuriating that it took getting a boyfriend for him to finally admit it. But that was where the speculation ended, because having feelings was one thing, but actually wanting to be with someone was another, and Jackson, most certainly, would never be with Cambria. It wasn't even something she envisioned or fantasized about because she'd always known it would never work. From the beginning, and without any concrete evidence, she knew. And she didn't *want* to be with him—she wanted to be with Finn.

Or did she?

"Why do you love me?" Jackson asked her later that evening. He'd now had the day to process everything. They sat in his backyard by the fire. For once they weren't drinking. Sober conversations weren't their forte, however, there were things that needed to be addressed.

She looked over at him. "I don't."

He laughed. "You just changed your mind?"

She laughed too. "I don't even know how to answer that."

He was quiet as he stared into the fire. "I'm not happy," he said. "About what you told me."

She looked over at him. "Which part?"

"That you have a boyfriend."

"I know."

"I don't think you should be dating someone," he said.

"Like now, or ever?"

"Ever."

At that she had to laugh. "You're crazy."

"You shouldn't be dating someone considering you're in love with me," he continued. "Those two things contradict each other, don't you think?" He finally looked at her.

"I don't know what you want me to do—break up with him?"

"Yeah."

She rolled her eyes

"It made me feel good," he continued. "What you told me."

"That I love you?"

"Yeah. It made me…happy."

This was huge. Not only was he talking about his feelings (unheard of), but he wasn't running away. Cambria had it ingrained in her brain that if he knew she had feelings for him, he'd retreat.

"But then the other thing ruined it," he continued.

She looked at him solemnly. "I'm sorry."

"I just don't understand how you can tell me that you love me and then tell me you have a boyfriend."

"Well actually it was the other way around. I told you I have a boyfriend, *then* I told you that I love you."

"Well actually *before* that you asked me if I'm in love with you."

"Yeah, but you didn't respond."

"It's the same shit, Cambria."

She went quiet. "What if I didn't?" she said. "Have a boyfriend."

"I don't know."

It was quiet again.

"Why are you even dating him?"

"Because I'm trying to get over you and move on with my life. I need someone who actually wants me. Someone who chooses me. And you, Jackson, will never choose me."

"I won't choose you unless you choose me. And you never have. From the beginning, you chose Theo."

"And you chose Natalia. And I had to sit back and watch. And wait. And I waited so long that I couldn't wait anymore. So, I chose him. Because I knew that you'd never choose me."

"You never even gave me a chance," he said, and he was right. "This is so confusing to me. How can you love a person and date someone else?"

"You should ask yourself the same thing."

"Would you date me?"

The question caught her off guard. "I don't know. It's not black and white; not as simple as yes or no." She paused a moment. "Would *you* date *me*?"

"I've thought about it," he said. "I've *been* thinking about it."

Cambria was quiet as she processed this information, thinking everything over. Then she said, "I think I would. Date you."

"I'm not looking for a relationship."

A slap in the face. He was maddening. Annoyed, she said, "then why are you asking?"

"Because I'm curious. Because I'd like to know."

"But you wouldn't date me."

"I just got out of a three-year relationship. With someone who was especially toxic. I need to be by myself for a bit."

"I never expected anything from you," she said. "I've perceived this as being unrequited."

"Well clearly it's not."

"So you admit it. You're confirming that you have feelings for me."

"Yes."

Finally—a concrete answer, confirming what she'd known all along. He was actually admitting it. *Astonishing.* But she couldn't even feel excited over the admission with everything else going on.

"I didn't intend for any of this," she said. "Everything just fell together serendipitously. But the timing sucks. Timing's never been on our side. We don't talk for six months, and then the *day* I meet Finn, the *day* my life changes, you come back. I was not expecting that. I didn't think I'd ever see you again. Then you just show up, out of the blue, here to ruin everything."

"*Ruin everything*," he repeated. "Is that how you really see it?"

"I don't know."

"Well I wasn't expecting you to have a boyfriend. And not only that, but to keep it a secret from me. That hurt."

"I'm sorry. I already told you—I was scared that if you knew about Finn, you'd pull away like you have in the past."

"When have I ever done that?"

"With Lawson! You got jealous and stopped talking to me."

"That didn't happen."

"Alright, well, I'm not trying to argue. I didn't do it with malicious intent. Quite the opposite. I didn't know it would hurt you."

"I know you didn't. You never do. But you still manage to hurt people all the same."

It was quiet again for a few minutes. And then she said, "to answer your question… Why I love you. I think it's because you're the only person I've ever been able to be my true, genuine self with. I'm constantly changing myself, suppressing myself, hiding who I am out of fear of judgment. I can never just let my walls down and be me. But with you, I can. You're the only person I can do that with. And I know that sounds cheesy and cliché, but it's the truth. Is that stupid?"

"No, not at all," he said. "It makes perfect sense."

"I have all these thoughts and perceptions about certain things, and you are the exception to all of them. Like how I'm an introvert and hate being around people, but not you. I could spend every waking minute with you. And I hate talking on the phone, but not with you. I want to talk to you every single day, every single night, until we both fall asleep. And then wake up the next morning to hear you're still on the other end. Basically, every rule I have, you're the exception. You're always the exception."

He was staring at her so intently. "And what do you feel when you're with him?"

"I don't know," she looked away. "Loved. Adorned."

"Does he make you happy?"

She hesitated, not wanting to say it to him. "Yes."

He nodded but didn't respond.

"You know," she said. "For three years I had to watch you be with Nat. And then you guys break up. You're single for the first time since I met you. And then I meet Finn."

"I know," he said.

She turned her body fully to face him. "Tell me what you want me to do."

"I can't tell you to do anything," he said. "That's your choice."

"But you won't be with me."

"I don't want to ruin our friendship."

"Can't you see?" she said solemnly. "We've already done that."

They spent eight consecutive days together after that. It was like they were in the honeymoon phase or something. Only when Cambria was with Jackson did she experience true elation. Not even Finn could elicit such a feeling. Finn was amazing in so many ways. But most importantly, he was kind, and he would take care of her. She knew he'd make a perfect husband and an exemplary father. But still, she couldn't deny how being with Jackson made her feel. And ever since the revelation, they'd only been getting closer.

She perceived him in a different way now, as did he to her. Now that they'd reached this point, there was no going back.

And while she knew it was wrong (so so wrong), she couldn't help herself. There was something about being with Jackson that made all logic and morals go out the window. He was a force to be reckoned with.

Their perfect illusion, however, was shattered after the eighth day, when Cambria had to inform Jackson that she had plans with Finn, who was taking her on a hike. Angry that she was spending time with Finn instead of him, he refused to talk to her for the rest of the day. Jackson, evidently, was not happy about the whole boyfriend thing. But at the same time, he wasn't ready to commit to her. Therefore, Cambria concluded, his anger was irrational and unsubstantiated. As long as she was with Finn, they would continue to exist in this weird limbo where neither of them was satisfied.

Still, Jackson wanted to spend time with no one but Cambria. And as soon as she was available again, they were together.

There had been a noticeable shift between them. He was being *nice* to her (for once), and even started giving her compliments, which nearly gave her a heart attack. One day, while driving in his car, he complimented her bra.

"You like *my bra?*" she said, dubious.

"Yeah," he glanced over at her from the driver's seat.

She raised an eyebrow. "What about it?"

He thought about this. "It's purple."

She rolled her eyes. "Good one, Einstein. But thanks, I guess?"

They stopped at a redlight. The car was silent, no music. Cambria hesitated, then said, "you told me you love me last night."

The night before, as Cambria was leaving Jackson's house, he said, "let me know when you get home. I love you goodnight."

Jackson didn't say anything for a moment, but she saw that he was trying to hold back a smile. "I did," he said. "Did that give you butterflies?"

"No," she said. "It made me want to die."

"Okay, I'll just say I fucking hate you then."

"I fucking hate you too."

When she was with Finn, things felt different, forced. She couldn't deny there had been a shift between them as well, ever since the revelation. She hated that this was happening, that these two huge events were coinciding. She tried her best to keep up appearances, but deep down, something felt *off*. When she looked at Finn, she didn't feel the same as she once had. He was still his same old self, the one she was supposed to love and adore. It was her who was changing.

When the time came for Cambria to meet Finn's family, she felt like a fraud. He reserved such an occasion for only someone he was serious about. Cambria was honored, but conflicted. While he was moving into next steps, she was distracted by her current predicament with Jackson. Her heart was being pulled in two different directions. She didn't know what she wanted. Because what she wanted, was both.

Dinner with Finn's parents couldn't have gone better. They were lovely and kind, much like their son. They asked her so many questions about herself, her family, her passions. And sitting there with them, she could envision a future. A future with Finn.

"They really like you," he told her afterwards.

She smiled. "I really like them too."

"I'm glad," he said. "I haven't felt this way in a long time. I don't think anyone's ever made me feel the way you do."

She wanted to jump in the ocean and drown.

Jackson was more than displeased to learn she had met his parents and ensured he made this known. "Cambria has a new boyfriend," he announced to his entire family while they sat in the backyard by the pool. "His name is Finn and he's a lawyer."

"A boyfriend?" his father repeated, flabbergasted. "Since when?"

Cambria covered her face.

"Wait," Victoria said, "I thought *you two* were dating?"

He began icing her out, acting cold, which left Cambria desperately trying to remedy the situation—which was kind of impossible as long as she was with Finn. She couldn't stand him being unhappy with her, and she would do almost anything to change that.

"You can't keep doing this," she said to him. "Are you going to get mad every time I'm with him instead of you?"

"Yes."

"You're being ridiculous," she threw her hands up. "And unreasonable."

"Am I?"

"Well, yes. You can't tell me you don't want to be with me and then get mad when I'm with someone else."

"Yes, I can."

"The only reason I'm with him is because I know I can't be with you."

"That's bullshit and we both know it."

"Why won't you be with me?"

"I can't give you what you want."

"I really don't understand you."

"I don't want to commit to you."

"Ouch. Thanks."

"If we date, we'd probably just fuck it up and never speak to each other again."

"You may be right. But what if you're not?"

"What if I am?"

"Trust me, I don't want to ruin our friendship either. But we already have, can't you see that? There is no way to go back to being friends after this." She stared at him desperately. "I can't keep doing this with you, it's exhausting."

"Well I can't keep doing this either, watching you be with him."

"You can't have it both ways," she snapped. "You can't have your cake and eat it too. You can't tell me not to be with him with no intention of being with me."

"Break up with him," he said. "And be with me."

"You don't mean that."

"I do."

"No, you don't. You're just saying that because you can't stand me being with someone else."

"You're right. I can't. So, break up with him. And be with me instead."

"You're not ready for that," she said. "You said it yourself, you just got out of a three-year relationship and want to be single. If we dated now, you'd end up resenting me for rushing you into something you weren't ready for."

"Okay, let's give it a few months."

"Give what a few months?"

"Us. Just take things one day at a time, see where things go."

"Okay… aren't we doing that now?"

"Not while you're with him."

"So you want me to break up with him on a whim, with only the *chance* that *maybe* sometime down the line we'll be together?"

"Yes."

She shook her head. "I don't think that's fair."

"How isn't that fair?"

"To me. How is that fair *to me*?"

"Well because what if we end up together?"

"If," she repeated. "You'd probably end up cheating on me."

"No, I wouldn't."

"Well you did it to Natalia."

"Yeah, with *you.*"

"I'm not going to just break up with him," she said. "I don't trust you."

"You have a choice to make," he told her. "Stay with him and lose me. Or lose him, and you can finally have me."

She should've known it would always come down to this.

THIRTY-SIX

Cambria, who once believed the universe was working in her favor, was now having doubts. Otherwise, how could it be so cruel? To hand her Finn on a silver platter, only to deliver Jackson on that very same platter.

The stars aligned when she met Jackson. Never had she felt such familiarity with someone. They were two halves of the same whole, but the timing had never been right—until now. Then she met Finn, and their fates, it seemed, had also been destined. Three years in the making, starting the very same night she met Jackson. Had she chosen Jackson that night rather than Theo, she never would have found the ring that would eventually lead her to Finn.

Everything was so confusing.

She had waited so long for a chance with Jackson, but at the same time, she was falling in love with Finn. Was it possible to love two people at once?

"You love Jackson?" her mother asked.

Cambria sat curled up on the couch with the phone to her ear, a cup of tea next to her. "Yes."

"Do you think you could love Finn?"

"Yes, one hundred percent."

"And you see a future with him?"

"Yes."

"Can you see a future with Jackson?"

"That's the thing—I don't know. It's been ingrained in my brain that we are friends, and to envision anything beyond that is almost incomprehensible."

"But surely you can *imagine* what it'd be like?" her mother said. "You two are best friends, you're thick as thieves. I saw how you two were when you were here, you're head over heels for each other."

"Really? You think."

"It's about what you *feel*, honey. How would being with Jackson make you *feel*?"

"Make a list," her father chimed in. "Pros and cons, weigh out your options."

Cambria considered this. "Pros for Jackson… He's my best friend, my person. He understands me better than anyone. We have this inexplicable bond that I've never had with anyone else. And being with him makes me the happiest I've ever been. But at the same time, my devotion to him makes me blind to his flaws, and trust me, there are a lot. Like his inability to talk about problems. Or express how he's feeling. He avoids conflict, preferring to pretend they don't exist. And he thinks he's always right. About everything. And he's so confident that it makes him cocky. He puts his pride and ego above all else, afraid to let his guard down and be vulnerable. It determines most of his decision making, which I personally think hinders him greatly. And he's entitled. Anything he's ever wanted has been given to him, and that has turned him into someone who expects the world. He can be so cruel sometimes, and it's not fair to me. But I'm in love with him. And when you're in love with somebody, you'll forgive just about anything.

"And then there's Finn, who's a breath of fresh air. Never did I think it'd be possible to find someone like him. He's charming and endearing, has a kind and gentle soul, wouldn't hurt a fly, treats me like a queen. He has his life together, has a stable career, has goals and ambitions. He wants to start a family someday. And when I told him that I wasn't sure if I want to have kids, he told me that wouldn't change anything, and that he'd be with me regardless. He wants me for me, not for what I could potentially give him. He's selfless, and caring, and puts others before himself, constantly. I see a future with him."

"But…"

"But he's not Jackson," Cambria said. "And that's his only shortcoming."

"It's a difficult decision," her father told her. "At the end of the day, I just want my daughter to be happy."

"I don't need anyone to make me happy," she said. "I make myself happy."

"I know you do, sweetheart. And I know you'd be fine on your own. I guess what I'm trying to say here is, no one can make this decision except you. But if you're asking for my opinion, I'd go with Jackson. I've seen how much his friendship has meant to you over the years, and I think you two could get past all this and find real happiness. And they always say, the best relationships start from friendships."

"I know. Thanks, Dad."

Her mother waited until after her father left and went to bed before continuing. "When I was your age," she said, "I found myself in a very similar situation."

Cambria was surprised to hear this. "You did?"

"I was with someone I had known a long time. We had been best friends growing up, but I always had a crush on him. When we were eighteen, we finally acknowledged those feelings and started dating.

"It was a crazy whirlwind love, like in the movies. I always thought I'd marry him. But then he cheated on me, and it was one of the hardest things I ever went through. Not just the betrayal, but self-blame, as if it were somehow my fault. I couldn't understand, and it did a lot of damage. But it was shortly after this that I met your father, and he was the light at the end of the tunnel. I saw so much potential with him. But I was conflicted, internally, because I still loved the other one. We had so much history together that I knew I'd never have with anyone else. And as much as he hurt me and broke my heart, I still wanted him. I believed he would always be the keeper of my heart." She paused for a moment. "What I'm trying to convey to you, Cambria, is that sometimes history isn't everything. And I know Jackson is your best friend, but we both know how he can be. And I fear that if you leave Finn and choose Jackson, he's going to blow it and destroy everything. And then you would have missed out on something wonderful, perhaps once in a lifetime."

"I had no idea," Cambria said, astonished. "You never told me."

"It's not something I talk about it. And just so you know, your father is very much aware—he doesn't have much of an opinion on the matter. He's just glad I made the right decision in the end and chose him. And so am I. Because it was the best decision I ever made. Choosing him, having you and Lincoln—I have no regrets. And I don't want you to have any either."

THIRTY-SEVEN

"I saw Jackson at Tap last night," Mara told her as they sat at the kitchen table drinking their morning coffee. "He was with someone."

"Again?" Her stomach sank. She wanted to die. Or kill him.

Mara was looking at her with remorse. "What's going on with you guys? I thought he told you to break up with Finn?"

"He did, but he's not ready to be with me right now. I think he just wants me out of this relationship. He said he wants to *take it day by day* and *see how the summer goes.* But that includes him seeing other girls. Like, he wants me to commit to him but he's not ready to commit to me."

"That's not fair."

"That's what I said. So why would I break up with Finn?"

"Well that's not fair to Finn," Mara said. "Don't get me wrong, Finn is an amazing guy, but he's no Jackson. You two are something else. I think it's huge that you've both FINALLY admitted your feelings. Now the next step is being together. You just gotta give it a chance."

Cambria didn't know how to respond.

"I know it's hard," Mara continued. "And I know you don't want to hurt Finn. He's been nothing but kind to you. But he doesn't deserve to be caught in the middle of this love triangle. You need to break it off with him before things get more serious and he gets hurt."

"He'll get hurt either way," Cambria said. "I see so much potential with him, that's why I can't bring myself to end it. I've never been so fucking conflicted about something in my entire life."

"Well you can't have both."

"I know. And Jackson's made that abundantly clear. Hence all the girls."

"You guys are messed up."

"Me!? This is *him*."

"No, neither of you are innocent, Cambria. You know what you're doing. And you know you have to choose."

Cambria dropped her head to the table. "I don't know, I can't decide." She looked up at Mara. "How am I supposed to decide?"

"How about instead of trying to make each other miserable, you just be together?"

"It's not that simple," Cambria said. "I feel like whichever decision I make is going to be the wrong one."

It'd be nice, right about now, to have that all-encompassing knowledge like in books and movies, where both choices are fully explored and brought to fruition. But unfortunately, she did not possess such a power. And was therefore left having an existential crisis instead.

Jackson, however, continued on with his antics, leaving Cambria in a manic state. She considered herself quite a sane person (was she serious?), yet how she felt when Jackson was with other girls made her want to check herself into a psych ward. She needed to get a grip or she was going to lose her mind. But because she could not control the situation—meaning she couldn't stop Jackson—she felt helpless.

Cambria, who didn't smoke weed unless she was with Jackson, resorted to smoking weed in order to cope with the mania. Her thoughts were overwhelming when she was sober—she needed to get out of her head. The weed calmed her. It stopped her tears and made her giggly.

Hailey's new boyfriend had baked them a batch of weed brownies and delivered them to the house. The instructions, which he scribbled on a sticky note, read: *take one bite, wait two hours.*

Cambria had an idea. She put a few brownies into Tupperware and headed over to Jackson's house.

"Wait two hours?" Jackson said as he read the sticky note. "Why two hours?"

"I don't know," she said. "I guess that's how long it takes to kick in."

By the hour mark, Cambria was buzzing, and after two hours, she was tripping balls. Never had she been so high—it felt like she was on ecstasy. "What'd he put in here?" Jackson asked her.

"I think crack."

Her plan had worked; they were back to normal. It was never too hard with him, but she hated that they even strayed from that in the first place.

"Grayson says you spend more time with me than your own boyfriend," Jackson told her.

"You're just telling everyone I have a boyfriend, aren't you?"

"Is that a problem?" he said. "Do you not want people to know you have a boyfriend?"

"What *else* does Grayson say?" she pushed.

Jackson laughed. "You don't want to know."

"Why?" she frowned.

Jackson stared at her. "He thinks you have feelings for me."

"Oh my God," she threw a pillow at him. "What are you telling people?"

"I'm not telling people anything. They just see it, Cambria, they're not fucking blind."

She covered her face. "I'm a horrible person."

"Stop," he moved her hands away from her face. "You're not."

Her eyes welled with tears. "I don't know what to do."

She wanted to keep talking to him about this, but she was too high. She was forgetting what she was saying midsentence.

The next morning, when they were sober, they tried again. "I feel like I want two opposing things," she explained. "The first thing is my friendship with you. You are my best friend and my favorite person. The dynamic we have is perfect. But the second thing is that I want to be more than friends. And so, you see, I can't have both, so I'm stuck in the middle. And I can't stand you being with anyone else, it's killing me."

"You're the one who's with someone, not me."

"You talk to *so* many girls."

"Yeah, but I'm not with any of them!" he said, exasperated. "You fully have a boyfriend!"

She didn't respond.

"How would you feel if the roles were reversed?" he continued. "And it was *you* who had to sit back and watch me be in a relationship with someone else."

"I HAVE," she nearly shouted. "Or did we forget that?"

"I meant now. After everything we know now."

She stared at him cooly. "If you had a girlfriend now," Cambria said. "I'd probably murder her."

"Yeah, that's what I thought. So just imagine how *I* feel. I've been pissed off all week. My mom said I'm on a rampage."

A smile engulfed her face.

"Why are you smiling?" he said, perplexed. "Does that make you happy?"

"Yes!" she exclaimed. "It means you care!"

He rolled his eyes.

"Do you remember," she said, "back in the summer of 1989 when Grayson had that party in July, and everyone left to go to the bar at the end?"

"Yeah."

"That's the night I was mad at Theo about the Dana thing, and I ended up going to the party with you. And there was this moment when we were all standing by the back door where I just had the urge to pull you into the bathroom and kiss you. And then… do you remember what happened?"

"What?"

"Nat showed up. Right then." Cambria laughed. "I had actually kind of forgotten about her."

"You never told me that."

"Yeah, why would I?" she laughed again. "But then we became best friends. Like, actual best friends. And then next thing I know, we're spending every day with each other." She was gazing at him. "You know, I think I can pinpoint the exact moment I fell in love with you. It was the last day of June 1990, one year from the day we met. That night at your house. Grayson and Ian were in the hot tub, and you and I were alone in the gazebo. And… I don't know if you remember this, I think you were kind of fucked up, but you were moving your hands all over my body, like across my stomach and legs. And I felt electrified, like I was going to explode at any minute. And I could just tell, somehow, that you were feeling the same way. And I think, or, well, know, that that's when I fell in love with you." She smiled. "And then you gave me a piggyback ride to the hot tub because I didn't want to get my feet wet."

"You remember everything," he remarked.

"I know, I told you I do. I never forget anything when it comes to us." She paused again. "When I started dating Lawson, you completely iced me out and distanced yourself. I know you were jealous."

"You're right," he said. "I was. I didn't want you dating someone."

Her mouth fell open. "I knew it. I knew it all along."

"It'll probably happen again," he said.

A shot to the heart. "Why would you say that?"

"Because it's true. I'll probably do it again the closer you get to your boyfriend."

"Don't say that. I don't like that."

"I'm sorry." He paused. "Two months ago, the thought of us being together would've never crossed my mind. But now..."

She was looking at him intently. "What changed?"

"I don't know, but something definitely did." He looked away. "We'd probably just fuck it up."

"Probably," she agreed. "I never told you this, but two months ago, Mara told me I need to choose. And I said I'd choose Finn because you'd never choose me. And she said, *Jackson will never choose you if you don't choose him.*"

"Yeah, exactly. How the fuck do you expect me to choose you when you can't even choose me? You went and got a boyfriend."

"YEAH, BECAUSE WHAT WAS THE ALTERNATIVE? I never thought you'd want to be with me, so why would I risk ruining things?"

He was quiet. "I still stand by what I said, I don't think you should be dating him."

"Well you won't be with me."

"I can't commit to you."

"Yes, I know, you've told me." She stared at him. "So does that mean you wouldn't date *anyone* right now, or just me? Because that would be a slap in the face."

"No," he said. "I wouldn't date anyone right now. If I was going to date someone, it'd be you."

This pleased her.

"I have two options," she said. "Option one, I stay with Finn, but I lose you. Option two, I break up with Finn, but then I still don't have you in the way I want. Either way, I lose you. And I can't lose you. I can't not have you in my life."

"Why can't we just take it day by day and see how the summer goes?"

"What does that even *mean*?" she asked. "You don't want to be in a relationship, but you also don't want to be exclusive."

"Yeah, we just take it easy."

"Easy? Meaning you can talk to however many girls you want?"

"Cambria, I just got out of a three-year relationship—I need to be single right now. I don't want to rush into something with you just because you want it right *now*."

He had a fair point.

"Okay…" she said, now somehow feeling guilty for putting pressure on him. "I understand." She paused while she thought it over. "So, we remain as we are; best friends, but also more. See what happens. We don't put a label on it. We just… take it day by day?"

"Yeah."

"But we're not exclusive?"

"No."

"See, I don't like that."

"And I don't like you dating another guy."

"I know! I get it." She felt defeated, like she didn't have much of a choice.

There was nothing else to say but, "okay."

He was grinning.

"But," she said. "We always put each other first. I know you're going to talk to other girls, but at the end of the day, it's me. *I'm* yours. No one comes before that."

"Of course."

She stuck out her pinky.

He linked his through hers and they shook on it.

"I have a feeling," he said to her, "that you'll probably end up being my wife someday."

THIRTY-EIGHT

While Cambria felt certain of her desire to be with Jackson, she didn't, however, feel that same certainty about ending her relationship with Finn. She didn't want to lose him, and still, regardless of her feelings for Jackson, could see a future with him.

She couldn't help but feel she was making a grave mistake.

She'd be breaking his heart, but in the process, would also break her own.

Her heart ached at the thought of hurting him. To hurt him would hurt her. He didn't deserve this. But perhaps it was for the best that Cambria removed herself from his life before she caused any further pain. She would only make things worse. For as long as she loved Finn, she knew she would love Jackson.

But alas, her hand had been forced.

When it was done, she felt pain, but also relief. For a great weight had now been lifted off her shoulders. Though wrong of her, she asked if they could still be friends, or something. She couldn't lose him completely and still wanted him in her life in some capacity. Finn was the perfect partner, but unfortunately, her heart beat for only one person. She hated that it had to be like this, but there wasn't any other way around it. She couldn't have both, though she would have *loved* that option. It felt like the perfect balance, yin and yang. With Jackson, she was bad, but with Finn, she wanted to be good.

But that was all over, and now, there was only Jackson.

They picked up vodka and got blue raspberry slushy's, driving around town with the windows down, music blaring, singing at the top of their lungs. They went back to Cambria's house and poured the vodka into the drinks, stirring it in with their straws.

This was only the beginning.

The curtain had dropped. There was no more boyfriend, no more relationship. They were free to do as they pleased.

Jackson couldn't get her clothes off fast enough. He took his time with her, caressing her entire body. When he tried to take off her bra, she refused.

"Why?" he asked.

"I don't want you to see me."

"I *want* to see you," he said. "You don't have to be self conscious with me." Then he reached behind her back and undid her bra, sliding it off.

Before he could get much of a look, Cambria pulled him to her.

They spent the next few days together, basking in their newfound freedom. Things still felt the same as they'd always been, just slightly different. They were still best friends. They still did everything together. The main difference now was the sex.

They couldn't get enough of each other. And somehow, it kept getting better and better each time. They'd finish having sex, and Cambria would think *surely nothing could top that*, only to be proven wrong the next time.

Despite this, the essence of their friendship remained. They'd hang out, just as they normally would. And then Jackson would say, "wanna have sex?" and she'd say, "yeah." And then he'd be putting a condom on saying, "this is my first time," and she'd go, "me too." They'd both laugh. And then he'd fuck her.

And then immediately afterwards, they'd go back to best friend mode.

That weekend, Jackson was invited to a friend's cottage, meaning they'd be apart for a couple days. When he told Cambria who was going to be there, her stomach sank at the mention of several girls. She knew there were no rules between them, meaning he could do whatever he wanted and she couldn't really say anything. But the idea of him touching another girl made her sick. And suddenly she didn't have a good feeling about him going anymore.

"Wouldn't you rather stay here with me?" she said to him as they lay in bed together Friday evening. He was leaving in the morning.

"We've spent all week together, silly."

"I know," she said. "But we normally don't like being away from each other. And especially now, when everything is so new."

"I'll be back Sunday night," he told her.

She pursed her lips. "You're not going to hook up with anyone, are you?"

He held her gaze. "I don't know."

Her stomach dropped. "What do you mean? You plan on hooking up with someone?"

"I'm not *planning* anything, but I don't know what's going to happen."

"So that means yes."

He sat up and shifted back from her. "We're not exclusive," he said to her. "You know that. We agreed on that."

"I know," she sat up too, tears forming in her eyes. "But I love you. And the thought of you with some other girl kills me."

"It's not serious," he said. "I don't plan on dating any of them."

Somehow, this didn't make her feel any better.

At ten o'clock, he insinuated that she go home, which was extremely out of character for him. Usually he was begging her to stay longer. Never did he *want* her to go.

"Is everything okay?" she asked, concern in her eyes.

"Everything's fine," he said. "I'm just tired, and I need a good night's sleep for tomorrow."

"Okay… Are we good?"

"Why wouldn't we be?"

She held his gaze. "Please be safe, okay? And check in with me if you can. I'll miss you."

"I'll miss you too."

She didn't hear from him all weekend. In fact, she didn't hear from him for days, even after he was home.

The knot in her stomach continued to grow the longer she went without hearing from him. She knew, without a doubt, that something was terribly wrong. She could try to deny it all she wanted and come up with excuses and justifications in her head, but the truth of the matter was that Jackson never did this unless something was wrong.

On Wednesday after she finished work, she went over to his house to talk to him. She could immediately tell that something was off. Still, she maintained her composure and tried not to think the worst.

They went to the backyard to sit in the gazebo. He grabbed two beers and brought them out, wordlessly handing her one.

She took a sip as she attempted to gather her thoughts. He wasn't saying anything, she wasn't saying anything. *What was happening?*

"Jackson," she said his name, turning his attention from the sky back to her.

"Cambria."

"What's going on?"

"What do you mean?"

She placed her beer on the table and sat up. "We haven't talked since Friday night, when I left your house. You were supposed to call me and check in. Or at least call me when you got back on Sunday."

"I was at a cottage, Cambria. I didn't really have time to call you."

"And what about when you got home?"

"It was late."

"So? When has that ever stopped you before? And also, it's *Wednesday*. What's your excuse for the last two days, hmm?"

He took a drink. "I've been busy."

She shook her head, hurt and fed up. "You're never too busy for me, Jackson. We're never too busy for *each other*. That's why I'm asking what's going on? What's changed? We were so good before you left."

"Nothing's changed."

"Then why are you acting like this?"

"I'm not acting like anything."

She stared at him. "What's going on with us?" she asked. "I need to know your stance on everything right now."

He held her gaze, a long moment of pause. And then he said, "I want to stay friends."

Her brain glitched. "You told me to break up with my boyfriend."

"Because you told me that you LOVED me."

"We had a discussion about this before I even did anything," she said. "You told me you wanted to see where things go over the next couple months."

"I'm not getting into a relationship right now."

"I agreed not to rush into anything."

"Okay."

"So now you're just going back on what you said? And telling me it's never going to happen?"

"What am I going back on?" he said. "There was never any guarantee."

She was dumbfounded. "I wish you would have fucking told me that a week ago. But no, it was probably your plan just to get me out of my relationship."

"I never planned it. If you want to get back together with Finn, that's fine, I understand. Just know that we will never be anything more than friends."

Those words would stay with her forever.

She was GOBSMACKED. "You can't act the way you do with me and say that we're *just friends*, Jackson."

"Well I just said it, didn't I?"

"You are so fucking hurtful. You just went back on everything we talked about."

"How?"

"You asked your family what they would think if we were together. You told me to break up with Finn and date you."

"Yeah, and I was seriously considering it. I said give it a couple months. It's been a week and you're asking for my stance on everything. How does that make sense?"

"I thought we were on the same page."

"There was never any promise for me to be with you."

"So that's where you stand then? Not *give it a couple months*. Just a definite no?"

"Yep."

"Why are you doing this?" She sat back. "I'm so fucking confused. I don't know what you want. And you're hurting me in the process."

"I'm sorry," he said. But he didn't seem sorry.

"Do you just want me out of your life?"

"No, I don't. I want you in my life."

"You don't act like it."

"Yeah," he said. "I'm good at that."

"I don't understand. Things were fine with us before. You actually acted like you cared. And we didn't fight or bicker or anything."

"Yeah, and I wonder why."

She stared at him, completely speechless. "So, this is it then? This is your final decision? That it's over between us? We'll never be anything?"

"Yep."

A moment of silence. "I can't believe I was so fucking stupid," she said. "I will never forgive you for this."

"Yeah, you will," he sat back, taking another drink of his beer. "You always do."

"Not this time, Jackson." She stood. "You've pushed me too far this time. And especially after everything we've just gone through? I broke up with my boyfriend for you. I chose *you.* And this is how you treat me? You're horrible. And you want to know the worst part? You just blew it with probably the only person who will ever love you like I do. You will never have a connection with anyone like you do with me. Try as you might, nothing will compare. You can go off into the world, get with as many girls as you'd like, and I can guarantee you won't find anything like what you have with me. It might take you some time to come to this realization—because clearly, right now, you think otherwise—but when you eventually do, it'll be too late. I'll be gone. So, congratulations," she said, forcing a smile. "You just blew the best thing you never had."

December 1993

THIRTY-NINE

It was Christmas time—Cambria's favorite time of year. She had spent the weekend shopping at the markets, buying more decorations than she needed. Her parents were flying in this week to spend the holidays with her. She sat in the living room, curled up on the couch with a book and a cup of hot cocoa. Finn sat next to her, flicking through the channels while absentmindedly stroking her thigh.

The telephone rang, and Cambria placed a finger on the page, prepared to get up, but Finn stood before she got the chance. He was always doing that, doting on her, making her life easier, even if only the slightest. She watched him walk to the kitchen, then readjusted in her seat. A moment later, he called her name. "It's Mara," he said.

She set her book down and stood, making her way to the kitchen. Finn passed her the phone, then kissed her cheek as they swapped places and he returned to the living room.

"Hi, baby doll," Mara's voice beamed through the phone.

"To what do I owe the pleasure?"

"How are you? How's Finn?"

"We're good, we just set up the tree. My parents are coming in this week."

"I still need to get that pie recipe from your mom. Tell her she owes me."

"She doesn't owe you shit."

"I beg to differ."

"I'll make sure you get your pie, don't worry."

"Good," Mara said. "I've lost ten pounds, I deserve a reward."

Cambria smiled into the phone. "How are you?"

"I'm fine. But I'm calling for a reason. Is Finn still nearby?"

"He's in the living room." Cambria peaked her head around the corner and watched him. "Why?"

"I need to tell you something."

Cambria took a few steps in the other direction. "What is it?"

"It's Jackson. He wants to see you."

The name, though no longer attached to her, still gave her the same reaction. "Does he know?"

"No, I don't think so."

"What did he say?"

"That he wants to see you. Needs to talk."

She lowered her voice. "What if I don't want to talk to him?"

"That's what I said. But between you and me… do you?"

Cambria hesitated. There was no point in lying to Mara; she knew her like the back of her hand. "Yes."

"Okay yeah, I figured. I already told him you'd say yes."

"Mara!"

"He asked if this week works."

"I'm busy."

"It sounded urgent."

"I'm sure it did."

"He said Tuesday. The Starbucks on Fifth. 6pm. Can you do that?"

She didn't hesitate. "Fine."

Of course Jackson would reach out now, after everything. He always did have the worst timing. And as much as she wanted to say no solely to spite him, she couldn't deny that she really did want to see him, despite how things had ended.

It had been a blessing in disguise what Jackson did to her. She couldn't see it at the time, but when everything was said and done, she realized it had needed to happen. Had it not happened then, it would've happened eventually. She always knew it'd be her who got hurt in the end. And therefore, she concluded, it was never Jackson she was supposed to end up with—it was Finn. It had always been Finn.

Real love wants you regardless of timing, not just when it's convenient to you. She needed someone who would choose her, and Finn always would.

It didn't take long to find their way back to each other; the universe couldn't keep them apart. By some divine intervention, they were meant to be together. Cambria had almost fucked it all up with her own intervention—Jackson's intervention. What a mistake that had been. It wasn't until later, with hindsight, that she could see everything for what it was.

A blessing in disguise.

At least, that's what she told herself. The truth was, Cambria still thought about Jackson—she never stopped. He was an omnipresent fixture in her mind, an obsession she couldn't shake. As much as she told herself she was happy with Finn and that everything worked out the way it was supposed to, even after all this time, she still couldn't help but wonder—what if?

What if things had been different? What if she'd never met Finn? What if she had chosen Jackson from the beginning?

But Jackson didn't choose her, despite her choosing him. And so rather than be stuck in the past, torturing herself with *what ifs*, she made a decision to move on and choose happiness. With Finn.

She told herself that she'd never loved anyone the way she loved Finn. It was a different kind of love, wholesome and requited. When she was with Finn, she wanted to be a better person. He was so good, and she wanted to be good like him.

He would never hurt her. He never yelled at her. He never even raised his voice at her. Scarcely did they have fights or arguments. Scarcely did they disagree. If an issue arose, they would talk it through, amicably and reasonably. He was so level-headed and calm. So reassuring and kind. He taught her what it meant to love, and to be loved.

He loved her feverishly, passionately, and unconditionally. He would've done anything for her; take a bullet for her, die for her. She knew it was an all or nothing kind of love. A love that only comes along once in a lifetime. She envisioned growing old together, dying together. It was the kind of love people only dream of finding. And it was hers. She had finally found it, at last.

Cambria had loved Jackson with reckless abandon, and that love made her blind to many things. She prioritized him over herself. He didn't inspire her to be better. His bad habits were her bad habits. They enabled each other. And at the time, she thought that was okay. She had never known someone who was like her in almost every way. They were two halves that made a whole. And she couldn't deny what being with Jackson made her feel. True elation to the highest degree. Something she knew she'd never achieve even with Finn. But that was a sacrifice she was willing to make to be better.

She had never really believed in soulmates, and still, to this day, struggled with the notion. Because if Finn was her soulmate, then what did that make Jackson?

If one thing was for certain, it was that she was meant to be with Finn. After all, she had found his ring on the sidewalk all those years ago. How else do you explain it?

———

On Tuesday at 6:00pm, she sat inside Starbucks at the spot that was once theirs. She fidgeted with her fingers nervously, picking at her nails, her mind a supercut of memories, flashing before her eyes.

She thought she might throw up.

And then he appeared, and something stirred from deep within. A myriad of emotions bubbled to the surface: resentment, longing, sadness.

"I didn't think you'd actually show," he said as he loomed over her.

She looked up at him and swallowed it all down. "I've always enjoyed proving you wrong."

He smirked, and she knew, then, that she still had him. Even after all this time, they were still Jackson and Cambria. They'd always be Jackson and Cambria.

He pulled out the chair and sat across from her. "You're blond," he remarked.

"I am," she replied.

"Very blond. It suits you."

"Thanks."

"Is this for me?" He nodded towards the coffee.

"No, they're both for me." She held his gaze. "Americano with brown sugar. Steamed hot. Extra shot of espresso."

"You remembered."

"Obviously."

He pulled the cup closer. "How have you been?"

"Let's cut the small talk," she said. "Why are we here?"

He was smirking at her, amused. "Because I wanted to see you."

"That much is clear. But why? Why now?

"Well, because I miss being friends."

"*Friends.*"

"Yes."

"And what happened with your girlfriend?" Cambria asked.

He held her gaze, presumably fuming that she knew about that. "We broke up."

"Mhm," she said. "Timing doesn't seem coincidental. You have a tendency of reaching out after break ups."

"That's not why I'm here," he said.

She studied his face. "Do you recall the last time we saw each other?"

"We don't need to rehash the past," he waved his hand. "What's done is done."

"Is it, though?"

"Classic Cambria, can never let go."

"Fuck you."

"Don't lie—you missed me." He had that stupid grin on his face.

She rolled her eyes. "Obviously."

He was smug, and she hated giving him the satisfaction. "And you've missed me, I presume, or we wouldn't be here."

"Yeah. I just said that I miss being friends."

"I think *friends* is a bit of an understatement," she said, "don't you think?"

"Semantics," he took a drink of his coffee. "Mmm, this is good."

"You're so annoying."

"You love me."

She held his gaze. "I hated you."

"I know."

"I want to talk about it."

"Why?" he said. "What's the point?"

"*Classic Jackson,*" she mimicked him. "*Always wanting to avoid everything.*"

"Is it so wrong of me to not want to dredge up the past?"

"Is it so wrong of me to want to talk about it?"

"Why, so we can continue blaming each other? I blame you, you blame me. It shouldn't even matter anymore."

"It matters to me." She stared at him. "I still don't understand why you did what you did. And it's been eating away at me, all this time."

"You're looking for an answer."

"Yes."

"Well, I don't have one."

"What do you mean?"

"I don't know why I did what I did. I'm just Jackson."

"That's not a good enough excuse."

"It's not an excuse. It's an explanation. And it's the only one I've got."

"You threw away everything," she said. "You ruined us."

"Did I? Or was that you?"

"I chose you. You asked me to choose you, and I did."

"But you chose him first."

"Oh my God, you're still on about that?"

He laughed. "You're one to talk."

"I'm trying to get to the bottom of this. Figure out where it all went wrong."

"You want to know where it all went wrong?" he said. "When you decided to get a boyfriend. And not tell me."

"But we moved past that," she said. "We still could've made it work. I *tried* to make it work."

"If that were the case—if you had really wanted to be with me—you never would have dated him in the first place."

"But even after that… I chose you. You told me to break up with him and I did. For *you.* And then for you to say, *we'll never be anything more than friends*, was so fucking hurtful. I don't understand why you did it. And I want an answer, I want to know why."

"You want an answer?" he said, staring at her. "I only told you I wanted to be with you because I didn't want you to be with him. I don't think I ever would've dated you."

The words hit, but they weren't even a shock to the system because, honestly, she had kind of suspected that. But still, hearing him confirm it stung.

"I knew it," she said. All this time she had wondered why. They had been *so* close. For him to throw it all away didn't make sense. What *did* make sense, however, was Cambria's blindness to his true nature. He'd probably intended on doing that all along, from the moment she first told him about Finn. "Do you know how fucked up that is?" she said, aghast. "You manipulated me."

"Why are we still talking about this? Can't we just move on? Be friends again?"

"I don't think I can ever be *friends* with you, Jackson."

"Why not?"

"After everything? Are you joking?"

He gave her a look that could only be described as *the classic Jackson look*. "Come on, Cambria."

She held his gaze. "You really don't know, do you?"

"Know what?"

She hesitated. "I'm with Finn. We ended up getting back together after all."

That was not what he was expecting. "Oh."

"Yeah."

"That's surprising."

"Not really."

"Does he know?" Jackson said. "That you're still in love with me?"

She didn't respond.

"I find it funny," he continued, "that you're settling."

"I'm not settling," she said. "He's the love of my life."

"I'm sure that's what you tell yourself."

"He is. He's a better man than you'll ever be."

"Yet I'm still the one you love."

"I don't love you," she said.

"Don't lie to yourself."

"Do *you* love *me*?" she asked.

He didn't respond.

"Let me ask you something," she said, leaning closer across the table. "Would you care," she said slowly and then paused, "if I married him?"

He laughed. "Hilarious."

"I'm serious. Would you? Answer honestly," she teased. "Remember what happened last time."

"Why would I care?"

"So you wouldn't care? At all?"

He held her gaze. "No."

She laughed. "You really haven't changed one bit. Still lying to yourself."

"I'm not lying to anyone."

"Alright," she sat back in her seat. "Because I am."

"You are *what?*"

"Going to marry him."

He laughed. "I'm sure you think you are."

Finally, she had the upper hand. She smirked, wanting to savor this moment, then placed her left hand out in front of her.

Jackson glanced at it for only a moment before returning his eyes to hers. "When did that happen?"

"Last month."

"That was quick."

"Well, what can I say? When you know, you know."

"You're actually going to do it," he said, the realization dawning on him. "You're going to marry someone just to spite me."

"Not everything is about you, Jackson."

"Of course it is. It always has been."

"You're so cocky," she said. "It's always gotten the best of you."

"You love it."

"No, I really don't."

He stared at her with an unreadable look on his face. "I hope your future husband knows what he's getting himself into."

"Your concern for my marriage is not needed. We'll be just fine."

"I'm just curious," he continued. "Do you think it'll last? How long will you go on pretending?"

"I'm not pretending," she said. "I love him."

Jackson laughed. "Whatever you need to tell yourself." He looked at her somberly, and they held each other's gaze for an extended moment, just how they used to, neither breaking away.

"Do you remember what you said to me?" Jackson asked her. "Back then? About never having a connection with anyone like I do with you?"

"Yeah," she said. "Was I right?"

"Well the same goes for you," he said. "You and I both know that. The only question is, when will *he* know that?"

June 30, 1995

FORTY

It was the thirtieth of June, the night before her wedding. She and Finn had spent the day at the spa, getting massages, bathing in hot springs, and wearing avocado face masks—the calm before the storm.

After dinner, they sat together on the sofa with their tea watching The Godfather. Her wedding dress hung in the spare bedroom upstairs. Her shoes sat by the door. Her jewelry was laid out on the dresser. Everything was ready to go. Everything, except her.

Once the movie finished, Cambria stood. "I'm going to go for a drive," she said.

He looked up at her. "Go for a drive, where?"

"I don't know. Anywhere. I just feel like driving."

"Okay, my love." He stood and faced her. "You alright?"

"I'm fine," she forced a smile.

He kissed her. "Be safe."

"Always am."

She grabbed her keys and left.

The last six months, she'd been so preoccupied with wedding planning that Cambria had never stopped to actual consider what it all meant. And now, suddenly, it was the eve of her wedding, and everything was hitting her all at once.

She thought she was so certain, but now, she realized, she was not. And what once seemed like a perfect fairy-tale happy-ever-after dream was now more like a perfect illusion.

They say *when you know, you know*, but what if you only *think* you know but actually don't? How are you supposed to *truly* know? Which test could she administer to be absolutely sure?

She would never admit it, but there was not a single day that passed that Cambria did not think of Jackson. Despite the wedding planning, and future planning, her mind was stuck in the past, stuck on *him*.

She thought she could escape him and evade her feelings forever, but she was wrong. She knew with great certainty that she would love Jackson Harding for as long as she lived, and nothing would change that. Not distance, not time—not anyone.

She was doomed.

He was living in a condo now. It took her nearly an hour to get there, giving her plenty of time to think, and at the same time, not enough time to think at all.

But she needed to do this, she needed to know.

She parked her car, walked to the lobby, found his number, and buzzed up, waiting in silence for someone to pick up. And then there it was, coming through the speaker—the voice she knew all too well. "Yes?"

She waited a beat. "It's me."

Silence.

A moment later, the door buzzed. She pulled it open and got in the elevator.

Once she arrived on his floor, she wandered down the hall until she found the number twenty-seven. She froze, staring at the door, trying to find the courage to knock. But before she even could, the door opened.

It was now or never.

There they were, face to face, after all this time. He still looked the same. He'd probably always look the same, just in different variations of himself. He had the same baby face, but it was older, more mature. He just kept getting better with age.

"Hi," he said.

"Hi," she replied.

He blinked once then said, "would you like to come in?" taking a step back.

Shc smiled coyly, then entered.

The lights were dim, just enough to catch a brief overview of the place. A spacious living room and an impeccable kitchen. And somewhere over there, a bedroom. It was neat and well kept. The air smelt faintly of smoke, and she wondered if that was from his clothes or something else.

Her heart was beating out of her chest. She felt like she could cry, or explode. "Nice place," she said.

He spoke softly. "What are you doing here, Cambria?"

She hesitated. "I don't know what to do."

"About what?"

"The wedding," she said. "It's tomorrow."

"And yet here you are."

"Here I am." They stared at each other. "Did you know?" she asked.

"I knew."

She held his gaze. "Were you going to say anything? Or were you just going to…"

"Going to, what?" he said. "Let you marry him?"

She didn't respond.

"What did you think I was going to do? Show up at the altar? Profess my love for you? *Speak now or forever hold your peace?*"

"I wouldn't put it past you."

He laughed. "Don't flatter yourself."

"Don't say you haven't thought about it."

"Is that the only reason you're marrying him?" he said. "To call my bluff?"

"Tell me you haven't thought about it."

"I've thought about it."

"I know."

"Is that why you're here?" he asked. "Because I was right all along? You're only doing this to spite me?"

"I'm not doing this to spite you," she said. "Quite the opposite. I'm doing this *in* spite of you."

"Because you actually love him?"

"I do."

"Then why are you here?"

"I don't know."

"Yes, you do. Just say it. Say what you want."

"I don't know what I want."

He rolled his eyes and walked away from her. "You're going to be miserable for the rest of your life, you know that?"

"I know." She stared at him until he faced her again.

"You want me to tell you not to do it but I'm not going to," he said. "You made your decision three years ago when you chose him. And you'll choose him again tomorrow."

What an inaccurate statement. "I didn't choose him three years ago," she exclaimed. "I chose *you*! I chose you, Jackson. You told me to break up with him and be with you AND I DID. And *you* didn't want me, remember? Or are we somehow forgetting that? It was *you* who destroyed us, not me."

"You chose him when you started dating him and didn't tell me."

"Oh my GOD!" she yelled. She was absolutely appalled. "AFTER THAT!" she yelled. "AFTER THAT, I CHOSE YOU!"

"It didn't matter," he said. "Because you already picked him."

"You're actually insane if you think that. I know what happened—I was there. You fucking betrayed me. And to be completely honest, I'm really not sure why you're even still going on about all this. It's in the past. You said it yourself the last time I saw you that you never would have dated me. You only told me that to get me out of my relationship with Finn."

"I only just said that."

She stopped. "What?"

"I just said that to get you to drop it. To stop talking about it."

"You told me," she said, "that you never would have dated me. And that you only told me otherwise because you didn't want me to be in a relationship with someone else."

"Yeah," he said. "I lied."

And just like that, her world flipped on its axis. She stared off across the room, in complete and utter shock, then put her face in her hands, shaking her head. "That was closure for me," she looked at him. "You telling me that a year and a half ago helped me move on. I've spent all this time thinking I was an idiot."

"You're not," he was looking at her so regretfully, and it broke her heart even more. "I was seriously considering dating you and seeing where things went over the summer. But then everything was happening so fast, all at once, and I wanted to be single, but I also wanted you. I just didn't prioritize the right thing. And then when you started pressuring me, asking me for a definitive answer—I felt rushed. And I knew I couldn't give you what you were looking for."

"So you just blew it all up instead?"

"I guess," he said. "That's what I do best."

A shocking revelation. All this time, and nothing had changed. It would always come back to this.

"Tell me not to do it," she said, looking into his eyes.

"I'm not going to tell you that."

"Why not?"

"Because that's your decision. I can't tell you what to do."

"You did before. And I did it."

"Yeah and look how that turned out."

She walked closer to him. "Do you want me to marry him?"

"It's not up to me."

"But what if it was?"

"It's not."

"I don't know what to do."

"You keep saying that, but I think you do, which is why you came here tonight. I think you've always known what you wanted, but you're too proud to admit it."

"I'm not."

"Say it, then. Say why you're here."

She held his gaze for a moment, then meandered towards the large window overlooking the city. She gazed out, staring at the skyline. "Beautiful view."

"Stop deflecting." He walked over so that he was next to her.

"Do you see it?" she said, looking up at the sky. "Polaris." He followed her gaze until he found it. "Tonight is the night we met," she said. "Six years ago."

"You think I don't know that?"

She faced him. "You were my best friend."

"And you were mine."

"How did we let it get to this?"

He was quiet for a moment. "I don't know."

She looked out the window again, and this is what flashed through her mind:

The night they met—shaking hands, smirking at each other, passing drinks across the table, spinning on the dancefloor. The entire summer of 1989—driving around in his car late at night, windows down, music up. All the nights in his backyard—sitting by the fire with a blanket wrapped around them, falling asleep with their feet tangled. Barbeques with his family. The way he'd tease her and pull her hair. Getting drunk and going out. Sneaking in, sneaking out. Staying up until four in the morning, puking while he held back her hair. Riding their bikes down to the beach. Dancing in the kitchen to no music, baking cookies, watching movies in his bedroom, falling asleep in his bed. Before her grandmother's funeral, standing in the bathroom at her parent's house, Jackson putting the necklace on her. The way he'd look at her, and how she'd look back—as though their gaze was everlasting, and it was just the two of them. The first time he kissed her, the rush she felt. And the second time. And the third. That night in the gazebo—the night she fell in love—his head in her lap, her fingers running through his hair.

She thought about the night they did ecstasy. How, to this day, it was probably the best night of her life. The elation, the euphoria, how tranquil she had been in his presence. How she wanted it to last forever.

She remembered giving each other massages, how she would've done anything to get his hands on her again. And how in those moments, lying next to him, she could've died and been content, as long as she was with him.

She remembered the night he returned to her after six months apart. How she knew, then, that he always would—the certainty of it. Talking for hours at the kitchen table, carrying her up the stairs, lying in bed next to him, whispering, *are you in love with me*?

And most of all, she remembered everything that came after—falling in love in a way they never had. How finally, after three years, they had reached a pinnacle. She had waited so long. But then just as suddenly as it had begun, it was over.

And then, she remembered everything else. How cruel he could be. How he would abandon her time and time again, cutting her off as if it were nothing. All the times he'd ice her out and push her away. Bailing on plans and cancelling at the last minute because Natalia was always his priority. The phone calls that went unanswered and unreturned. The periods of drought expanding. The slow dwindling of a friendship she once thought was unbreakable.

She remembered the highs and the lows, how she was addicted to him like a drug, and that he wasn't good for her. *Oh, but how good it felt.* She remembered feeling on top of the world. She remembered feeling the lowest she'd ever felt. She remembered thinking that she couldn't survive without him.

And finally, she remembered that day in his backyard, the words he said: "Just know that we will never be anything more than friends." How they stayed with her—haunted her—for years to follow.

How they came so close, and how he threw it all away.

Then, she thought about Finn—how he came out of nowhere, at exactly the right time. She pictured his blue eyes, so sensitive, and how they'd look into hers. She thought about how ever since overhearing him in a coffee shop, she'd felt that something mystical was at play. She couldn't believe her luck, and never imagined she'd find anyone like him. How he put her on a pedestal and worshipped the ground she walked on. His softspoken demeanor and gentle disposition. She thought about his family, and how they welcomed her as their own. And how she had known so early on that he was the one. She remembered moving in together, and all the time they'd spend with each other, sometimes doing nothing, but always content. She thought of him proposing, the excitement she'd felt—that she had found her forever person, who would always love her, support her, and take care of her. With him, she felt safe. Safe and protected. And knew, with great certainty, what kind of husband and father he would be. She knew they'd grow old together, and die together.

She could choose Finn—the man who would choose her, every single day. Together, they'd build a happy, healthy marriage, and a life that was not only successful, but more than enough. They'd start a family. He'd work hard to support them, giving her everything she could ever want. She knew they'd last—effortlessly, endlessly. A seamless existence. They would be the epitome of the perfect couple.

But there would always be something missing.

Or she could choose Jackson. It wouldn't be easy—it would be messy and complicated. They'd fight all the time. She'd tell him what to do, and he'd put her in her place. They'd drive each other crazy, and fight about things that didn't even matter. But it would be love. It would be passion. It would provide the highest form of elation possible. With him, there was nobody else. Her life would be complete.

Would she choose a love that made sense, or a love that made her feel alive?

She looked at Jackson. "I think I'll love you for the rest of my life."

He held her gaze, and his smile was sad. "I know."

FORTY-ONE

She stood outside the church doors, clutching her dress, waiting for her cue to go inside. Her palms were sweating, her heart was pounding. The sun was luminescent, a beautiful summer day.

The music started to play. The doors opened slowly.

Suddenly, it was time. Everything came down to this moment, the day she had always anticipated—the one they say is the best day of your life.

She didn't feel nervous and she didn't feel scared. She felt surprisingly calm, given there were about to be a hundred set of eyes on her.

Her father looped his arm through hers, and together they stepped forward, one slow step at a time. She did not think about everyone who was awaiting her. Instead, she thought about the only person that mattered—the man waiting at the front for her.

She saw his face as he watched her walk down the aisle. Tears formed in his eyes, and she knew she had made the right choice.

She reached the altar, and at last they were face to face. The love of her life. The man she would spend forever with.

"Dearly beloved," the minister began. "We are gathered here today in the sight of God, and in the presence of family and friends, to join this man and this woman in holy matrimony."

As he spoke, Cambria tuned everything else out. His words blurred into white noise. All she could focus on was Finn—his eyes, staring directly into hers.

And then before she knew it, she heard the minister say, "do you, Finn Patrick Whitaker, take Cambria Annabelle Nickson, as your lawfully wedded wife, to have and to hold, from this day forward, for better, for worse, for richer, for poorer, in sickness, and in health, until death do you part?"

His smile was relentless, engulfing his face. "I do."

"And do you, Cambria Annabelle Nickson, take Finn Patrick Whitaker, as your lawfully wedded husband, to have and to hold, from this day forward, for better, for worse, for richer, for poorer, in sickness, and in health, until death do you part?"

She was smiling back just as hard, her cheeks sore from grinning. "I do."

"May the Peace and the Unconditional Love of God surround you and remain with you now and forevermore. By the powers vested in me and the highest power of the land and sea, I now pronounce you husband and wife. You may now seal your vows with a kiss."

THE END

EPILOGUE

Years would go by. Cambria would slip into this new skin of Finn's wife. They would live together in perfect harmony, never yelling at each other, never causing a stir. They vowed to love each other for better and for worse, through sickness and in health.

Cambria knew that Finn was the right choice, regardless of the conflicting thoughts she had immediately after the wedding, knowing she had just sealed her fate. Finn was good for her—he was stability, longevity, loyalty. And that was everything she needed.

But with that being said, fate cannot be fooled. It cannot be hoodwinked, and it cannot be evaded. Cambria knew deep down that choosing Finn on her wedding day did not mark the end of her and Jackson. Nothing could stop them—not discipline, not time, not destiny. Just as the sun would rise each morning, Jackson and Cambria would find their way back to one another.

Cambria knew, years after the wedding, two or three kids later, living her idyllic life with Finn, that he would show up. And she would let him. He would always return to her, just as she would always return to him.

The wedding did not mean *the end*. It simply meant, *until we meet again*.

She knew, without a doubt, that her heart would yearn for Jackson as long as she lived. Until the day she died. And perhaps even after that.

One lifetime would not be enough.

Discussion Questions

Core Identity

1. Throughout the story, Cambria describes herself as an outsider who never truly fits in, adapting like a "chameleon" to match those around her. What psychological dynamics drive this behavior, and how does it reflect her struggles with belonging?

2. Cambria's low self-regard subconsciously draws her to toxic relationships and self-sabotage. How does this mindset influence her decisions, especially given her belief that “we take what we can get, even if it’s far from what we deserve”?

3. The narrative states that the primary difference between Cambria and Lawson is that Lawson acts on impulses while Cambria suppresses them. Do you agree or disagree, and why?

4. Cambria repeatedly frames her connections to Jackson and Finn as workings of "fate" or "destiny." How does this lens enable her to rationalize poor choices, and what does it reveal about her avoidance of personal accountability?

5. Is Cambria a good person, a bad person, or somewhere in between? Support your view with evidence from the text.

Relationships and Patterns

1. At the end of part one, after their kiss, Jackson misinterprets Cambria's surprise as reluctance, halting their progression. How might the story have unfolded without this miscommunication?

2. Jackson questions Cambria about her feelings for him twice: in December 1989 and May 1991. What motivates each instance? Are the motives the same, or different. Why?

3. Jackson's accusation in December 1989 that Cambria has feelings for him instills in her the fear that such emotions risk losing his friendship. How does this impact her choices throughout the story?

4. Each time Jackson and Cambria stop being friends, Jackson is the one to reach out to reconnect—except the final time, when she seeks him out. What prompts this reversal?

5. Similarly to *Wuthering Heights* when Catherine ultimately chooses status over Heathcliff, how does Cambria prioritize societal success and stability at the expense of her authentic passion for Jackson? Does this echo of calculated ambition reveal a deeper flaw in her character, or a universal human desire?

ABOUT THE AUTHOR

A.R. Tyler, who is based in Toronto, was drawn to storytelling from a young age. She graduated from Trent University in 2018 with a bachelor's degree in Cultural Studies, specializing in film, video, and media. Drawn to stories about growth, relationships, and personal transformation, A.R. Tyler crafts fiction that explores the complexities of life. Follow @author_artyler on Instagram, Threads, and TikTok, and @AbbyRoseTyler on Wattpad.

www.ingramcontent.com/pod-product-compliance
Lightning Source LLC
LaVergne TN
LVHW041107080826
845145LV00007B/1712
* 9 7 8 1 0 6 9 6 0 0 7 0 7 *